ROYALLY EXPOSED

HER ROYAL HAREM, BOOK TWO

CATHERINE BANKS

Turbo Kitten Industries™

P.O. Box 5012

Galt, CA 95632

www.turbokitten.us

Catherine Banks

www.catherinebanks.com

www.turbokitten.us/catherine-banks

CHAPTER 1

The four males I inadvertently fell for, were all still asleep when I opened the door to my apartment. We had been up until four o'clock in the morning trying to beat the new raid in *Ghost 2*'s second expansion. My body decided it was ready to get up, and for the first time, the guys didn't wake when I climbed out of the giant bed Deryn had had custom made for us. It was large enough to fit eight people, side by side, which gave us plenty of room since there were only five of us. The mattress was plush and heavenly, as though lying on clouds.

I set the coffee carafe on my kitchen counter and arranged the four boxes of donuts, one dozen in each, lids opened. Before the smells could reach the guys, I grabbed my two favorite donuts, put them on a plate, and took the cup of hot chocolate I had purchased to the couch and set them all on the coffee table.

"Coffee," Deryn grumbled, half asleep, as he stumbled into the living room.

"Good morning," I greeted him and smiled as I enjoyed the view. All of them slept in pajama bottoms and nothing else, their chests and abdomens, rippling with muscle, naked for my viewing pleasure.

He bent down and kissed my cheek as he passed by, mumbling what sounded like good morning.

"You left alone again," Rhys growled at me half-heartedly.

They had been getting better about letting me out on my own now that I could tap into their powers, if needed, and protect myself. However, their protectiveness as my guards, and lovers, still made it difficult for them to be okay with me going out alone.

"I wanted to surprise you with donuts," I told him and sipped on my hot chocolate.

He kissed my cheek and slid his hand along the back of my neck. "It's a good surprise," he said. Rhys hated mornings more than any of us, but said getting to wake up with me was making him start to like them more. I knew that was a lie, but I enjoyed the flattery.

"Donuts!" Foxfire yelled and raced into the kitchen, grabbing a box, and running over to sit beside me. "Thanks, Jolie," he whispered and kissed my cheek with a wide smile. Fox loved mornings. Well, Fox loved almost everything. He was almost always in a good mood and his attitude was infectious.

"You're welcome," I replied and leaned into his shoulder with mine.

"Did you use a shield?" Nico asked, rubbing his eyes and then stretching to give me a nice view of the muscles over his hips that formed a V and led down to a very fun area.

"No," I admitted.

Four sets of eyes turned to look at me.

"I couldn't figure out how to do it with my hands full," I explained quickly. "But I had scales on the back of my head and over my heart, so if I had been shot at they couldn't have killed me."

It had been months since the last time someone had tried to

kill me. You would think stopping a war would endear you to those who had been fighting, but some people had been pretty upset about it. Most of them had been thankful. Hell, they'd made me a princess of the dragons, mages, wolves, and elves and given me a necklace with power stored inside from the kings and princes of each race. I still couldn't believe it.

I touched the necklace and felt the energy thrumming within, a constant reminder of the power I could now use.

"That's good," Deryn praised me. "I wouldn't have thought to use scales on the back of my head."

"That's because you don't have scales," Rhys said with a grumble. "I'm glad you've figured out how to use the scales beneath your hair."

"It wasn't easy," I mumbled. The first few times I had tried to do it, I had covered my entire head with scales and freaked out because I thought I was going to be bald afterward.

"How long can you keep the scales on?" Nico asked around a bite of sugar coated donut.

I waited until I'd finished eating my chocolate bar before answering. "I can hold the scales in a small area, like over my heart, for an hour. If I put it in several small areas, I can hold it for half an hour. I can cover my entire body for fifteen minutes at most."

"The more you use it, the easier it becomes," Rhys said. He gulped down a mug of coffee and added, "It will become second nature and you won't even have to think about it."

That sounded like a great thing to have the ability to do. Instead of focusing and putting scales in the spot you wanted, you could just automatically have it there. I had seen Rhys use scales when fighting hand to hand with Deryn, and Rhys said it just happened automatically for him.

"What are our plans today?" Deryn asked.

"I'm going to the dragons' den today," I told them, waiting for Rhys to blow up...again.

"What?" Rhys asked quietly.

Uh oh. Quiet was bad.

"King Emrys invited me over. He promised me safe passage and that I would be allowed to return whenever I wanted to."

"They aren't faeries," Fox whispered.

"When were you going to tell me?" Rhys asked, his voice a deep rumble from the kitchen where he was standing, his grip on the mug he was holding so tight, that I could see cracks forming already.

"Now," I said with a smile.

"I told you why I didn't want you-"

"I've been ordered to come by my king," I said and stood up, shoving the rest of my donut in my mouth.

"I can talk-"

"If I disobey him now, that's setting a bad precedence with your clan. I can't disobey him. I'm going. So, you need to decide whether you're coming with me, or not."

Without giving him a chance to respond, I hurried to my bedroom to change clothes. Emrys had warned me to wear something comfortable and to bring a jacket. That should have made me nervous, but I knew Rhys would go with me and wouldn't let anything happen to me. They'd told me before that even though their fathers were their alphas, they could withstand their orders, because they were so high in the hierarchy.

Once I was satisfied with my appearance, I went out to the living room where Rhys sat alone. The others had snuck out without me hearing the front door open or close. Rhys sat on my couch, his arms draped across the back, giving me time to take in his new appearance. He had put on jeans and a t-shirt that said, "Unicorns do exist and they're tasty."

Instead of talking, I walked straight to him and sat in his lap, straddling him with my face level with his. "You're mad at me for leaving this morning," I guessed.

One of his warm arms snaked around my lower back, and pulled me forward so that our chests were touching.

"I don't like waking up to find you aren't in bed with me. I don't like knowing that someone could have hurt you while I was sleeping. I also don't like the way you keep hiding things from me." I opened my mouth to say something, but he squeezed me and then sighed. "However, I know you need to obey my father. I don't think anyone will hurt you while I'm by your side, but I can't help but worry. You're my light, Jolie. I can't lose you."

I kissed him deeply and thoroughly, his erection almost immediate beneath me.

"We don't have time," he growled and nipped his way down my throat.

"He isn't supposed to be here until one o'clock," I told him and ground against him.

"He said he was ten minutes away," he said and nodded at his phone.

"Then we better hurry," I said, wrapped my hands around his neck, ground my hips into his, and licked his neck. Rhys's hot button was licking his neck. One lick and he was ready to go.

Rhys carried me to the bed, stripping his clothes off as he walked. The amount of strength he possessed, to carry me with one arm, while stripping with the other, was a big turn on.

"Later, I'm going to make love to you until your legs quiver so much that they can't hold you up," he murmured in my ear and then thrust into me.

My back arched up and I screamed his name. He stretched and filled me perfectly, his strokes perfectly positioned to hit the spot deep inside of me that built my ecstasy. His strokes built the pressure until I screamed my orgasm and tightened around him with my inner muscles.

He growled and covered my nipple with his mouth, flicking his tongue across it with each pump of his hips.

"Yes!" I gasped and matched his hip movements with my own.

"You're beautiful," he told me as he loomed above me, up on his arms.

"You're perfect," I gasped as another orgasm hit.

"Your ass is perfect," he growled and flipped me over, grabbing my hips and jerking them upright so that the top of my body was down on the bed and my lower body was up on my knees.

He entered me slowly, grunting in pleasure as he did. He reached down to rub my clit with one hand while he gripped my hips with the other. His fingers moved quickly back and forth and it wasn't long before I was gripped by not one, but two orgasms.

"Yes!" Rhys yelled, slamming his hips into mine harder and faster.

His phone rang and he growled, but ignored it, leaning forward to grasp one of my breasts while he finished.

We cleaned up and got dressed, making it down to the car just as the driver was getting out.

"Sorry for making you wait," Rhys apologized, opened the door, and ushered me inside.

"No problem, Prince Rhys," the driver replied stiffly and got back into the driver's seat.

"I should have eaten more than donuts," I grumbled and rubbed my hungry stomach.

"We'll eat when we get there," he promised and slid his hand along my stomach.

"Anything I should be warned about before we do get there?" I asked him. His hand was now rubbing my arm, up and down, slowly. It was relaxing me and turning me on at the same time.

"Stay by my side the entire time," he said. "The females are just as aggressive and possessive as the males, sometimes more so. Don't turn your back on a dragon, it's rude and tells them that you think they're not a threat. Don't ask to ride any of them. Don't approach any of them without them approaching you first."

"Geez," I chuckled. "This is a super serious clan."

He nodded. "We can be."

"Eye contact?" I asked.

"Meet all of their stares. You're a princess, so we want to make sure they don't view you as weak."

"Okay."

The gates to the dragon's den were ridiculously high, stretching up so far that if I were standing in front of them, I would have to lean my head all the way back to see where it stopped. They slid open as we approached and the driver took us down the black asphalt driveway. At first, there was nothing to see. Trees and bushes, but no houses of any kind. A half mile later, we finally approached a mansion with two massive dragon statues on each side of the driveway, one wing of each stretched over to create an archway for us to drive beneath.

"Wow," I whispered as I admired the statues.

"Compliment Dad on those," he told me. "He loves bragging about the statues."

We stopped at the mansion where Emrys stood, waiting for us. I hurried out and walked up to give him a hug. "Sorry we're late."

"Did he have a fit?" he guessed as he hugged me back.

"A bit," I admitted and pulled back as Rhys approached.

"Son," Emrys greeted Rhys.

"Father," Rhys replied.

"You look well," Emrys commented.

"You're not getting out of this with compliments," Rhys told him and folded his arms across his chest. "I'm pissed."

Emrys chuckled. "Of course you are."

"Will we be eating?" Rhys asked him. "We're rather famished."

"I have snacks ready," Emrys said with a nod. "Come on, let's get this tour started." He held out his bent elbow and I slid my arm through his. "Did you know that Rhys used to hate wearing clothes. As a child, his mother and nannies used to chase him around the steps here, trying to get him back into clothes."

"He still hates clothes," I said with a chuckle.

Emrys howled with laughter. "I suppose some things don't change."

"I'm dressed now, aren't I?" Rhys mumbled.

I joined in with Emrys's laughter at that comment, but stopped when I saw the beautiful woman standing just outside the door to the mansion. She had the same dark brown hair as Rhys and the same eye shape. She was tall, willowy, and beautiful. Most of all, she's was intimidating. Something about her screamed at me to run the other way.

Emrys patted my hand, released me, and went to the woman to kiss her cheek. Some of her ferocity diminished at his touch, but not much.

"Jolie, please meet my mate and Rhys's mother, Adelaide. Adelaide please meet Jolie, Queen of Rhys's and Princess of the Four Clans."

That was a lot easier to say than to name each clan. I'd have to remember that.

"So, you're the human who thinks she's good enough for my son?" she asked, a snarl on his lips.

"Mother!" Rhys growled.

"No," I answered immediately. "I don't think I'm good enough. That's one of the reasons that I haven't taken him as a mate."

Her composure broke and she frowned in uncertainty. "What?"

"Jolie," Rhys whispered and moved closer to me.

"I'm human. I'm pretty, yes, but I'm not gorgeous. I have no abilities, aside from the ones I inherited from my guards. I have a decent paying job with some job security, but not enough for retirement. My savings is reasonable and I increase the amount every month, something I plan to continue until I retire. I'll die before Rhys, unless he does something stupid trying to protect me, which I will do everything within my power to prevent. I also have three others who want me to be their mate. I'm not an ideal mate for Rhys. Not by a long shot. However, I love Rhys. I love him more than my own life. I've given him opportunities to leave, to free himself from me, but he loves me too. I'm not worthy of him or the others. I'm not and I know it, but I can't give them up, because I'm selfish."

Rhys turned me and tilted my chin up, tears in the corners of his eyes. "You are more than worthy of me and are the most self-less person I know."

"She's right," Adelaide said.

"Addie," Emrys chastised.

"Well, she is. It's good that you know this. Know this and understand how lucky you are to have Rhys not only give you attention, but warm your bed," she said and then went inside the mansion.

"Forgive her," Rhys whispered and kissed my cheek. "She's overprotective of me. Always has been."

"That's because you're her favorite," a baritone voice said to my right.

I turned and stared at Rhys's brother. I knew without a doubt that was who he was. They looked similar, but the symmetry of his face was slightly different than Rhys. He was also taller and larger, something I couldn't believe without seeing for myself. His jeans looked painted on and his tank top was stretched to its limit.

"I didn't know you had siblings," I growled softly at Rhys.

"There are seven of us," his brother said with a smile and then bowed. "Greetings, Princess Jolie."

"I'd reciprocate the gesture, but I'm afraid I don't know your name. Since someone never said he had siblings," I grumbled. Why had he kept this from me?

"Jolie, meet my younger brother, Andras. Andras, please meet my queen and the Princess of the Four Clans, Jolie," Rhys introduced us.

I held out my hand to shake Andras's, but he pulled me forward with it and hugged me. "Handshakes are for acquaintances. You're family now, Jolie."

Rhys growled low and took a step forward, but Emrys punched his shoulder and reprimanded him. "She's perfectly safe with your siblings."

"He's not worried about me hurting her, Father. He's worried I'll steal her like I did his last girlfriend," Andras said and took a step away from me. "Don't worry, I know better than to try anything with this one. You've made it clear that you love her."

"Oh, your brother stole one of your girlfriends? I should hear this story," I said and smirked at Rhys.

He folded his arms across his chest and glared at me. "My pain brings you joy?"

"Do you wish to have her back?" I asked, smirk still in place.

His arms lowered. "No."

"So, Rhys was sixteen," Andras said, instantly launching into the story, and draped an arm across my shoulders as we walked into the mansion. This mansion was even more luxurious than the Elders'. The chandelier above us looked like it was made with real diamonds and not crystals, but I didn't want to ask for confirmation. The hallways were bustling with activity, but everyone stepped aside as we walked, most bowing to us.

Would I ever get used to this?

"Rhys's girlfriend was always into me. I tried to tell him that when he first introduced her as his girlfriend, but he didn't listen. He caught her flirting with me, and me reciprocating, and lost it."

"You mean Rhys got mad at another female for flirting? So, I'm not special?" I teased and gave Rhys a fake pout.

He rolled his eyes in response.

"Ah, but for you, I think he might challenge me. For her, he just told her to have fun and left."

"And what happened to this girl?" I asked Andras, sensing they were not still together.

He shrugged. "Who knows? That was more than a decade ago."

We turned down a hallway and I stopped at the first picture I saw. It was of Rhys and eight others in dragon form posing together.

"That's the entire family," Rhys told me.

"This is your mother," I guessed pointing towards a dragon who looked just as fierce, but less muscular, and had the same piercing gaze.

"Yes. How'd you know?" Andras asked.

"She's a tad less muscular and her eyes are the same," I said.

"Which is Rhys?" Andras asked.

Immediately, I pointed to Rhys. "There."

"That's pretty impressive," Emrys said.

"Why?" I asked. "Rhys has distinct markings on his face. There are two small black spots on the edge of his snout." I reached out and touched the right and left side of Rhys's nose.

"Which is me?" Emrys asked.

I had never seen him in dragon form, but I looked at the picture and pointed at the one on the far left, the opposite side of the family from Adelaide. "Here."

"Holy shit," Andras said. "Which one is me?"

This was harder. I studied Andras' face and then looked back at the picture. I was having trouble between two of them and finally just admitted it to them. "You're either this one or this one," I said and pointed at the two on either side of Rhys. "I think you're the one on the right, but I can't be sure."

"Dad," Rhys whispered.

"I know," Emrys whispered back.

"Why do I get the feeling that most people can't tell dragons apart?" I asked them. "I mean, you're all different colors."

"What?" Rhys asked.

"All of you have slightly different mottling to your colors," I said. "It makes you all different colors despite having the same color scheme."

"That's something only dragons are able to discern," Rhys told me. He looked at his dad and asked, "Do you think it's another ability from being bonded to me?"

Emrys shook his head. "No, I've never heard of anyone outside of a dragon being able to see that much and tell dragons apart without having seen them as a dragon before."

"Well, you keep telling me I'm special," I teased Rhys to try to break some of the tension that had built between us. Just one more thing to mark down as odd about me.

"Come, let's eat," Emrys said and led the way.

"Am I in trouble?" I asked Rhys softly.

He chuckled and linked hands with me. "No, my queen."

"I feel like you've replaced 'Love' with 'Queen' just because you know it makes me uncomfortable," I mumbled.

"I would never do such a thing, my queen," he replied and kissed my cheek.

"Liar."

"You're the liar," he shot back in a high-pitched tone.

I rolled my eyes at him. "Real mature."

"I'm rubber and you're glue-" he said and was cut off by Andras's laugh.

"You two are adorable," Andras said.

I looked at the other pictures, all family pictures, and was surprised that there were none of them as children. Did they only leave up the newest pictures? Why not leave up one from each decade?

The dining room we entered was unlike any I had seen before. There was a large table on one side and couches on the other side situated in front of a giant fireplace, the mantle at least six feet tall. The table had silver settings and a full feast.

"Didn't he say he had snacks for us? This is a feast," I whispered as softly as possible to Rhys.

"This is a snack for us," he told me. "You forget how much I eat alone. Now, picture nine of us plus you here. How much food do you think we need for us to have even a snack's worth?"

That did make sense. The Others ate a ton of food, and ever since I started using their powers, I had begun eating a ton as well. Nico said it was necessary to keep the magic reserve in our body. That they required a lot of fuel to keep the storage going. I asked if starvation would cause the reserves to shrink and he nodded.

"Please, sit," Emrys said and pulled out a chair for me next to his at the head of the table. I sat and he pushed me in before taking his place. Rhys sat next to me and Andras sat across from me.

"Food!" Emrys bellowed, the silverware and plates shaking briefly from the rumble that felt like an earthquake and tornado approaching at the same time.

"Coming!" a few different voices yelled. Soon, four males and one female came into the room and took seats at the table. The female was a teenager, or very early adult. One of the males was also a teenager, and the other two ranged between Rhys and the teenagers. They were all wearing sweatpants and tank tops, which made me wonder if they had been training. The female and one of the males looked like Rhys and Andras, but the other two looked much more like their mother.

"Oh, a guest!" the teenage boy said happily. "I didn't know we were having a guest!"

"Quiet," Emrys ordered him.

The boy didn't say anything, but he was still smiling wide and practically bouncing in his chair.

"Swear an oath of silence," Emrys ordered them.

The four newcomers gasped and looked at each other as well as Rhys and Andras.

"Really?" the female teenager asked. She swept her long black, curled hair over her shoulder and studied me. "Is this human pregnant with one of these idiots' kids?"

I laughed hard, getting a disapproving look from Andras. "I like her already," I told Rhys.

He smirked. "I knew you would. You two are similar in several ways."

"Who is she?" one of the middle males asked.

"Obey!" Emrys snapped angrily, his power shooting through the table and making me gasp in pain for a brief moment as it went through me.

"Sorry," Rhys apologized quickly. "I didn't realize he was going to do that or I would have shielded you."

"It's fine," I whispered and rubbed my chest.

"We swear an oath of silence on all things to be said henceforth. Our tongues shall not work to reveal the secrets divulged and our hands will fail should we try to bypass words," all of his siblings said as one.

"I'm sorry, Jolie," Emrys apologized after giving his children one more hard stare. "I forgot that you would be affected by my powers."

"I'm fine," I assured him. "It just stung a bit."

"Father," the female whispered. "We swore."

"Jolie, I'd like you to meet the rest of my children. The impatient female is Rhian. She is the youngest. The fidgeting teenage male is Gavin. He is one year older than Rhian. To Rhian's right is Mawrth and to his right is Brenin. Children, this is Jolie. Jolie is the Princess of the Four Clans and Rhys's Queen."

"Queen!" Rhian gasped. "Why? What? She's *human*!"

"Rhian!" Rhys growled. "Show some decorum. Humans are not less than us."

"When did this happen?" Brenin asked calmly. His eyes were cool and calculating, measuring me in in a way that was slightly unnerving. Whatever weaknesses I had, I was certain he could see them all.

"At the meeting when she returned the necklace to us," Rhys answered.

"She's also the other three's queen, isn't she?" Gavin asked, his smile still in place. Was he like Fox and perpetually happy?

"Yes," Emrys replied before Rhys could.

"Are you mates?" Mawrth asked.

"Ew," Rhian whispered.

"No," I answered.

"Not yet," Rhys mumbled under his breath.

"Why is she here?" Mawrth asked.

"I invited her so that she could come see our clan and learn more about us. Also, because I want her to show you something," Emrys told them.

"Dad," Rhys groaned.

"They need to know everything about our clan that they can," Emrys said and I knew that was his way of telling Rhys the discussion was over.

"Let's eat," Emrys said. "Jolie will answer your questions after she eats."

Rhys took my plate and piled it high with food and his siblings watched in silence. As soon as he set my plate down, everyone began scrambling for the food at the same time. Apparently, it was common practice for them to allow guests to get food first. I was perfectly fine with that. The food looked amazing and smelled even better. Roast, mashed potatoes, gravy, rolls, green beans, brussel sprouts, tri-tip, and some kind of fish were all on my plate.

My stomach demanded it be filled with the food, which turned out to taste just as amazing as it smelled. When I scraped the last food off my plate, Rhys took it and added another roll, green beans, and some more potatoes and gravy. He had been doing things like this a lot recently, knowing what I wanted without me saying it. Obviously, it was the bond, but it felt incredibly one sided since I never knew what he wanted unless it was poking me. Heh.

He set the plate down and then chuckled. "I did it again, didn't I?" he asked.

"Yes," I said and patted his hand. "Thank you."

"It's not a conscious decision," he said.

"I know."

I ate my food, enjoying the buttery goodness of the roll slowly.

"She eats a lot for a human," Rhian muttered.

"You'll see why," Emrys told her. "Make sure you drink that glass of water," he told me.

I obeyed, chugging the entire glass before wiping my mouth and smiling at him. "Thank you. That was delicious."

"I'm glad you liked it. Now, let's go outside," he said and stood. Rhys pulled out my chair, but Emrys took my arm before he could.

"Even my own father," Rhys said with a sigh.

Andras laughed and patted him on the back.

We went out a door that I had not seen in the corner of the living room. It led to a rose garden, and just beyond that, a huge fighting arena. A fenced in area large enough for two fully shifted dragons to fight.

"Clear the area!" Emrys ordered everyone.

This time, the order didn't touch me.

"Thanks," I whispered, not sure if it was him or Rhys.

"I can direct it if I think about it," Emrys told me.

"That's handy," I said.

"Especially when you have this many children," he grumbled.

"How do you feel?" Rhys asked me.

"I feel great. Why?"

"He wants you to shift," Rhys said, meaning his father wanted me to shift forms.

"Dragon or wolf?" I asked.

"You can shift forms?" Andras asked.

Emrys's orders had been carried out and only the family and I were at the arena now. "Please, show them," he requested.

Rhys picked me up and jumped over the arena fence in one leap, landing on bent knees on the other side. He set me down and leaned back against the fence.

I walked farther away from him, still not sure of my exact size, and then focused on Rhys through our bond. The bond I had, forked off four different ways, all connected to my heart. I followed the line to Rhys and the magic he carried, which was wild, like Deryn's, but more fierce, and with a lot more fire.

I closed my eyes and let the change come. When I had finished shifting, I opened my eyes and Rhys walked to me. I lowered my head and he set his hand on my snout. "You're gorgeous," he whispered and stroked his hand from my nostril, up over my eye, down my neck, and stopped at my shoulder.

"Holy shit!" Rhian yelled. "She turned into one of us!"

"I've never seen scales that color before," Andras commented. "Can I come in?"

I thought he was asking me, but it was Rhys who nodded. "Yes, you are all welcome to come."

Emrys jumped in first and walked to me, staring into my eyes. "Even her eyes are different. They're very similar to yours though, Rhys."

"How is this possible?" Mawrth asked. "She smells like a human."

"She is a human," Rhys explained. "Since she is human, when we made her our queen, she joined our bond instead of us making a true queen's bond with her. This allowed her the ability to access our powers."

"Can she fly?" Rhian asked.

"She can, but she isn't fond of it, yet," Rhys said with a smirk.

"Can she breathe fire?" Gavin asked.

I huffed smoke out of my nostrils and Rhys chuckled. "Yes, she can."

"You can shift back," Emrys told me.

I shifted back and then covered my body in scales. "I can also do this, and this." This time, I half shifted, a warrior's shift. I enjoyed Rhys's equally surprised face, a replica of his siblings'.

"I didn't know you could do this," Emrys said and poked at my scales.

"Neither did I," Rhys growled at me.

I let my body revert and exhaled, tired from using so much energy. "It's a lot harder to hold," I told them.

"When did you discover you could do this?" Rhys asked.

"Last night," I admitted. "On accident."

"When the boss killed you the third time we tried to beat the raid, right?" he asked.

I nodded. How had he known that? I mean, I know I had cussed up a storm on the mic.

"I felt your anger and thought I felt you more distinctly in our bond, but wasn't sure," he admitted.

"I can't even do that," Brenin grumbled.

"Can you shift into the wolf warrior form?" Rhian asked.

I nodded. "I can, but I used up a lot of my energy taking the dragon warrior form just now. I need at least five minutes to recover."

"You don't need to shift anymore," Emrys told me.

"So, if one of us takes a human as a queen, they'll have our abilities," Brenin said while looking at Emrys.

Emrys nodded. "Yes."

"So, this was to show us, so that we don't make the same mistake as Rhys, right?" Mawrth asked.

"No, this is just to let you know this is possible," Emrys said with a soft sigh. "I swear I raised them to be polite children, Jolie. I blame their mother."

"This was not a mistake," Rhys said.

"Sort of," I whispered under my breath while looking up at the sky.

Rhys growled, but didn't rise to my bait.

"They are very cynical," Emrys said. "It is good to understand the negative in everything, or the possible negatives, so you are prepared for all circumstances. However, they should also understand that some things are shown so they understand what happens, not in a negative way."

"It's okay," I told him and smiled at everyone. "I don't take offense."

"It doesn't excuse them from being rude," Rhys growled at them.

"We're sorry," all five of the younger siblings said.

"Come on, let's show her the rest of our den," Andras suggested.

"Why did we have to swear an oath of silence?" Rhian asked.

"Because it is not public knowledge that Rhys and the other three princes have a queen. We are keeping it quiet. We don't want the media finding out," Emrys told them. "So, you are forbidden from telling anyone. As far as anyone knows, she is simply the Princess of the Four Clans. Understood?"

"Yes, Father," all six of Rhys's siblings said.

CHAPTER 2

We ended up flying to the next part of the den, which was fun because I got to ride on Rhys's back and look at everything as we flew. The den was huge-- hundreds, maybe thousands, of acres in size. They had their own city within the city of Jinla. Amazing.

There was a large building in the very center, which Rhys said was like their city hall where the family heard disputes and prosecuted those accused of crimes. Each clan was allowed their own legal system, but if the crimes were serious enough and happened in the human city they turned the dragon over to the human courts. Rhys said that it had only happened a few times in fifty years.

There were several apartment complexes, housing tracks, and a few other houses far out in the wilderness areas. They raised their own animals for food and grew their own crops too. That explained the real reason he had never been to a human grocery store before.

I still needed to take them on trips to all of the human places I discovered they had never experienced. It was important for them to understand humans, even if I hadn't met them. Even though they had gone to a grocery store already, I needed to show them the joy of grocery stores with bulk food areas. The second place I wanted to take them was the movie theater, though I hadn't decided between the regular theater and the drive-in theater. I knew that they would get a kick out of both of them. Third was the zoo. We just had to be sure to keep Rhys and Deryn a distance away from the animals so that they didn't frighten them.

We landed in the center of their market area. There were vendors selling produce, meats, seafood, crafts, jewelry, and some cooking various foods and treats.

"You have to try the sweet bread," Gavin said and jogged towards one of the vendors selling pastries.

"It's a whole other world here," I whispered to Rhys.

"Yes. There are many who never go out into Jinla," he whispered back to me.

"So, they never meet anyone outside of dragons?" I asked. That didn't seem like a great way to raise children, never introducing them to the other beings that were out there. Yes, there was evil, but there was also so much to learn from the other races.

"We encourage them to venture beyond our gates, even offer field trips for those schooled here, but there are many who choose to stay here," Emrys told me. "We discuss all the other races and ensure they understand that there are good and evil in all races and no one race is all evil."

"Except vampires," I whispered to myself.

Rhys put his arms around me and hugged me into his chest. "I'm sorry," he whispered.

"Don't be sorry. You saved me from them multiple times," I mumbled into his chest and wiped my tears on his shirt.

"Here," Gavin said, pulling me out of my reverie.

I stepped back from Rhys, reminding myself that we were

supposed to be keeping our relationship secret. "What's this?" I asked and accepted the pastry Gavin held out to me.

"Take a bite," Gavin encouraged me.

Rhys nodded that it was safe.

I took a bite and moaned. "This is amazing."

Gavin, Emrys, and Rhys smiled at my reaction.

"I told you," Gavin said with a wide smile and took a huge bite of his.

"I guess I'll need to start ordering these for delivery," Rhys said.

"Lots," I replied and finished eating the one Gavin had given me.

"Oh, let's try the meat stick next!" Gavin said and started to rush off, but looked back at me expectantly.

I squeezed Rhys's forearm, then ran with Gavin to get in line for the next vendor.

"I don't have any cash," I told Gavin.

"Don't worry," he assured me. "I've got money."

It was strange to see Gavin and think that Rhys may have been like him as a teenager. Rhys had been raised in this very area.

"What's your favorite thing to do in the den?" I asked Gavin.

"The festivals," he answered immediately. "They're full of fun and action. You should come to our next one! Our fall festival and is in just a few weeks. You would enjoy it, I know you would. If my eldest brother won't bring you, just talk to Dad. I'm sure he'll let you come. I'll show you around if Rhys isn't here," he offered.

"That is a very generous offer," I said with a smile.

"Well, I can tell that my brother cares for you. That must mean you are a special female. He never really showed affection for other females. But, it's like he's drawn to you. Like magnets."

That was partly due to our bond. One of the reasons I considered breaking the bond was to see if they really were in love with me and drawn to me because of me and not the bond.

"I'm pretty drawn to your brother too," I whispered and glanced at Rhys who was watching me with a smirk on his face while Emrys talked to him.

The line finally moved and we were at the front. Gavin ordered for me and then handed me one of the sticks that had a few different types of meat on it, with some with sauce dribbled on them.

"Go on," he encouraged.

I tried a bite from each of the meats and smiled at him. "These are great!"

His smile widened and his chest puffed out a bit. "I told you."

"Can we go look at the vendors?" I asked. "Christmas is coming up and I think I saw something that would work great for one of my friends."

"Sure," Gavin said and led the way. People moved out of his way without him even saying anything, which made it much easier for me to get through them. Rhys caught up to us and walked behind me.

"What's up?" I asked him, glancing back.

"Nothing. I just wanted to walk with you. If that's alright?"

I reached out and squeezed his hand. "Great." A few females glared at my hand touching Rhys, so I lowered it and faced Gavin again, as he made his way to the first vendor who sold hand-crafted items.

"Good afternoon, Princes," the woman behind the table greeted them. She looked to be in her late sixties, but that could mean she was two hundred years old since she was a shifter. "And greetings to their friend."

"Hello, Estella," Rhys said and smiled at her. She picked up a bag that had some tissue paper in it and handed it to Rhys. "Is this my full order?" he asked, peeking into the bag.

She nodded. "Yes. I made sure to follow your guidelines and specifications exactly."

He handed her some money and bowed his head respectfully to her. "Thank you."

"Thank you, for your patronage."

The items she sold were mostly knitted and crocheted beanies and gloves. I eyed one of the knitted scarves, but reminded myself that I was not supposed to be here buying things for me.

"Your items are lovely," I told her with a warm smile.

She smiled in return. "Thank you."

We moved on to the next booth with a younger man selling daggers. I picked up one of the smaller, thinner daggers and admired the design etched into it. "This is gorgeous," I whispered and showed it to Rhys.

"Rhys," the man greeted him.

Rhys nodded at him. "Afternoon, Felix."

"Who have you brought to my booth? You rarely have visitors," Felix said with an arched eyebrow.

"Jolie, this is Felix. Felix, this is Jolie, Princess of the Four Clans."

Felix's eyes widened and he dropped his head in a bow. "Apologies, I didn't know-"

"Please, don't treat me any differently than you do Rhys," I said quickly. "Though, I would like to know how much this dagger is."

"Fifty," Felix said right away.

"What are you going to do with that dagger?" Rhys asked me.

"It's not for me. I was thinking it would make a good present for Fox," I admitted to him.

Rhys smiled. "It would make a good present for him."

"Can you bring me back tomorrow?" I asked Rhys. "I didn't bring cash with me, since I didn't realize I would be shopping."

"You can pay me back when we get home," Rhys offered and handed Felix money. Felix took the dagger from me and wrapped it up, put it into a wooden box, and then put that into a small brown paper bag.

"Thank you. This is just what I was looking for, for him," I told Felix.

He bowed his head. "I'm glad to have been of service."

"I'll just make you a tab and you can pay me back or work it off," Rhys whispered so softly into my ear that I almost didn't hear him.

I gaped at him, shocked that he would flirt with me to that magnitude in the den…in public. "You're shameless."

He winked. "I thought you knew that by now."

"What did you say to make her blush like that?" Gavin asked.

"Nothing," I gasped and hurried to the next vendor.

Rhys picked up a few more orders from vendors we went to, and I found a few more Christmas presents for the other guys. I still had no idea what I was going to get Rhys. Honestly, if I hadn't known that the guys would be happy with whatever I got them, I would have zero idea what to get them. What do you get four rich princes who can purchase whatever they want?

Rhys bought a basket of strawberries and we shared them as we perused more vendors. One jewelry vendor in particular caught my eye and I was mesmerized by the rings she had. Not the rings for women though, but the rings for the men. They were made of a gorgeous, dark metal that shone in the sun.

"Thinking of proposing to someone?" the vendor, a man who looked about thirty, asked me.

"No," I said quickly, not glancing at Rhys. "I just find these incredibly beautiful."

"Thank you," he said with a wide smile. "I make them myself from a type of metal that will never break and so, you can't get them resized ever. You have to make certain that the ring you buy is in the correct size."

"How much are they?" I asked out of sheer curiosity.

"Hello, Paul," Rhys greeted the vendor. "What's she hounding you about over here?"

"Nothing," I replied quickly. "Just telling him how much I admire his work. The jewelry is gorgeous."

Rhys nodded. "He has some of the best jewelry."

"Can you get me something to drink?" I asked Rhys. "I'm really thirsty after all of that food."

He nodded and went towards one of the food vendors who had bottles of water.

"Four hundred per ring," Paul whispered quickly to me. "However, since you're a friend of the Prince's, I will drop the price to three hundred."

"They're gorgeous, but I'm not sure if they're going to work for what I have in mind. Do you have a website or something?" I asked and glanced quickly back to see Rhys heading our way.

"Here's my business card. It has my website, email address, and phone number," Paul said softly. Then, louder, he said, "I hope to see you again soon, miss. Have a wonderful day."

I tucked the card into the bag of my other presents and smiled at him. "Thank you."

Rhys handed me my water and I took a huge drink of it, glad I had asked him to get me some because I truly was thirsty after eating a bunch of sweets and meat.

"I still haven't decided what to get you for Christmas," Rhys told me as we headed toward Emrys, who was waiting on the outskirts of the market area.

"You don't have to get me anything. I've got all I want at home," I said and glanced at him with a smirk.

"I'm going to get you a present. I'm just trying to figure out what is the best gift to give you," he said with a smile and put a hand on my back as he guided me around a small crowd in front of a vendor.

"Something under a hundred dollars," I muttered.

He laughed loudly, his head thrown back, and eyes closed for a moment. "That's hilarious."

I put my hands on my hips and glared at him. "What is so funny?"

"There's no way that you're going to keep us from spending what we want on you. I know the amounts some of the others have spent already, and let's just say that your number is miniscule."

"It's not fair," I whispered. "I don't have a lot of money to spend on you guys."

"We don't need anything."

"Neither do I," I growled and faced him.

"She's talking back to Prince Rhys," someone said in the crowd.

"Does she not know who he is?" another person asked.

"I'm sorry," I whispered to Rhys and walked towards Emrys, feeling like an idiot for forgetting that we were in his clan's home, with tons of people watching our every move. I shouldn't speak to him like I do at home.

Rhys grabbed my arm, spun me around to face him, dipped me to the side, and kissed me deeply. There were gasps, shocked murmurs, and some laughs.

When he pulled back and set me upright, I stared at him in disbelief. "Why did you do that?" I whispered softly to him.

"I just felt like kissing my girlfriend," he told me and took my hand in his.

Girlfriend? Royalty didn't usually have girlfriends, especially not Other royalty.

"Girlfriend?" someone asked.

Rhys tugged on our joined hands and I stumbled after him, looking at Emrys in shock and worry.

"That's one way to go with things," Emrys whispered and chuckled. "Now, they will just think that you're taking the human route for your relationship, since she's human. And it will allow you to touch her more in public. Pretty smart, kid."

"I have my moments," Rhys replied and stroked his thumb across the back of my hand.

"I don't understand what happened," I whispered. "You guys don't do girlfriends."

"Well, we *do* girlfriends, but not like you're talking about," Rhys teased.

"No, we generally don't, but Rhys has never done things like the majority of us," Andras said. "Normally after we graduate, we don't have girlfriends any longer. Girlfriends are more of a teenage experience for us, since we aren't allowed to have sex until after we graduate. But, since Rhys said you're his girlfriend now, it will spread around the clan and you won't have potential suitors coming after you. Or females, who want Rhys, coming after you for your head."

"I thought we were keeping our relationship secret?" I asked Rhys and glanced at Emrys.

"We were, but I am tired of not being able to touch you. This was an easy way around all of that," Rhys explained and shrugged his shoulders. "Plus, aren't you my girlfriend?"

"I guess," I whispered. "I hadn't really thought about it in those terms."

"Well, now you have," 'he said with a wide smile.

"Why didn't you think of it before?" I asked. "It seems like such a simple solution."

"I'm not perfect," he said with a smirk. "No matter how many times you tell me I am."

"I meant your body was perfect, not you," I teased and spun away from him with Andras and Emrys laughing behind me.

Rhys followed me, his presence causing the hairs on the back of my neck to rise since there was a predator stalking us now.

"Still hungry?" Gavin asked from the line he was standing in.

"What are you getting?" I asked him, ignoring Rhys.

"Sweet bread," he said and licked his lips.

"I want two," I said with a wide smile.

"I'll pay," Rhys told Gavin. "She'll eat your savings dry."

"Did you just insinuate that I'm fat?" I asked and spun to face him.

He startled me by grabbing me and pulling me against him, his face inches from mine. "You know I didn't, you brat."

"You're in so much trouble when we get home," I whispered to him, trying very hard to swallow my arousal and failing miserably.

He chuckled, the deep sound vibrating through my body and traveling south to cause a warmth I didn't want to experience with his teenage brother right next to us. "You're the one who is in trouble," he told me and nipped the tip of my nose.

"Ouch," I grumbled and rubbed my nose as I pushed away from him. Arousal gone.

"Can I get a dozen breads now and two dozen to go?" Rhys ordered.

"Certainly, Prince Rhys," the baker replied.

"Are you staying for dinner?" Gavin asked me.

I looked at Rhys. "I don't know. Are we?"

"No, we have plans tonight," Rhys told Gavin.

"We do?" I asked, not remembering us making plans.

"We're going out with the guys tonight," he informed me. "Didn't Fox tell you?"

He might have told me, but I was most likely a few drinks deep when he did. "I think he told me something around the middle of the raid, but I was drinking by then and…"

"Ah, you were drunk," Rhys chuckled.

"She plays video games?" Gavin asked, his mouth popped open.

"More than I do," Rhys said.

"That's so hot!" Gavin exclaimed.

"Little brother, you need to work on your inappropriate

comments," Andras chastised him and gently tapped the back of his head.

"I'm right," Gavin told him. "You know I am. Finding a girl who plays games instead of trying to get you off of them is super rare."

"She's a rarity, alright," Rhys said and winked at me.

"Here you go," the baker said and held out a bag with the two dozen he had ordered to go and a box with the one dozen for now.

I opened the one dozen and took three before handing the box to Gavin. Rhys snagged the rolls from me and I pouted at him. "Hey!"

He held them up over his head, way too high for me to be able to reach. "You have to pay for these," he said and walked back towards his father.

"What price?" I asked and tried to jump up and grab his arm to force it down, but he easily dodged my attempt.

He turned and bent so that his face was level with mine. "One kiss."

"If I must," I said with a dramatic sigh. I pecked him on the cheek and managed to grab one of the rolls from him and run behind Emrys to eat it.

"Cheater," Rhys said, but he was smiling wide and his family was amused as well. Before I could respond, Rhys shoved both of the rolls in his mouth and chewed them up.

"Those were mine!" I gaped at him.

He shrugged. "Maybe next time you'll pay the toll."

"I'm going to come back without you one of these days and buy them. Then you won't be able to stop me," I threatened him.

"I'll keep her company when she comes," Andras said and draped an arm across my shoulders. "She'll be perfectly safe."

Rhys growled and his eyes shifted to his dragon's eyes.

"Rhys," Emrys growled a warning at him.

"And I thought Deryn was bad," I grumbled.

Andras hadn't moved, more accurately, he had frozen at Rhys's growl.

"Sounds like we've got a plan," I said with a wide smile. "I'll come back, Andras will keep me safe, and I'll eat all the sweet bread I can without making myself sick."

Rhys blinked twice and his eyes reverted. "Sorry."

"When do we have to leave today?" I asked Rhys, hoping the subject change would keep him from getting angry about Andras *still* touching me.

Rhys looked at his phone and said, "We should probably head back now."

"Already?" I sighed. I stood up on my tiptoes and kissed Andras's cheek. "Thanks for an entertaining day."

His mouth opened for a moment, but he quickly recovered and smiled. "Come back whenever you want."

I hugged Emrys. "Thanks for forcing his hand, so I could visit. I had a lot of fun learning about your clan today."

"I'd like you to come back and train with us," he told me. "There's a lot of skills we can teach you that Rhys can't show you when the others are around."

That sounded slightly terrifying.

"Okay."

"You're serious?" Rhian asked, appearing out of thin air.

"Rhian, what have we discussed about you questioning me?" Emrys asked her.

"I'm not questioning you, father. I'm questioning that you're actually going to teach her family secrets. She's not his mate."

"Rhian, come here," Rhys ordered her.

I thought she might argue, but she followed him as they walked away from the crowds to a secluded area that was still within our sight. She had her arms folded across her chest defiantly, but as Rhys spoke to her, she slowly lowered them. He didn't appear to be yelling at her or angry, since his face was relaxed and he kept occasionally smirking. She glanced at me and then looked back at him and nodded once. I thought she would come back, but instead she shifted and flew away.

"What was that about?" Andras asked Rhys.

"Just some brother sister heart to heart," he told us. "You ready to go?" he asked me.

I nodded.

"If he tries to keep you away again, just text me and I'll send a team in to steal you," Emrys called after me.

"Thanks!" I called back and waved to him.

Rhys sighed and handed the boxes of bread to me. "You fit in way too well here."

"You should be happy that your family likes me so much. Well, not your mom." It actually stung quite a bit that she seemed to hate me, even after I had opened up to her.

"She'll learn to love you. She's very protective of me."

He shifted and we flew back to the apartment instead of taking a car from the mansion. I was going to ask him why, but relaxed on his back and watched the city fly by beneath us. Millions of people lived here with different lives and different circumstances. What would they be doing if I hadn't moved here?

The wind pressing against me was cold, and I was glad I had worn a jacket, but it wasn't helping my face any. Rhys's body beneath me grew warmer and I lay down on my stomach, pressing my cheek to his warm scales.

"Thank you," I called as loudly as I could. A deep rumble beneath my cheek was his response. He landed on the roof of the apartment building and I slid down his foreleg, landing on my feet with the boxes still safely in my arms.

"That was fun," I told him as I waited for him to shift back. "I think they'd be fun to be around, once they aren't so negative."

"They're always negative," Rhys said and tried to grab the boxes.

I spun away from him with a smirk. "No. You have to pay the fee."

He caught my body with his arms, caging me in against his body. "Okay."

I tilted my head back and he brushed his lips across mine gently.

After releasing me, he took the boxes I offered, opened the door and started down the stairs to the second floor toward my apartment.

"Jolie," Rhys called.

I stopped in front of the door that opened to my floor. "Huh?"

He set the boxes down and asked, "Did you mean what you said to my mother?"

I nodded.

"Are you still considering breaking the bond?"

His fists were clenched, and he stared into my eyes with a frightening intensity.

I turned and took his hands in both of mine. "I know I'm not worthy of you four. I know this, but I am selfish. I don't want to give you up. The thought occasionally flitters across my mind, but I've decided that I will not break the bond. I love you and hurting you by breaking the bond is not something I want to do. To you or to me."

"How can I show you that you are worthy of us? What do I need to do to prove that to you?" he asked. Gently, he stroked his knuckles down my cheek.

"Self-esteem isn't usually an issue for me," I admitted to him. "I like to think that I am practical about how I look. But, when it comes to being the mate of not just one prince, but four? I'm just a weird human girl who plays games too much. That doesn't sound like someone fit to be your mate."

"What should my mate be like?" he asked.

"Strong. Fierce. Powerful. Someone who will produce heirs for you. I don't know if I want children. And if I do decide to have children, I'm going to have to worry about there being four of you who need heirs."

"Heirs aren't a deal breaker," he told me.

"It's still something to consider. Right now, it might not be a deal breaker, but what about in five years or-"

"I love you. I want you at my side for the rest of my life. I want you as my life partner."

"Well, the rest of my life. You all live much longer than me. That's the other issue. If we become mates, my death is going to be so much more painful and-"

He stepped back from me and sighed. "I really wish you wouldn't talk about your death like that."

"Like what?"

"Like it is a sure thing."

"Everyone dies, Rhys."

"Yes, but you make it sound like you're going to die soon."

"I could. You know what my life has been like. I'm always in danger."

He picked up the boxes and opened the door for me. "You are a handful."

I expected to find at least one of the others in my apartment, but it was empty. "Where is everyone?" I asked Rhys.

He set the boxes on my counter and I quickly stole two more pieces of bread while he dialed one of their numbers. He held the phone up to his ear for a bit and then looked at it strangely before dialing another number. He repeated the process again.

"They're not answering. That's not like them."

"Do you think something's happened?" I asked nervously.

"Yes, but the issue is figuring out what has happened," he whispered and then began furiously typing on his phone. After a minute of silence, he said, "Oh, shit."

"What is it?"

"There's a monster attacking the city. They're out there trying to stop it." He showed me a photo of the three of them standing in front of what looked like a huge ogre with tusks as big as their bodies.

"We need to go help them!" I yelled and moved towards the door.

"You're not doing anything. We can't risk you getting hurt," he told me.

"I'm not staying here. If you try to leave me behind, I will just follow you at a distance."

Our defiant stares met and I could practically see sparks between us.

"Fine, but you have to promise to use your scales and shield. And stay out of the way," he ordered me.

I nodded. "Yes, sir."

He growled, and we hurried back to the roof where he shifted and we flew to the park. Rhys set me down a few blocks away, but still within eyesight of the fight. I stood against a building and set scales over my heart and the back of my head and formed a shield like Nico had taught me.

Deryn was in warrior form and I watched in disbelief as he used his claws to crawl up the back of the giant ogre and began tearing into his back. The ogre bellowed and tried to grab Deryn, but he dodged the ogre's attempted grabs easily.

Nico fired a few different spells at the ogre, making it drop to one knee. Fox used his sword to cut at the ogre, but I could tell that the sword wasn't doing much damage, despite Fox's skill.

Rhys dropped from the sky in his dragon form and wrapped his mouth around the ogre's throat. The ogre yowled and tried to pry Rhys's mouth open, but his sharp teeth dug in. The other three increased their work, taking advantage of Rhys's immobilization of the ogre.

A small child wandered by me, mesmerized by the fight and out into the street. I ran out to the child as her mother screamed and grabbed her. I glanced up and screamed at the hell hound's snout right in front of my face.

What was a hell hound doing here? They were only able to

come to this side with a demon's summoning, but I didn't see any demons around.

Deryn slammed into the side of the hell hound and sent it flying into the side of the building where I had been. I wrapped my body protectively around the child and then picked her up.

"Hey, beautiful," Deryn said, then ran to continue fighting the hell hound, which was definitely not down yet.

"Don't get hurt!" I ordered him.

"Yes, my queen!" he called back and punched the hell hound on his nose. The hell hound made a terrible, high-pitched squeal of pain, sounding just like a dog when it's hurt.

The child's mother ran to me and I dropped my shield so she could take her. "Thank you!" she yelled and hugged her child to her. "Thank you, so much."

"Jolie!" Nico screamed at me.

I spun around and had just enough time to put up the shield around the mother, child, and me before the ogre slammed into it with his fists, trying to squash us.

"Fuck you!" I screamed at him.

"Let us out!" the mother screamed.

"I'm protecting you, you moron," I growled at her and backed up slowly, keeping her within my shield as we moved towards the building's entrance. Once there, I dropped my shield so she could carry her child inside to safety.

The ogre grabbed me in his giant hand and screamed in my face.

"Jolie!" Nico yelled.

"I'm fine!" I yelled back and stared into the ogre's eyes. "Put. Me. Down."

The ogre snarled at me and tried to tighten his grip around my body, but I'd changed everything below my neck to scales. He looked confused a moment and then threw me as hard as he could towards the park.

"Rhys! Incoming!" Deryn yelled and ran slightly behind me.

Rhys shifted just in time to catch me and wrapped his body around mine, so that when we landed, I landed on top of him. We slid several feet and then he released me.

"You okay?" I asked him.

"I told you, you should have stayed home."

"That child would have been killed!" I yelled at him.

"Now is not the time!" Nico reminded us, his staff glowing as we faced the ogre, the hell hound who had tried to attack me, and two goblins.

"What the hell is going on?" I demanded.

"A portal was opened to the other realm," Nico said. "I've been trying to close it, but it's taking me a while."

"Can I help?" I asked him.

"Come touch me," he ordered me.

"This is not the time for that," Rhys growled at him.

"Jolie," Nico grunted.

I rushed to his side and placed my hands on his bare forearms. Our connection opened and suddenly, I felt Nico use the connection to take magic from me. I gasped in shock and my grip tightened on his arm.

"Protect them!" Rhys ordered Deryn and Fox.

"You don't have to tell us," Deryn growled and punched the hell hound back.

"Almost there," Nico whispered and I could see it. It was a faint, shimmering oval in the air in front of us. It looked like a tear, but on the other side, I could see fire and several dark bodies moving. How many more would come if we didn't close the portal?

"Nico," I whispered, feeling lightheaded.

"Almost," he grunted.

I would pass out if I let him keep taking my power. I had to do something.

The necklace! I took one hand from Nico's arm and wrapped it around the necklace. Instantly, the power poured through me and into Nico. It felt like lava pouring through my veins, and I would have screamed if I had been able to breathe. His back arched and he gasped, but quickly recovered and used the power to close the portal. Once it was closed, I dropped my hand, breaking contact with Nico, and fell in the grass onto my butt.

"Shit, that hurt," I growled.

"Not out of hot water yet," Rhys growled.

I turned my head and watched Deryn and Rhys pummeling the ogre with their fists, pushing it further and further away from me.

"I got this," Nico said, his eyes glowing with power and his feet floating above the ground. He pointed his staff at the ogre and it disintegrated instantly.

"What the-" Rhys gaped.

"Did he just-" Deryn asked.

"Yeah," Rhys replied.

Fox picked me up and carried me away from the park and towards our building. "Are you alright?" he asked me

"Tired," I whispered and leaned my head against his shoulder. "Siphoning the magic from the necklace to Nico hurt. A lot."

"Are you still in pain?"

"No."

"How was your day at the dragon's den?" he asked.

"No. No. You had a giant ogre attacking you. You tell me what happened first."

"Not much to tell," he admitted. "We were walking home from Deryn's pizza parlor and the ogre and hound started attacking people. We kept them from hurting anyone, but we weren't really making any headway until you and Rhys came."

"His mom doesn't like me," I told Fox softly.

He kissed the top of my head. "She hates everyone, especially if they have contact with her precious baby, Rhys. She's always favored him and in her opinion, everyone is worthless and has no business talking to him."

"Emrys had me show them that I could shift into a dragon and his family thought it was to explain the consequences of the mistake Rhys had made, so that they wouldn't repeat the mistake."

I hadn't realized how much their reactions had hurt my feelings until talking to Fox. He was great at listening and I could really open up to him about anything.

"You're not a mistake," he told him firmly. "I'm sure Rhys already told you that his family is super negative in general."

"Gavin was the only one who liked me."

"I'm sure Andras liked you too," Fox replied.

I looked up and saw his smirk. "Rhys went all 'Deryn' on him for draping his arm across my shoulders and saying he would protect me if I visited without Rhys."

"'Went all 'Deryn'?" Deryn asked. "Why is my name being used as a verb now?"

"Because you were the first one to get super jealous," I explained.

"I have every reason to get jealous," Rhys said, the rest of them having caught up to us at some point.

"No, you don't."

"If I didn't set the ground rules now, he would be doing everything in his power to steal you from us," Rhys assured me.

"Oh, yes. Because I'm such a prize," I said and rolled my eyes. "You're all so ridiculous."

"He's most likely right," Fox said.

"Hey, you're supposed to be the neutral party here," I grumbled.

"Right. Sorry. So, what else happened?"

"I ate a ton of food. I bought a few presents. And, Rhys announced me as his girlfriend."

Fox stopped walking so abruptly, I almost fell out of his arms, but he held on to me. "You did what?" he asked and spun around to face Rhys who was looking rather sheepish at the moment.

"Well, it just sort of happened. I wasn't planning it or anything," Rhys admitted.

"You announced her as your girlfriend?" Nico asked.

Rhys nodded.

"You asshole," he growled.

"What's wrong?" I asked them.

"We can't all claim you as our girlfriend," Nico informed me. "So, right now the clan, and whoever they tell, thinks you're just his girlfriend."

"Which means, that we aren't supposed to touch you as freely as we usually do," Fox said and set me on my feet with a scowl at Rhys.

"I'm sorry. She was walking with my brothers and I wanted to touch her, but I couldn't and it was driving me insane," Rhys told them.

"How do you think I feel every time she comes to the pack?" Deryn growled at him.

"Guys, this isn't a conversation for outdoors," I whispered, noticing that we were growing an audience.

All four of them resumed walking, storming by me and glaring at each other, even Rhys was glaring. *Oh boy.* I'd definitely stirred the pot on that one. I had no idea they would react that way or that what they said was true. *Whoops.*

CHAPTER 3

"How could you do that?" Deryn growled at Rhys as he paced back and forth in front of my television.

"I apologized and told you that it wasn't on purpose or premeditated." Rhys said again.

"This changes everything!" Nico yelled at him.

"No, it doesn't," he said. "You three can announce her as your girlfriend too."

"That lie will crumble faster than elf bread," Fox snapped.

"It's not technically a lie," I said, finally joining into the conversation.

"What?" Fox asked.

"You guys are all, technically, my boyfriends. We aren't married. We aren't mated. Yes, we're bound, but aside from that, we are dating. So, really, we are boyfriend and girlfriend." Not that I liked the idea of people hearing that I had four boyfriends. The humans would definitely get the wrong idea.

"If we tell them that, we might as well tell them that you're our queen," Nico argued. "It will spread to the news faster than wildfire."

"He's right," Rhys agreed solemnly.

"And why aren't we telling people that I'm your queen, again?" I asked softly, waiting for one of them to blow up.

None did.

"Because, it could make you an even bigger target. By hurting you, they'll be hurting us, and they will use that to their advantage," Nico explained.

"Won't they do the same with me as Rhys's girlfriend?"

"No, they won't think it will hurt him. Piss him off, sure, but it won't physically or emotionally hurt him for a girlfriend to be killed," Nico said, blunt as ever.

"Glad girlfriends don't count for anything," I muttered and reached for a sweet bread, but Fox smacked my hand.

"We're going out to eat. You'll ruin your appetite," he told me.

"Fine. I'm going to shower," I grumbled and then spun around and said, "and none of you can join me!"

They laughed behind me until I started the water. They were probably still laughing, but the water drowned them out. There was more dirt on me than I realized. I had to wash my hair three times to get it clean. After changing and putting on a bit of makeup, I was finally ready to go and came out to discover all of them gone.

"Hello?" I called. They didn't usually leave me alone without telling me where they were going or where I could find one of them.

I grabbed my ID card and bank card, then peeked my head out into the hallway, but they weren't there either. None of them answered their phones or returned my texts. I sat in my apartment for five minutes, fretting, then finally decided to go search their apartments. We'd recently given each other copies of our apartment keys, so we could get into all of the apartments if there was an emergency. Fox's apartment was empty. So were Nico and Deryn's. I went to the first floor and knocked on Rhys's apartment.

"Hello?" I called.

"Looking for us?" Rhys asked behind me.

I spun around and my jaw dropped open. The four of them wore tailored-to-fit tuxedos. They also all had half face masks on.

"What?"

"You're a bit underdressed," Deryn commented.

"We took care of that though," Rhys assured me. "In my bedroom, you'll find your gown. Hurry, or we'll be late and all the food will be gone."

"Where are we going?" I asked, still drooling over their appearances.

"To a masquerade ball, obviously," Nico chuckled.

"But-"

"No more talking. Go!" Rhys ordered me.

I obeyed, hurrying into the apartment and to Rhys's bedroom where a gorgeous emerald dress hung on the back of the door. It fit perfectly, reminding me of the dress Fox had purchased for me. I slipped on the matching shoes and picked up the mask on his dresser. My mask only covered my eyes, but had gorgeous swirls with diamonds accenting the corners. I tied it on and admired myself in the mirror. I looked amazing. Like a real princess.

I hesitated just a second before walking out of Rhys's apartment and doing a slow twirl for the guys, who all looked appropriately pleased.

"You look perfect," Rhys said and kissed the back of my hand.

"You look like a goddess," Deryn said and bowed to me.

"Come on," Nico urged us. "Our ride is here."

Nico took my hand and placed it on his arm, escorting me outside to a long, black limousine.

"A limo?" I gasped. "I've never ridden in one before."

"Oh?" he asked. "Well, next time I'll have to make sure it's just you and me, so I can show you the real fun to be had inside of a limo."

"If only we didn't have plans tonight," Deryn teased me, "we could show you a good time now."

"Ah, but then the dress would be ruined," Rhys sighed. "So, we must restrain ourselves."

"You guys don't share, remember?" I told them with an eyeroll.

"We might if you were the only one being pleasured," Nico whispered into my ear.

I shivered and felt my cheeks warm. *Oh. My. Goddess. Did he? They had!* They never discussed doing sexual things together. I wasn't really into guy on guy action, but the thought of more than one of them touching me at the same time was a *huge* turn on. I clenched my legs together tightly as I sat inside of the limo, trying to keep my hormones at bay. I took a deep breath, and grew serious.

"Should I be prepared for an attack at this dance?" I asked them softly.

Nico patted my arm. "No. This time, you do not need to be worried about anyone attempting to hurt you."

"That's what we said last time," Fox muttered. "Then she got stabbed."

"You'll only be dancing with the four of us," Rhys said. "So, no one will get close enough to hurt you."

I nodded, feeling the tension slip away. Once focused on the task at hand, excitement began building in my stomach.

"I've never been to a masquerade ball!" I told them and tried not to bounce in my seat.

"They're a lot of fun," Deryn assured me. "Lots of eating and then lots of dancing."

"We go to this one every year," Nico said. "It's a fundraiser for one of the orphanages."

"Oh, that's nice," I said, wondering why I didn't know they donated and did events like this.

We arrived at the Galleria, a huge building used for events

that cost thousands of dollars to attend. I shuddered, thinking how much money they had paid for all of us to go. Rhys stepped out first, standing on a red carpet with media on each side, cameras flashing as they snapped pictures. Deryn got out next, then Fox, and I realized they were forming the diamond of protection, as I lovingly named it. Their formation shielding me from potential attacks and kept me hidden within their towering heights.

"Ready, beautiful?" Nico asked and kissed my cheek.

"Is my mask on right?" I asked and checked the bow I had tied and the bobby pins I had used to secure it.

"Everything about you is perfect," he whispered. "Now, get out before I tear that dress off of you."

"That's not exactly motivation for me to leave," I muttered, but climbed out with the help of Deryn's hand.

Nico climbed out last, taking the rear position of protection. They didn't always take the same spots in the diamond, except Rhys who always took the front. The other three took different positions depending on the situation.

"Move," Nico whispered.

The guys moved as one, walking down the carpet with a wide smile on each of their faces, turning to the cameras to let them take their pictures. Surrounded by my guards, no one could get a clear picture of me. Someone with wings tried to fly up to get a picture, but Nico discreetly used his powers to knock the person down before they could click their camera.

At the door, a man in a tuxedo and a full-face mask held out his hand. The guys set tickets in his hand, Rhys handing him two tickets, one for me. The man bowed and stepped to the side to let us enter.

The Galleria looked like a ballroom in a movie and intricately decorated for the masquerade ball. Thick, dark drapes hung around the room. A giant chandelier hung over the ballroom. On one side of the room, there was an orchestra playing soft music.

The rest of the room was dominated by tables of people snacking on hors d'oeuvres.

We went to one of the empty tables and Rhys pulled out a chair for me. "My Queen," he whispered.

"Thank you," I told him, then opened my napkin and put it in my lap.

Rhys sat on my left, Fox on my right, Deryn to Fox's right, and Nico sat across from me, on Rhys's left.

"Did you guys ro-sham-bo for seats?" I asked with a teasing smirk.

"No," Fox answered, avoiding my eyes while picking up his napkin.

"Arm wrestling," Rhys said with a grin.

I looked at Fox next to me. "You beat Deryn?"

Fox scowled at me. "I am an elf."

"I still say he cheated," Deryn grumbled.

"I beat you twice, with both hands," Fox replied with a happy smile.

"Fox, I think you just upped your hot points," I told him.

"My what?" he asked with a tilted head and a frown that made his brows furrow slightly in the middle.

"You know the number given based on how hot you are. Women do it a lot. Sometimes it's like a game and we give points to random guys we see walk by us."

"Women do that too?" Fox asked with a laugh. "I thought only men did it."

"What's my score?" Rhys asked.

"I can't tell you that," I said and scoffed.

"You're a perfect ten," Fox told me, picked up my hand, and kissed my knuckles.

"Only a ten?" I asked and stuck out my lower lip in a pout.

"Oh, that's a good pout," Nico commented. "Judges?"

"Seven," Deryn said. "I've seen her give much better pouts."

"Eight, but only because she's doing that glistening eye thing even through the mask," Rhys said.

"Ten is the highest you can go," Fox said.

"Women give men bonus points," I informed them. "Tattoos add two points. Well, good tattoos. Sometimes tattoos can be worth negative points, but that's very rare."

"I had no idea that you liked tattoos," Nico said. He had one beautiful tattoo on his chest and one on his shoulder. I constantly ran my fingers over them when he was shirtless, so I was surprised that he hadn't put two and two together.

I nodded.

"What else gives you bonus points?" Deryn asked.

"Accents. Super deep voices. Unique eye colors. Being an alpha, but not overbearing. Basically, an alpha who submits in the bedroom on occasion and isn't one of those super assholes. Doing heroic things, like saving kids or me. Those veins that stick out on your arms when you're muscular. Dimples. Being a kind person in general. Slaying my enemies."

"So, we're like, what? Twenties?" Deryn asked with a smirk. "Since we possess most of those traits?"

"I can't reveal your scores," I told them, "but I can tell you that you all have several bonus points."

"Looks like I need to get a tattoo," Rhys said and winked at me.

"Mm," I purred at him. "Yes, please."

The four guys laughed at me, which I found annoying since I was being serious.

"Every girl is different in how they assign bonus points. For example, tattoos are a plus two, while slaying my enemies is a plus four. Dimples are a plus one. It's all about preference," I explained.

"Good evening, princes," a tall, stork looking man, said as he stopped between Fox and Nico.

"Evening," they returned the greeting.

"Dinner will be served in just a few minutes. Would you like something to drink?" he asked us.

"Champagne," Rhys ordered, gesturing the number four with his hand. "Bring us a few bottles."

"Of course, sir. Anything else?" he asked.

"Princess?" Rhys asked me.

"I'll have the champagne with you," I replied.

The waiter nodded and disappeared in a hurry.

"Let me fill your water," Fox said, took my glass, and filled it with water from the pitcher on the table.

"Thank you," I replied and sipped from the glass.

"Boys," a distinctly feminine voice crooned. "I was hoping you would be here."

Resisting the urge to spin around and glare at whoever she was, I took another drink from my water glass. Then, I almost spit it out when all four of the guys, *my* guards, rose and walked to her to kiss her on the cheek, just below her mask. They each laid a hand on her arm as they leaned to kiss her cheek, and I felt my anger boiling within me. Who the fuck was she? She had on a bright red dress with lace on the ends of her sleeves and down her cleavage. Her lips were perfectly plump, perfectly shaped, and her lipstick was applied perfectly. I hated her. Okay, that was wrong of me to think, but I was feeling very territorial.

"See you on the dance floor," she told them with a smirk in my direction before she sauntered away.

The guys sat down and I returned to drinking my water, trying to pretend I didn't care to know who she was.

Rhys leaned close to me, his breath tickling my neck. "You realize, that even if you learn to control your expressions, it doesn't matter since we can feel your emotions?"

Shit. I'd forgotten.

"I don't know what you're talking about," I replied in an even tone that impressed me.

"Oh?" he asked and straightened. "Then I guess I won't tell you who she is, if you don't care."

"Not in the slightest."

Of course I cared! Tell me, you bastard!

"Your champagne, sirs and madam," the waiter said as he pushed a cart towards our table. It had four buckets of ice with four champagne bottles inside of them. He opened the first bottle, filled our glasses, and then set the four buckets in the center of the table.

"A toast," Fox announced and raised his glass.

We raised our glasses as well.

"To friends, now and forever."

"To the clan!" I said and clinked glasses with Fox and then the others.

"The clan!" the four said and clinked glasses before drinking the champagne.

Nico refilled the glasses and our food came out on real silver platters with silver lids. It was magical, everything I had dreamed princesses did.

A team of servers set a plate down before each of us with the waiter overseeing. Once they were finished, the waiter nodded and they disappeared in the crowd.

"Enjoy," the waiter said and then scurried away after the servers.

"Oh my god," I whispered, wiping the drool from my mouth as I looked over my plate. "This is amazing."

"We thought you would enjoy it," Rhys said and began eating.

Steak cooked to a perfect medium rare, rosemary potatoes, and asparagus with mushrooms sat in perfect proportions on my plate. I had never been one for taking pictures of my food, but at that moment, I wanted to take a picture to document how beautiful the plate was presented. The food tasted even better than it looked. None of us spoke until we were finished ravaging our food like it was the first we'd eaten in days.

"That was phenomenal," I told them and wiped my mouth with my napkin.

"Their chef is world renowned, so I hoped it would be amazing," Fox said.

As if he had been watching us, immediately the waiter brought out dessert, crème brûlée. I had never had it before, but after taking one bite, I vowed to have it again very soon.

"Once you have finished your meals, please make your way to the sides of the room so that we may clear the tables to prepare for the dances," someone announced from behind us.

Fox pulled out my chair and held a hand out to me. I gratefully accepted his hand and assistance standing up. We walked to the side and the guys surrounded me.

People were looking at us and whispering to each other. How could they tell who the guys were with their masks on? I could tell who they were, but I contributed that to being intimately involved with them.

I leaned against the wall with Fox on my left, Nico on my right, and Rhys and Deryn in front of me, but thankfully facing me.

"Who gets the first dance?" Deryn asked.

"We could arm wrestle and find out," Fox taunted him.

"Ro-sham-bo," Rhys said before Deryn could say whatever retort was on the tip of his tongue.

They faced each other, fists held between them.

"Ro-sham-bo," they said in unison, raising and lowering their fists with each word and then on the last one, they make a sign. The signs are either rock, paper, or scissors.

Rhys slapped his flat hand, paper, over Fox's closed fist, rock.

Deryn hit his closed fist, rock, over Nico's two extended fingers, scissors.

Deryn and Rhys turned to each other, closed fists in the center between them.

"Ro. Sham. Bo," they said again, enunciating each word while moving their hands.

They both left their hands in closed fists, rock, so they had to do it again. The same result occurred again. The third time, Deryn switched to an open hand laying parallel to the floor, paper. Rhys hadn't changed, so Deryn won.

"Ha!" Deryn shouted victoriously.

"We all get to dance with her still," Rhys reminded him.

"Yeah, but I get the first dance with her at her first masquerade ball," he reminded them.

"No bragging. That's poor sportsmanship," I chastised him.

"Gentlemen," a deep male voice said in greeting behind Deryn. His voice was one of those that I would have given extra points towards his hot score for.

Deryn stepped to the side, so I could see the newcomer. I knew instantly who he was, Fox's brother. The pointed ears were a big giveaway.

He smiled when he saw me, picked my hand up, and kissed my knuckles. "Princess," he said in greeting.

"Prince Silverowl. It's nice to see you again," I replied.

"You look stunning," he said, eyeing me in silence for several long moments.

So did he.

"What do you want, little bro?" Fox asked through a tight-lipped smile.

"I came hoping to get a dance with the Princess," he said while staring at me.

"Her card is-" Fox began, but I interrupted him.

"I'd love a dance, Silver, but my first must go to Deryn."

"I would never presume to take the first dance," he said with a smirk. "I look forward to seeing you on the dancefloor." He bowed and walked away.

"Jolie," Fox grumbled, pouting. "Why did you agree to that?"

"I have to get along with your families. Dancing one dance with your brother is hardly any inconvenience."

"You can't add him to our harem," Fox said adamantly.

I gaped at him. "What? I didn't...harem?"

Our arrangement was a harem, I supposed, but reversed since it was many men with one woman. That did not make me feel any better though. It made me feel like a terrible person.

"I didn't mean it as a bad thing," Fox whispered and pulled me into a hug.

I let him hug me, but his power wasn't working on me for some reason, so I still felt sad.

"None of us are here against our will, right?" Nico asked.

Fox released me so I could turn around to face him. "I'm fine," I lied and waved my hand at him. "Just emotional lately." I really was extra sensitive lately.

The orchestra was set up again and the dance floor was cleared. Right when the music started, a giant hand took mine and spun me out onto the floor.

I gasped in shock and looked up the massive body to the mask. "Dan!" I yelled. "You scared me."

"Hey! I get the first dance!" Deryn growled.

Dan set my hand on his shoulder and held my other hand. "Not tonight, junior!" Dan told him and joined the rest of the dancers seamlessly. After a short while, I finally noticed Dan's eyes studying me intensely. "What's wrong?" he asked as we continued dancing.

"Sorry," I mumbled and shook my head, pushing away all of my negative thoughts. "I've been extra emotional lately. Thank you for dancing with me."

"Have you been practicing shielding yourself from their emotions?" he asked, concern in his eyes and voice.

"Yes. It's not them."

"Well, we all have off days. A lot has happened to you recently.

Your life has been drastically changed. It's okay to be overwhelmed, but it is best if you talk to someone about it."

"Yes, sir."

The song ended and he dipped me, making me laugh and smiled wide. He was always so happy and playful, just like Deryn.

"Keep my son in line, okay?" he said and kissed the knuckles on my right hand.

"I'll try," I replied.

Deryn took my hand from his father's grip and bowed over it. "May I have this dance, my queen?"

"I'd be honored," I replied.

He pulled me close, his arm wrapped around my waist and kissed me gently, at complete odds with the roughness of his movement and the raging desire in his eyes. "I love you, baby," he whispered.

My heart felt so full, it could have exploded. "I love you too, my wolf."

We waltzed around the room with happy smiles and my worries melted away. The dance ended and Deryn kissed my knuckles before passing me off to Rhys.

"Hello, handsome," I greeted him, standing close to him.

"Evening, gorgeous," he replied, setting one hand on my lower back and taking my other in his free hand.

Our dance was flawless, my eyes never leaving his as we twirled amongst the other dancers. I had no idea how he was able to keep us from bumping into anyone else when his eyes were glued to mine, but it was awesome. I was very glad I'd taken ballroom dancing lessons as a teenager, or this night might have been a disaster.

I saw a flash of red as the woman from earlier spun by us, Deryn her dancing partner. Jealousy surged through me, hot and strong.

"What?" Rhys asked and looked around.

"Nothing," I replied and squashed my feelings.

"May I cut in?" Prince Silverowl asked.

Rhys hesitated, but then nodded and let him take me into the next dance.

"I'm surprised you would dance with me when there are so many other females here," I told him.

"My brother is never possessive, but when it comes to you, he's as bad as a werewolf with a bone."

I laughed, picturing Deryn and Fox fighting over a bone. "He's not that bad."

"He's gotten stronger since he met you. He has learned new powers and trains constantly. All so he can protect you," he told me.

The guys trained a lot, but I had no idea he was learning new powers too.

"You're good for Foxfire. He was beginning to neglect his duties and responsibilities and seemed to be falling into a funk. But, he's much better now. Thank you."

"Uh, you're welcome. Really, I haven't done anything. Fox does far more for me."

The music shifted, signaling the end of the song. "Time's up," he whispered. "See you around."

He disappeared into the crowd and Fox took his place.

"What did he say to you?" Fox asked, entering the dancers' area.

"He said he thinks I'm good for you," I answered honestly.

Fox blinked in stunned silence a moment. "Oh."

"You look great in that tuxedo," I complimented him.

"I look even better out of it," he replied with a cocky smirk and a wink.

I laughed and shook my head at him. "Conceited."

He shrugged. "Honest."

"Well, I happen to like how you look in the tuxedo," I told him.

"Thank you." The music shifted again.

Nico cut in and sighed, "Finally! It's my turn."

I giggled and kissed him. "Hello, Sparkles."

He tensed, hating the pet name I had given him after he had tried to do a new spell and all that happened was some bright sparks coming out of his fingertips.

His hand slid lower, his fingers brushing the top of my butt as we danced. "My fingers are known to make you see sparkles while your head is thrown back and screaming my name."

Heat rushed to my core and I stumbled in my dance with him as my muscles clenched.

"Tease," I growled at him, suddenly out of breath.

"You're so easily worked up tonight," he commented with a frown. "When was the last time one of us pleased you?"

He was always so blunt, never beating around the bush. Sometimes, it still caught me off guard.

"Two days ago," I answered honestly. I had become a bit of a sex addict, wanting it, no *needing* it once a day at the very least. Or, I ended up like this, starved and almost uncontrollable. Despite their assurances that they didn't care if I took one of them away for sex when we were all hanging out, I just couldn't do it. It felt too awkward and wrong to do.

"Come on," he ordered me, dragging me by the hand away from the crowd. The other three pushed off the wall they had been leaning on and followed us.

"Where are we going?" I asked, trying not to trip on the dress with the longer strides I had to use to keep up with him.

"Every male here can smell your arousal now," he explained. "I doubt any of them would try anything, but I'd rather be cautious than continue dancing." We exited the ballroom and entered the foyer. "Plus," he stopped and kissed me fiercely, his arms pulling me against him and his tongue sliding along mine. When he pulled back, we were both breathless. "Plus, we have special plans for you tonight."

"What?" I asked, my brain still stuck on his amazing kiss. He had tasted like champagne.

Our limo pulled up and we all climbed in. Once inside, the four sat together across the limo from me.

"Why are you all over there?" I asked. Normally, we all sat together.

"If we touch you before we get to the apartment, our plan will be ruined," Rhys said.

"I thought you were going to take me in this limo?" I asked, leaning my elbows on my knees and my chin on my hands, giving them a nice view of my cleavage.

All four groaned and averted their gazes.

"Rude!" I gasped at them, sat up, and folded my arms across my chest. "Maybe I'll just ruin your plan and lock myself away to have some alone time."

"No, you won't," Fox said with a smug smile. "You're insanely curious, too curious for your own good. And we won't tell you what it is. So, the only way to find out, is to go along with our plan."

"I don't like when you guys push me away," I mumbled while staring up at the roof of the limo. Self-esteem had always been an issue for me, especially as a preteen. It had gotten better when my boobs finally came in, and even better when Martin and I started dating. But, there was always this little voice, who I lovingly named Bitchtits, who assured me in moments like this, I still wasn't good enough. I blamed Bitchtits for my negative thoughts about other women too. I tried really hard to be supportive and positive to other women. Women needed to stick together in the gaming community. The industry was heavily dominated by men.

"It'll be worth it," Deryn promised.

My body was wound tight, liquid heat pooled between my legs, and I clamped my knees together.

"Fuck," Rhys growled, his eyes now dragon's eyes. "She smells amazing."

"Her pheromones are exceptionally enticing," Fox agreed and

licked his lips, my eyes tracking the movement. He could do some amazing things with that tongue.

All four groaned again and I could see their erections jerk inside their pants.

"Hurry up!" Deryn ordered the driver.

"I'm trying," the driver responded in a growling tone. "I can smell her too, you know?'

"Sorry," I gasped.

"You can't control it," the driver replied, "but maybe think sad thoughts instead?"

CHAPTER 4

Deryn rolled up the window that separated us from the driver.

"Who was that woman?" I asked them, anger and jealousy replacing my horny desire.

"I thought you didn't care," Rhys smirked.

"Rhys," I growled.

"She's the President's daughter," Nico told me.

"How many of you slept with her?" I asked, ignoring the voice telling me I didn't really want to know.

"None of us did more than dance with her tonight," Rhys replied, misinterpreting what I wanted to know.

"I'm not talking about tonight." Though, it was good to hear.

They didn't respond for several heartbeats.

"I did," Rhys admitted.

"I did too," Nico said.

"Me too," Deryn said.

Everyone looked at Fox. "Yeah, okay. I did too. Just once, though."

All four of them. I was a bit surprised, but had expected this.

"I see," I said and nodded. Strangely, I wasn't mad or upset. I was sort of numb.

"You're not mad?" Rhys asked, head tilted to the side and nostrils flaring.

"Or sad?" Fox asked.

"I expected that response," I told them and shrugged.

"Now you're sad…no…irritated," Deryn said.

"How would you have felt if I got up to kiss some guy on the cheek who I'd slept with. Oh, wait, I know since I experienced your reactions to Martin."

"Sorry," they all mumbled, satisfyingly guilty looks on their faces.

The limo stopped and I climbed out before they could get to the door, almost hitting the driver with it as it opened.

Our elevator ride was silent, my hormones squashed. Why was I so moody lately? My period had just ended four days ago, so I wasn't PMSing or pregnant. Was it them? Was I not shielding well enough?

I dropped my shields to allow the guys' feelings to reach me. All of them were worried.

"Why are you all so worried?" I asked in a strangled voice, swallowing thickly.

I put my shields back up and sagged against the elevator wall.

"We are worried about you," Fox said, drawing closer. "Your emotions have been all over the place, my powers aren't working, and you're not talking to us. You've been sad a lot lately."

"I'm not sure what's going on," I admitted.

The elevator opened and we all filed out, going to my apartment. I went to my room, stripping out of the dress, fully aware that I had an audience.

"Peeping Toms," I accused them without turning around. I put the mask on my dresser, smiling at how thoughtful it had been for them to remember that attending a masquerade ball was on my bucket list.

Rhys spun me around, claiming my mouth with his and

sliding his tongue in. His left hand gripped my butt while his right hand slid into my hair to cradle my head.

"Whoa," I whispered when he pulled back. I thought we would be alone, but the other three were still here.

Rhys threw me onto the bed and took his tie and shirt off. The other three followed suit, removing their ties and shirts and then all four climbed onto the bed.

"Guys, what's going on?" I asked, fire rushing through my veins and pooled in my core.

"We wanted to try sharing," Nico said.

"Sharing?" I asked breathlessly. Four insanely hot men, shirtless, and seated around me was making it hard to breathe or think of anything except touching their bare skin.

Fox pushed me on my back and began kissing me, his tongue slow and precise in its movements, driving me crazy.

Someone removed my thong, the last piece of clothing I had been wearing. All four gasped when my scent hit them, Fox stopped kissing me to look where the others were looking.

"She's so wet already," Deryn said. He bent forward and licked my clit, making me gasp and arch up off the bed.

Rhys latched onto one of my nipples, sucking and nipping. Nico took my other nipple into his mouth, swirling his tongue around my already hard nub.

I screamed out, and Fox took my mouth again, forcing my moans into his mouth.

Deryn sucked and licked me expertly, pushing me closer and closer to the cliff of euphoria.

Having all four of their mouths on me at once was a new experience that I thoroughly enjoyed.

Before I could orgasm, Deryn sat back and wiped his mouth with the back of his hand. "She's really close already."

Fox kissed my neck and bit down just hard enough to make me moan, but not enough to leave a mark.

"Go ahead," Rhys nodded and smirked at the whine I made when his mouth left my body.

Nico sucked harder on the nipple he was playing with and I moaned loudly.

I thought Deryn would finish me, but he removed his pants and thrust into me instead.

"Yes!" I screamed, throwing my head back and my hands grasped Nico and Rhys's thighs.

Rhys, Nico, and Fox removed their pants too, and I immediately grabbed Rhys and Nico, stroking them in time to Deryn's thrusts. Fox turned my head and I eagerly opened my mouth to accept his fully erect penis.

"Yes," he groaned, arching his back.

I screamed as an orgasm hit, tightening around Deryn, who orgasmed with me.

He pulled out and quickly rubbed my clit, making me orgasm in a few strokes.

Suddenly, all of them were gone, none of them touching me.

"Hey," I started, but realized they were switching positions.

Fox entered me slowly and used a steady rhythm. Deryn cupped my breast and flicked his tongue across it. Rhys stood by my head, and gripped my hair as he pushed into my mouth.

I stroked Nico slowly, wanting to keep him hard, but not finish too early. It wasn't until Fox that I realized they were slipping condoms on right before entering me.

Fox's movements were normally slow, but he gripped my hips and began to slam into me hard enough for our skin to slap loudly. He orgasmed before I did, pulling out to let Rhys take his spot.

I flipped over onto my hands and knees. Nico laid on the bed so I could give him head while Rhys gripped my hips and slid into me until he was fully buried.

Deryn continued pleasuring my breasts and Fox reached under me to rub my clit.

I orgasmed several times before Rhys finished, my legs shaking. Since it was just Nico left, and he was already on his back, I sat down on him. He moaned and his eyes rolled into the back of his head.

"What do you want?" Rhys asked as he kissed my neck.

I rode Nico and said, "Just touch me."

Rhys, Fox, and Deryn moved closer to me, kissing my upper body.

My walls fell and the euphoria and love they felt poured into me. I gasped and gripped Nico's chest to keep from falling forward.

"Yes," Nico moaned. "Now we can fully feel your emotions."

"I love all of you," I whispered, resuming my riding.

"You're our world," Nico told me, adding his own thrusts to meet mine.

"You are the only one that we want," Rhys whispered in my ear, his hot breath making me shiver.

"We will always love you," Fox whispered against my neck.

"We will never leave you," Deryn said.

Nico flipped me on to my back and took control. "Which do you love?" He asked as the pressure grew and grew.

"You all."

"You know the answer we want," he chastised and slammed into me faster and harder. "Who did you love?"

The orgasm was the strongest one I had ever had, shooting fire through my veins. "My princes!" I screamed the answer they wanted to hear and Nico joined with his own orgasm.

Nico fell to my side, panting happily.

"I love my guards," I whispered.

After cleaning up and dressing in pajamas, we cuddled on the couch to watch movies. I was high on euphoria and smiling like a fool.

I never thought they would have sex together with me. I

would be lying if I said that it had been anything other than magical.

"Jolie," Fox whispered, drawing my attention to him. He sat on the floor between my legs.

"Yeah?"

"We need to ask you something."

My euphoria vanished as fear took its place. "What?"

Rhys rubbed my arm. "Calm down. It's nothing bad."

"We have an important trip coming up," Fox said. "We'll be gone at least two weeks."

"That's right before Christmas," I whispered sadly. It was supposed to be our first Christmas together.

"We would be back on the twenty-fourth, so we would be home for Christmas," Rhys chimed in.

"Okay, so you want me to stay with the pack?" I guessed. They'd all gone on an overnight trip and the only way they had felt okay leaving me was because I had stayed with the pack and Martin had stuck next to me.

"No, we would like you to go with us," Deryn said.

"I can't leave work for two weeks."

"You're just writing. Can't you telework and send them your updates electronically?" Fox suggested.

I doubted it.

"Please," Nico begged from my right side. "I don't want to be separated from you for two weeks. I might go insane."

I felt the same way.

"I don't know. I'll have to think about it."

"We're going to Mascrol," Fox said with a smirk.

"You're going out of country?" I asked, my palms slick with sweat at the thought of them thousands of miles away, across an ocean from me.

"Easy," Rhys said, pulling me into a hug and rubbing my back. "Calm down."

"You'll be across the ocean from me," I whispered into his chest.

"Come with us," he whispered into my hair. "I can't stand the thought of being so far away from you. Plus, we know you've always wanted to visit Mascrol."

"Please," Deryn begged.

What could I say?

"I'll talk to my boss tomorrow. When would we leave?"

"Sunday the tenth," Fox said with a bright smile.

"It's not a yes yet," I reminded them.

"But it's not a no," he replied and went to the kitchen humming.

Sometimes he was so childlike. It was "serious" Fox that always threw me for a loop.

"Pizza?" Fox asked, phone in his hand.

I yawned and stretched with my arms above my head. "I'm going to call it a night."

Nico followed me to my bedroom and climbed into bed right behind me, wrapping his arms around me to make a safety net of warmth. "I can't stand the thought of being away from you," he whispered and kissed the top of my ear. "It hurts just imagining it."

"Same," I whispered back, stroking one of his forearms where it was wrapped around my chest.

"I'm not trying to convince you," he whispered. "I'm just sharing my feelings with you."

"I appreciate that," I said honestly. "And I know being apart for two weeks, even if you were in the next town over, would still put us all on edge. Or, possibly lose our shit. Not being able to touch any of you for two weeks?" I shuddered.

"Same," he whispered and kissed my head.

"Can I talk to you?" I asked Justin, my boss, popping my head into the doorway of his office. He was in his mid-forties with graying temples and a gnarly scar on his right cheek. Rumor around the office was that he got it in a bar fight when someone suggested that video games were only for children and adults who played were childish.

He looked up and waved me in. "What's up?"

I closed the door and sat in the chair in front of him. His office was covered in video game memorabilia that I drooled over every time I walked by. So many of the items were rare and super valuable.

"I need to talk to you about-"

"Wait, let me guess. You're here to talk to me about the Summit," he said with a smirk. "The two week trip the princes are going on."

"How did you know?" I gaped.

He laughed. "I'm a werewolf."

Then, he did something I had never seen before. He grew wolf ears out of the top of his head, complete with fur. It reminded me of several anime shows I watched and before I could stop myself, I leapt up and touched one of them.

He didn't growl or snap at me, which I took as a good sign. Coming to my senses, I plopped back down into my seat, my cheeks warm. "Sorry."

"You're a princess to our pack. You're allowed to touch us without worrying we will bite you," he said with a smirk. "Though, I doubt Prince Deryn would like seeing you do that."

"Deryn's never done that," I whispered and pointed at his ears.

"I started doing it for conventions. It's easier to let my wolf ears out than to purchase some fake ones," he admitted. "I get a lot of girls wanting to touch my ears and even more when I let my tail out."

I bet he did.

"So, about the Summit?" I said to bring us back on topic.

"You're good to go. Just make sure you email me your work, so I know you're working," he said. "If I declined your request, I know I'd have an angry prince visiting me, and I'd rather avoid that. Plus, you are ahead of schedule on all of your projects and all of your work has been stellar. So, I don't see any harm letting you go."

"Thank you!" I screeched and stood up. "Thank you, so much."

"You're welcome, Princess."

I flinched. "Please, don't call me that here. People will think I'm getting special treatment. I don't want that. I want equal treatment. I want to earn my place in the gaming industry."

"You are," he assured me. "I would have booted you out of here a while ago if your writing wasn't so great."

"Thanks," I said, shocked at the huge compliment. As soon as I left his office, I sent a message in our group chat.

Me: I can go with you.

Deryn: Really?

Rhys: Good.

Nico: Sweet.

Fox: Yes! Woohoo!

Me: Yes, Deryn. My boss okayed it since I'm ahead of schedule on my projects.

Rhys: I'll get the paperwork all in order.

Nico: We should celebrate tonight. Pizza and party games?

Me: Sounds great!

Deryn: You touched another wolf's ears?!!!

Damn, how had he found out so fast? Had Justin really called and let him know? Why?

Me: He grew wolf ears out of the top of his head! Like in that show I've been watching. I just leapt up to touch them without thinking. He's part of the pack, so I'm allowed to touch him. Plus, it wasn't like I touched him inappropriately. It was just an ear.

Deryn: -_-

Me: Jealous monster.

Fox: You're ruining our happy mood! Jolie is coming with us on our trip! We won't have to be separated from her!

Nico: I agree with Fox.

Deryn: We'll talk later.

Me: *static* what's that? *static* you're breaking up. *static* I think I'm going into a tun-

Fox: XD

Deryn: >:(

Rhys: lol

Nico: o(ˆoˆ)o

Me: BYE! xoxox <3

When I got home, Deryn was waiting for me in the lobby.

"Hey, handsome," I greeted him and kissed his cheek.

"Show me how you touched him," he ordered me and folded his arms across his chest.

"Grow ears," I ordered him back.

Shockingly, he did as I asked and two ears popped out of the top of his head. I reached up and rubbed one of his ears and then stepped back. "That's what I did."

"No wonder he called me," he growled, his eyes now his wolf's eyes.

"What do you mean?"

"That goes into my top three turn on spots," he told me, his body crowding mine as he moved closer. "Touching me like that makes me want to take you right here."

"He hadn't seemed flustered," I told him. "He said he does it at conventions all the time."

"Yeah, and I'm sure he walks around with a hard-on all day."

"I didn't know," I whispered weakly. "I wouldn't have done it if I'd known."

"You grow ears," he ordered me.

Me? I could shift, but I wasn't sure I could just grow ears. "Can we go to my apartment first?" I asked. There wasn't anyone else in the apartment lobby with us, but I still didn't want to do it here.

He nodded, the ears disappearing, and we went to my apartment, which was empty.

We faced each other and I focused on the image of a girl with wolf ears and a wolf tail, but a human body. It wasn't difficult, since I had watched a ton of anime movies with characters like that. My scalp began to tingle and my lower back throbbed.

Suddenly, they just popped out. I screeched since my tail was stuck in my pants and hurriedly pushed them down in the back, to let it out.

Deryn groaned and growled at the same time, something I hadn't ever heard before. "That is so hot."

Hurrying towards the mirror in the bathroom, I looked at myself and had to admit, it was sort of hot.

"Come here, please," he requested.

I walked to him, sashaying my hips so that my tail swung side to side.

His eyes darkened and he got a hungry look, one I recognized all too well. With one hand, he reached up and touched my ear like I had done to him.

Holy fangs! It felt amazing and I moaned out loud, tilting my head so he could rub it more.

"See?" he asked, stepping forward and continuing to rub my ear. "It feels amazing."

"I'm sorry," I moaned. "I didn't know. I won't do it again."

"I know you didn't know. I'm not mad at you. I was at first, but once I realized that you weren't aware, my anger disappeared. However, it is important that you learn about things like this, so you don't repeat your mistakes."

"Deryn," I whispered, "does it feel as amazing when you touch my tail?"

He dropped the hand that had been touching my ear and I

whimpered at the loss of his touch. His chuckle quickly followed my sound and then he gently stroked my tail.

A gasp wrenched out of my throat. It caused warmth to flow low in my stomach, a sensation I had not been prepared for. Wow.

"Whoa," he whispered. "I've never done the tail before."

"Too much," I whimpered. "It's so sensitive."

"Did you orgasm?"

I shook my head and swallowed thickly. "Almost," I admitted and reverted back to my human form.

Deryn's phone rang. He ignored it, eyes still darkened.

"You should answer that."

He groaned and put his phone to his ear. "What?" A moment later, he said, "fine," and hung up. He grabbed my hand and pulled me towards the doorway. I followed, just glad to shake off the sexual tension from a moment ago.

We met the rest of the guys for pizza and games at Deryn's apartment. He released my hand with a smile.

"Jolie!" the three guys yelled when I walked in. Clearly, they had started drinking before we arrived, but I was okay with that. They were all happy drunks.

"Guards!" I yelled back and raised my arms in the air.

Fox popped the top on a bottle of hard cider for me, which I gratefully accepted. They came over and we held our bottles up.

"To a wonderful adventure," I said.

"Adventuring!" Deryn yelled.

"Adventuring!" the five of us yelled at the same time.

Yeah, we were nerds, and we were perfectly okay with admitting that. How I had lucked out to find four hot nerds was beyond me, but I knew better than to look a gift horse in the mouth.

We took a big gulp of our drinks and then went to the couch to play games. These games were serious, but we were still having fun. Once we got a few more drinks in us, they would be hilarious and ridiculous to watch. We had recorded ourselves one night and watched, as many of us couldn't keep our kart on the track since we were so drunk. The amount of cussing and swerving karts was one of the most hilarious things I'd ever seen. I had saved that video to my hard drive, ensuring I kept it forever.

The pizza came and we ate while sitting at the table together. It always made me happy to eat at the dining table with them, like we were a family.

"We are a family," Deryn grumbled at me.

I jerked my head up and asked, "What? I didn't say that out loud, did I?"

"I didn't hear anything," Fox scowled.

"Me neither," Nico admitted.

"I heard her," Rhys said.

I have a third nipple, I thought in my head.

Rhys and Deryn rolled their eyes.

"Still nothing," Nico said.

"Me neither," Fox said.

"What the hell?" I growled.

Now I couldn't even have my thoughts to myself?

"It's not like we did it on purpose," Rhys reminded me. "Why did this suddenly start? What changed?"

"I don't know," I whispered and shoved more pizza into my mouth. Sometimes, I was a stress eater. This was one of those times. Who wouldn't be stressed when two of the four men you were dating could suddenly read your mind? Nothing would be secret anymore.

"Got a lot of secrets to hide?" Rhys asked with a smirk.

I glared at him.

"Stay out of my head."

"You're yelling your thoughts at me," he accused.

"We need to talk to the Elders tonight," I said urgently.

"Tomorrow. None of us are in any shape to see the Elders," Rhys countered.

The guys continued eating, drinking, playing, and having a good time, but I just wasn't into it anymore. Slinking off during one of their epic battles, I climbed into Deryn's bed and stared up at the ceiling.

If they all ended up able to hear my thoughts, what was I going to do? Not that I *could* do anything. It would change everything. There would be no freedom. Everything I thought of would be on display for them. I could never surprise them. How were they going to react to hearing my thoughts about the others? Oh, Goddess! I couldn't have sex with the other two now! They would hear everything I was thinking about and, uh, this was so unfair. Just once, it would be nice if just once my fucking curse didn't make things worse.

I jolted up in bed.

"That's it!" I shouted.

"What?" Nico called from the living room.

"Nothing!" I shouted back. Had the two not heard my thoughts? Were they too busy playing or too drunk now?

Rhys likes fingers in his ass. I thought as loud as I could.

No laughter.

No growling.

They couldn't hear me. Perfect. My plan was in place and I just had to keep them from hearing my thoughts until I completed it. Step one, go to sleep now!

"WHY IS SHE SINGING CHILDREN'S SONGS IN HER HEAD?" RHYS growled from the back seat of the SUV.

"Stop!" Deryn begged, leaning forward to set a hand on the back of the passenger seat.

In order to keep them from hearing my thoughts, I'd resorted to singing all of the catchy songs that I knew. Children's songs were the best because they were easy to remember and often repetitive with few breaks. Less time for stray thoughts to slip in.

Deryn growled and rubbed his temples. "Martin, please drive faster."

My other two guards sat in silence, barely knowing what was going on.

Martin chuckled from the driver's seat next to me. "You're torturing them for something, aren't you? What did they do?"

"They didn't do anything," I answered and just as a stray thought started to slip in, I started singing my favorite rhyme, over and over. And over.

The SUV stopped and we all leapt out, racing into the Elders' room where they were waiting for us. I slid to a stop and bowed low, keeping my songs up.

"What's troubling you so much?" Dragon Elder asked.

"Rhys and I can hear her thoughts now," Deryn told him.

"We can't think of any reason why we could suddenly start hearing them, but we can," Rhys agreed.

The Elders looked at me.

"Walls are up. No idea how it's happening," I replied and went back to rhyming.

"What is it you wish to ask us, Jolie?" Elf Elder asked.

Damn. He was so good at reading people!

"Break my curse!" I shouted. "I-I mean, please break my curse, Elders."

"Jolie! No!" Rhys yelled.

"I thought we had discussed this?" Deryn said.

"Please," I begged and dropped to my knees in front of the Elders. "I'm sure that the curse is what did this. I'm sure the curse will continue doing things to ruin my life. No more. I can't have it ruining things anymore. Everything is going so well and I can't risk it. I can't lose anyone else."

Tears streamed down my cheeks, but I didn't move to wipe them.

"Jolie," Deryn whispered in shock.

I could feel the four of them wanting to move closer, but they held their ground out of respect for me and the Elders.

I have to do this. If my curse takes one of you... I couldn't even finish that thought.

"Very well," Wolf Elder agreed. "We will break your curse."

"It is going to hurt and you might very well die, so speak with your guards and then we will take you to the room we use for this sort of event," Dragon Elder told me.

"Thank you," I gasped. Part of me had been sure they weren't going to do it.

The Elders left and I spun around to find a mixture of anger and worry on four gorgeous male faces.

"I love you," I whispered. "I love all of you, individually and together. Thinking of a life where one of you is missing...it's torturous. This curse is always hurting me in the worst way possible. You are what matters most to me now and I know it will target you next. I have to do this."

"What if you die?" Rhys asked, pulling me into his arms and burying his face in my hair above my ear. "What will we do then?"

"You will become kings. You will find mates. You will do what you did before you met me," I whispered and hugged him tightly. "You will do all this knowing that I loved you more than anything and will always be part of you. I'll always be in here," I whispered and touched his chest.

"No!" Deryn yelled. "No!" He flipped a chair over and growled loudly, his body shaking and fists clenched.

Without hesitation, I went to him and wrapped my arms around his back. "It's okay, Moon Moon. I love you, too."

"Please, don't. Please reconsider," he begged in a tight voice. "If I lose you, I lose everything."

"You won't lose me," I whispered, trying to put as much assurance into those four words as I could.

I hugged Fox who hadn't said a word and he hugged me back, drawing my scent in deeply before he pushed me to Nico. "I'll see you once your curse is removed," he whispered and turned his back on me.

"Stay strong," Nico ordered me, grabbed my chin, and tilted it up. "You're strong and powerful. You carry a piece of each of us in you. You can survive the curse breaking."

I nodded and kissed his cheek. "Yes, sir."

With one final look at the four men I loved, I went into the room the Elders had gone to.

"It will be alright," Dragon Elder assured me. "We will do everything within our power to keep you safe during this."

Nodding, I went to the bed he was pointing to. Well, not a bed, more of a cot. It was the only thing in the room we were now in. Bare walls, stone floor, and one single cot.

I sat down and they pushed my shoulder, guiding me down onto the cot.

"Close your eyes," Dragon Elder ordered me.

I followed his directions.

"Center yourself."

Done.

"You're going to feel tingles along your stomach and chest. Just stay relaxed. After the tingling ends, you'll feel burning, and immense pain. Stay strong and it will be gone, never to bother you again."

"Okay."

I could do this. I would do this.

The tingling wasn't so bad, and the burning was uncomfortable. The pain, wasn't immense. The pain was *excruciating*. I screamed and thrashed on the cot.

The Elders were chanting and their powers funneled into me at an alarming rate.

My skin was being peeled off. My muscles ripped apart. My soul torn with claws and knives.

The chanting grew louder, as did my screams.

Nico's words came to me. My soul contained pieces of all of them. I was strong. I had a lot that I wanted to do with my life. I wanted to become an award-winning writer. I wanted to become known in the gaming community. I wanted to claim my mates.

CHAPTER 5

Pain coursed through my body, so I was fairly certain I was still alive.

"When will she wake up?" Fox asked.

"Soon," Dragon Elder answered. "Remember that her experience was painful."

"We know," Rhys grumbled. "We all felt it."

"Not like she did," Dragon Elder said. "You felt one hundredth of the pain she felt."

"You're joking, right? Over exaggerating?" Deryn asked.

"No, we're being honest. She had up solid walls between you all and we added our own as well to protect you," Elf Elder explained.

"I can't imagine dealing with that amount of pain," Fox whispered.

"It must have felt-"

"Like my skin was ripped off, my muscles ripped apart, and my soul shredded," I whispered and opened my eyes.

The four of them sat around my cot, scowls on their faces.

"Who died?" I asked with a small smile.

"You almost did," Dragon Elder told me, coming to stand at the end of the cot so I could see him. "It was very close."

"It worked, right? The curse is gone? I really don't think I could do that again."

He smiled and nodded. "Yes, your curse is gone. We successfully removed it."

"Thank you," I said as tears built and dripped down my cheeks. It was gone. My curse was gone!

"We can't hear your thoughts anymore," Rhys informed me.

"Thank you," I sighed.

I was so glad that I didn't have to deal with trying to hide my thoughts from them.

"Can you sit up?" Fox asked and held out his hand.

I took it and let him pull me up into a sitting position. "I'm so sore," I moaned.

"Can we take her home?" Rhys asked.

Dragon Elder nodded. "Stay safe on your trip," he told me. "Keep your ears open and eyes scanning."

Was he warning me that there was going to be an attack? Was I in danger going with them?

"Thank you. Please, thank the other Elders for me."

He nodded and Rhys picked me up and carried me out to our waiting SUV.

"What happened?" Martin asked. "You've been in there for hours."

"Jolie decided to become suicidal," Deryn growled and climbed into the front seat, slamming the door shut.

"What?" Martin asked.

"I had them remove my curse," I told him with a smile. "It's gone!"

"Your curse is gone?" he asked.

I nodded.

"Why is he upset about that?" Martin asked Rhys.

"Because there was a high likelihood she could have died. They told us that she very nearly died," he explained.

"But she didn't," Martin said.

"Exactly!" I yelled and kissed Martin's cheek as we walked by him. "Glad someone understands."

"Drive," Deryn ordered him, snarling and sitting in his seat with tense shoulders.

There was no point in talking to him in the car, so I would wait until we were home to talk to him privately. He was mad that I had risked myself. I understood that. However, it was my decision and I had done what I thought was right.

"I need to buy luggage," I told Rhys, settling onto the seat beside him.

"Okay, we can go out tomorrow, if you want," he offered.

"Why not tonight?" I asked him.

"Because we need you to be with us tonight," Fox told me. "We need time together without outside distractions."

"Okay."

I could understand their need to reassure themselves that I was okay.

Before we climbed into our cuddle puddle once back at the apartment, I grabbed Deryn and dragged him into the hallway. He was stiff and kept turning away from me and folding his arms across his chest.

"I'm sorry you were worried. I don't like worrying you. But, this was something I had to do for myself," I told him.

"You almost died," he growled.

"But, I didn't."

"I almost lost you," he whispered.

"I'm right here," I whispered back and stepped forward, so that my breasts were pushing against his folded arms.

He dropped his arms and then pulled me against his chest and hugged me tightly. "The pain you experienced was too much. Then, we felt you slipping. We felt you dying. I couldn't do anything. There was no enemy for me to kill. There was no way for me to protect you. I was helpless. All I could do was sit there and wonder if the woman I love was going to survive or not."

"It's over. My curse is gone. I'm alive and well. I'm so happy. I never meant to cause you pain or worry. I had to do this. I had to get rid of this curse before it took you from me."

"It almost took you from me, though."

"Deryn, please don't be mad at me any longer. I love you. I love you so much that I would rather put my life on the line, than endanger you," I explained to him.

He picked me up until we were eye level and kissed me lightly before he whispered, "Don't ever do that again. Okay?"

"No problem," I said and smiled. He set me down on my feet, but kept his hands on my arms.

"Please, don't endanger yourself to keep me or the other guys safe. It is our job to protect you. You are my queen. You are the one who matters. Keeping you alive is what is important."

"Do you think the Elder was warning me to expect an attack at the Summit?" I asked. The warning was really bothering me.

"No, I think he was just reminding you not to let your guard down. There are always threats and dangers. If you let your guard down, you will open yourself up to attacks."

"Are we good?" I asked him and looked up into his eyes.

He was frowning still, not a twitch of his lips at all. "Yes. We're good."

"Still love me?"

He rested his hand against my cheek and whispered, "I will *always* love you, Jolie."

"Good," I said with a wide smile and spun around to walk inside.

"Jolie," he said, stopping me.

"Yes?" I asked and looked over my shoulder at him.

"You are my world. I will do whatever I can to keep you safe.

Even if you decide we aren't going to be mates, I will still watch over you."

"I will always be grateful to have you in my life. I am beyond grateful to have a place in your heart. I will never take you for granted," I told him. "I love you."

"I love you more than you'll ever know," he said.

He pushed open the door and we joined the others on the couch to cuddle and watch movies.

Tomorrow, I would try to find my final presents for them. I wanted this to be the best Christmas ever. I wanted to ensure that this would be a Christmas no one would ever forget.

I couldn't wait to go to Mascrol. It would be my first long distance travel with the guys. It was going to be the longest I had been on vacation in my entire life. Normally, I only took two or three-day trips. Two weeks was going to be insane. How many pairs of pants would I need to bring? How big of a suitcase was I allowed?

I didn't want to be like some girls, carrying sixteen bags and making others take care of them for her.

"You're chewing on your lip," Rhys whispered. "What are you worrying about?"

"What size bag I'll need and how many pairs of pants I'll have to take for a two-week vacation."

He chuckled softly and patted my knee. "We'll take care of it all tomorrow. Don't worry."

WHAT HE DIDN'T TELL ME, WAS THAT I ONLY NEEDED LUGGAGE BIG enough for my bras, underwear, pajamas, and a few pairs of pants. Everything else was being provided for me. Whatever the hell that meant. Part of me suspected I was going to be forced to wear dresses quite often.

"What will I be doing while you're stuck in meetings?" I asked the guys while packing my bag.

The four of them were lying around my room, two on the floor, one on the bed and one across the chest at the end of my bed. The chest was wooden with an ornate symbol, a symbol I had never seen before, and that Rhys, who had given me the chest, said was something I would learn about later. No matter how much I pestered him, he wouldn't tell me what the symbol was, and neither would the others.

The chest had a few weapons, a thick quilt, and a few dragon scales from Rhys inside. Every few weeks, he would add another scale to the chest. He said it was important to him that I keep them in the chest, but didn't explain the significance.

"Martin will be guarding you while we are there," Deryn told me. "He will take you anywhere you want to go within the grounds."

"So, I won't get to go explore?" I asked.

"We'll take you when we can," Deryn promised.

"I'm surprised that you guys are okay with Martin watching me," I teased them.

"We trust you," Fox said.

"We had a long talk with him. So, he understands our expectations," Deryn said with a smile that held no warmth.

"So, you threatened him," I said and shook my head. It wasn't surprising. Alphas in general were protective, but because he was my guard, and I was his queen, it made him even more protective.

"We will come get you every opportunity that we can," Nico assured me. "We would prefer to be with you than attend the meetings. They are always boring."

My phone rang and I quickly answered when I saw it was Martin. "Hello, handsome."

"Hello, beautiful," he replied.

Deryn growled softly, able to hear both sides of the conversation.

"Are you here?" I asked in a sultry voice.

"Yes. So, why don't you slip past your four guards and get down here. We can run away together."

"Martin," Deryn growled.

Martin laughed loudly. "He is so easy to rile up when it comes to you. It's almost like he loves you or something."

"I know, it's weird, right?" I said and winked at Deryn. "We'll be down in a few."

"I'll count the seconds until I'm honored with your presence, Princess."

"I'm going to punch him," Deryn said calmly, merely stating a fact.

"Let's go. We've only got a ten-hour train ride to endure," Rhys said, glancing at his watch.

"Ten hours of torturing you four. Yay!" I cheered.

"She's sadistic," Fox sighed while he stood from the bed. "Why must you enjoy torturing us?"

"Stop being so jealous, and I will stop teasing you so much. You four should know that I am not going to leave you for anyone else. My heart belongs equally to you four."

Fox kissed my cheek, his normal, radiant smile back in place. "That was all I wanted to hear."

Rhys grabbed my bag for me and headed out. Fox followed.

I stopped Deryn with a hand on his arm. "Hey."

He turned and smiled at me, a dazzling, happy smile. "Hey."

"Are we good?" Things had been strained between us since I removed my curse. He had been affectionate, but seemed far away whenever he was with me.

He rested his hand on my cheek and nodded, smile still in place. "Yes, baby. I'm sorry if I've been acting weird. I'm just worried about you." He kissed my lips and then linked our fingers.

They were all worried about me, which I didn't understand. The curse was gone, so they shouldn't have been worried any longer.

Nico had held the elevator for us, so we quickly got in.

Martin had the backdoor of the SUV open and helped load the bags before walking to me and bowing. "Princess."

A couple people walking down the sidewalk slowed to look at us.

I smacked his shoulder. "Stop that."

He pulled me into a hug and rubbed his cheek against mine, the stubble on his chin scraping me slightly. "This trip is going to be a ton of fun."

"I hope so," I replied with a tight smile.

Honestly, the Elder's warning still bothered me. Plus, my life had never been quiet or easy.

When we boarded the train, the guys argued over seating arrangements for a minute before resorting to ro-sham-bo.

I took the window seat so I would be able to look at everything as we went.

Nico sat beside me with a victorious smile and draped his arm around my shoulders.

Fox sat in front of me, Rhys next to him, and Deryn and Martin behind us.

"Nico," I whispered.

He leaned close to me. "Yes?"

"How much did you spend on my Christmas present?"

He jolted backward as though I had shocked him. "I'm not telling you that."

I smirked. "You haven't even purchased anything yet, have you? Don't worry. I'm not done shopping either."

"I have your present already," he said. "I'm just not going to tell you how much I spent. That's not something that you share with each other."

"More than one hundred? Two hundred? Three hundred?"

He didn't react to my questions at all.

I tapped Rhys's shoulder. "What about you?"

"Not saying."

"Fox?"

"Nope."

"Deryn?"

"I haven't gotten it yet," he admitted. "But, I am not telling you what I think I am going to spend."

"It's not fair," I grumbled and folded my arms across my chest. "How do I know how much to spend on you, if you won't give me an idea of what you are spending?"

"We wouldn't care if you spent absolutely zero on us. You could put a bow on yourself and lay on the bed, and we would be fine with that present," Nico whispered huskily in my ear.

"Sounds like a great present," Deryn whispered behind us.

I groaned and gave up.

The train whistle blew and it lurched forward. Our journey had officially begun.

Nico pulled me closer to him, pushing the arm of the seat that separated us up and out of the way. I rested my head on his chest, getting comfortable.

We were the only ones in this car of the train, but I felt like someone was watching me.

"What's wrong?" Nico asked. "You tensed up."

"I feel like I'm being watched," I whispered as quietly as possible.

"Do you want to switch seats?"

I shook my head and snuggled closer to him. "No, I'm fine. I know you'll protect me."

He put a shield around us. "Better?"

I nodded, feeling immensely better with the shield around us, and allowed myself to doze on and off.

After two hours of silence, Deryn stood with a groan and paced the aisle.

"Wouldn't you be more comfortable in your other form?" I asked him. I was considering it myself.

"Yes, but it's more boredom than a comfort issue bothering me right now."

"Let's play a game," I suggested.

"What game?" Rhys asked, standing and stretching too.

His shirt rode up, revealing the V of muscles that made women weak in the knees and brought to mind all sorts of fun things.

Martin inhaled deeply and then, sighed happily.

All eyes turned to him and Deryn stood beside him again with tensed legs, ready to jump on him.

I rolled my eyes.

"Don't fret," Martin told Deryn. "I've learned to lock down my hormones when it comes to her. We wouldn't have finished high school if I had let that delicious smell overpower me."

"We almost missed graduation," I reminded him softly.

"We made it, didn't we?" he said and smirked.

"You're really not affected by it?" Rhys asked.

"It's delicious to smell, but a perk to being mated is my mate's scent is super enticing and mutes other females' scents to allow me to resist easier."

"Good to know," Deryn said.

"You're like a teenage boy," Martin accused me. "You saw Rhys's skin and got all worked up."

"First of all, I am glad I'm not a boy because I know I would get boners way too often. Second, it wasn't just skin. It was the V. You know that drives me nuts."

"I really don't enjoy hearing about how much he knows about your turn-ons," Nico grumbled.

"You should be thanking me. A lot of her likes and dislikes are because of me," Martin teased.

"You mean you guys didn't ask him about me or things I like?" I asked, eyebrows raised. If there was a female who could tell me about them, I would have asked. Well, except for the President's daughter. Definitely not her.

"Part of the fun of new relationships is figuring out what the other likes," Fox said.

"Let's play a card game," Nico suggested.

"Only if you swear not to cheat," Fox said immediately.

"I never cheat when we're playing for fun," Nico replied with a devious smirk.

"Aren't most card games only four players?" I asked. I didn't really know much about card games, since I rarely played them.

"We will take turns, like we do with everything else," Deryn offered.

Deep in my heart, I felt a twinge of regret. Before me, they wouldn't have had to take turns. Before I came into their lives, they had four, which was the perfect amount to play almost any game. It was just a good, even amount in general. With me, I brought them to an odd number of five, which wasn't good for anything.

"What's wrong, cupcake?" Martin asked me softly, leaning against the top of my seat.

"It's nothing," I whispered and shook my head.

"Come on, you know you can't lie to me," he chastised.

"I don't want to talk about it," I whispered and glanced at the guys who were discussing which game to play.

"Want to go for a walk to the dining car? We can get some food and bring stuff back for everyone. I'm sure we're all hungry by now," he suggested.

He was trying to get me away from the guys so that I could talk to him. I *really* appreciated that.

"Okay," I agreed, climbing over Nico to get into the aisle, then pushing past Rhys and Fox to the door leading to another car.

"We're going to get some food for everyone," Martin told them.

"Oh, I'll come too and-" Rhys started, but there was a quiet conversation, too quiet for me to hear, and then Martin was pushing me through the door.

Part of me wanted to glance back at them, since it was dead silent now, but I kept my eyes forward and walked with Martin down the aisle of a car filled with passengers. Every single seat was taken and I felt bad we had an entire car to ourselves. The guys probably paid for all of the seats, but I still felt bad for all the people crammed into this one car.

We went into the next car and delicious scents filled the air.

"Food," I whispered and headed forward.

"So, what's going on?" Martin asked. "And don't say, 'nothing' or I'll pinch you until you tell me."

"I was just thinking about how much I've changed things for them. Before, they wouldn't have had to take turns playing games. They didn't have to take turns with a woman. They didn't have to take turns going out on dates. Now, they have to take turns, make schedules, and ro-sham-bo just to determine what fucking seat they're going to sit in."

A woman in a fancy suit, turned and gaped at me for my language. I rolled my eyes at her and focused back on Martin who smiled at me.

"Why the fuck are you smiling when I just poured my deep, inner thoughts out to you?" I growled at him.

"Sometimes you are so dense, cupcake. They love you. They do all of those things because they want to make this work with you. If they didn't want to do it, they wouldn't. They're fucking princes. They don't take orders from anyone, except their king, and sometimes not even them!"

"I should let them go, so they can go pursue other females, but I'm too selfish for that. I can't imagine my life without them. I can't imagine having to see them with another female. It hurts so much, just imagining it. Which then makes me feel worse, since they have to see me with other males."

The woman looked like she was about to faint now.

"If you don't want to hear us, then hurry up and get out of line," I snapped at her.

She gasped and spun around with a harrumph.

"Again, if they wanted to do that, they would. They don't want to pursue other females. And you're not being selfish. You love them."

"What's going to happen at the Summit?" I asked.

"All of the Other races get together and discuss peace agreements, trade requests, and any orders of business the kings might have to bring up. The princes are there to give advice to the kings and assist in making decisions. Really, they just have to listen to all the boring crap and nod once or twice at their fathers. It's *super* boring."

That sounded awful.

"So, you and I are going to be holed up in a room for hours on end, with nothing to do," I said.

"Yeah, too bad we aren't single," he smirked at me. "Then, we could fill the hours with lots of things to do."

"There are children," the woman gasped at us.

"And we didn't say anything bad. Your dirty mind was the one that supplied what you thought we were talking about," Martin pointed out. "We could have been talking about playing two-person video games for all you know."

"Do you think I should take them as my mates?" I asked Martin as quietly as possible. I never knew when someone from the media would be around.

"I can't answer that for you. That is something that you have to figure out for yourself."

"I think I already have," I admitted. "And I need your help."

"My help?" he asked with raised eyebrows. "I can't mate with them for you."

I laughed loudly, throwing my head back at the ridiculousness of his statement. "No, you idiot. I need you to help me get their mating gifts." Like humans gave each other engagement rings,

Others gave each other gifts. Normally, it was jewelry, but shifters couldn't wear rings because they would get in the way when they were shifting. I had heard that one shifter lost a finger because she had forgotten to take off a ring before shifting.

"Oh!" he said, drawing out the word. "That, I can help you with."

We grabbed a ton of food and headed back to our car, where the four princes were huddled together, whispering conspiratorially, but stopped when we walked in.

I rolled my eyes. "Oh, I wonder what you were talking about. It couldn't have been me."

"You're always on our minds," Deryn replied smoothly with a sweet smile.

"That was sweet," I told him and kissed his cheek.

"That's not enough food," Rhys grumbled.

"Well, that's all we could get. So, why don't you go get more, if you think we need more," I suggested. "I'm going to sit down, look at the scenery, and eat my blueberry bagel."

"Martin," Deryn called. "Come with me."

Martin set our haul onto a table and went with Deryn and Rhys to get more food.

"You okay?" Fox asked, sitting next to me in the seat. "You felt sad for a bit while you were gone."

"I'm fine," I assured him with a smile. "Just talking with Martin about some stuff."

"Stuff like?" he probed.

"I love you, Fox, but there are some things that I can't talk to you guys about."

"Why not?" he asked with a scowl. "I talk to you about everything. You're one of my best friends. Aren't I one of your best friends?"

"Yes," I replied immediately. "But, I don't feel comfortable talking with one of you about one of the others. You guys are each other's original best friends and I refuse to cause a rift or issues between you. If I have problems with one of you, I am not going to go complain to someone else about it. Remember what happened when Rhys made me sad that one day? He got punched in the face and it wasn't even something that he deserved to get hit over."

"I get your point, but I wish you would talk to me more," he pouted.

"Plus, you guys talk to each other about everything. So, if I told you something about Rhys, you would either tell Rhys or tell one of the others who would then tell Rhys. It would get back to him and then he'd come talk to me about it and want to know why I didn't just talk to him about it in the first place."

"See, you already know that you should be talking to us first anyway. All of us wish you would talk to us about your feelings more. We want to know what is going on in that beautiful head of yours. We want to know when we do something that makes you happy. We want to know when we do something that makes you mad. And we especially want to know when we do something that makes you sad. We hate when you're sad. It creates this pressure in our chests that won't go away. It's incredibly uncomfortable and all we can think about is making you happy again."

I felt bad, but I meant what I had said to him. I wouldn't complain to them about one of the others. It wouldn't be right.

"I'll try to get better about that," I promised.

We ate and played games for a few hours, but I was tired again. I grabbed Deryn away from the game, pulling him to one of the chairs and lay my head on his lap. He pet my hair and hummed a song that I thought sounded familiar, but couldn't place as I fell asleep.

My sleep didn't last long, though. The train slammed to a halt, throwing us forward and onto the floor. Deryn had managed to keep me from hurting myself and helped me get up.

Our food was now all over the floor, chips strewn all over.

"What the hell happened?" I asked.

"Stay here," Rhys ordered Deryn. "Martin and Nico, come with me. Fox, stay with them."

"Stay safe!" I ordered them.

They didn't respond, just walked out of the car to find out what had happened.

A second later, the train rocked wildly as an explosion hit.

Deryn picked me up and curled his body around mine.

"Status?" Deryn asked.

"No answer," Fox growled, putting his phone away.

"Decision?" Deryn asked.

"Out the back," Fox said. "I'll go first."

Deryn nodded and we headed out the back end of the train. Fox took point, throwing open the doors as we went, but as we looked out the rear of the last car, we hadn't found anything except scared people. Fox leapt out of the last car, onto the train tracks, and then leapt up onto the top of the car.

"Oh, fuck," he said, loud enough for the sound to make it down to us.

"Status!" Deryn growled, growing impatient.

"It's a god damn Cthulhu!" Fox yelled. "It's got the first few cars of the train in its tentacles.

"That's not a real creature. It was created by H.P. Lovecraft," I reminded Deryn.

"Well, then how do you explain that?" Fox asked.

Deryn leapt up onto the top of the train car, me still in his arms, and we both stared at the creature attacking the train. It sure as hell looked like Cthulhu.

"Well..." I didn't know how to finish that.

Rhys, Martin, and Nico were battling with the Cthulhu-like creature, trying to save the cars from its tentacles.

"Fox?" Deryn asked.

"I'll go. You stay with her," Fox said. He kissed my cheek and raced across the top of the train cars.

"Do you guys do things like this a lot?" I asked Deryn.

He smirked. "You'd be surprised how often things like this happen to us."

"So, maybe you guys are the problem and not me," I teased.

"Oh, you definitely attract your own danger," he replied. "But, so do we."

Rhys, Martin, Nico, and a few additional Others were fighting the creature, trying to save the people inside of the cars.

"We need to do more training," I whispered. "I could be useful in situations like these."

"Too dangerous. We will never allow you to face something like this," Deryn said, shaking his head.

"I can shift into a god damn dragon," I reminded him angrily.

"We don't care. You're not going to jump into battle. You only need to do things like that to protect yourself. And yes, your nieces or children on occasion," he said.

"Overprotective," I grumbled.

"There's no such thing. We are supposed to keep you safe. Letting you jump into a fight is not a way to keep you safe. Our entire being is set to keep you safe. All we can focus on is keeping you safe. So, no, there is no such thing as us being overprotective. You are the most important thing to us."

"I wasn't looking for a lecture," I grumbled at him.

He smirked and kissed my cheek. "Well, too bad. You got one."

The train shuddered beneath us, the monster pulling on it, forcing Deryn to jump down off of it and onto the train tracks.

"This is not looking good," I commented. So far, my guys seemed to be able to stay out of harm's way, so I wasn't too worried about them. I was worried about all of the people on the train though.

"This is such a pain in the butt," a guy said as he stepped out of the back of the train in front of us. He had long, golden hair, piercing blue eyes, and was carrying a huge sledge hammer.

"Thor? What are you doing here?" Deryn asked.

Thor? Like, God of Thunder?

"Yo, Deryn. I was sleeping on the train when it slammed on its brakes and sent me flying. Now I'm pissed and I'm going to take it out on the squid thing," he explained. His eyes fell on me, in Deryn's arms, and they widened. "Who is this? Did you find a mate?"

"This is the Princess of the Four Clans," Deryn introduced, but his grip on me tightened.

"I'd stay for a longer introduction, but as a resident god, I've got to go handle this," he said, winked at me, and then leapt up and ran down the train cars towards the monster.

"Is he really a god?" I asked.

Deryn scoffed. "In his own mind."

Thor leapt from the train, hammer raised, and gave a mighty bellow. The sky filled with clouds and lightning struck his hammer, alighting it and with a swing, the lightning went from his hammer to the monster.

Rhys and everyone else who had been battling it, leapt away just before the lightning struck, saving themselves from electrocution.

"Thor! Warn us first!" Rhys yelled at him.

"I bellowed," Thor countered and together they all watched as the monster twitched and then sank back into the water from where it had come. The cars righted on the tracks and everyone cheered.

"Great, now he's going to be made out a hero again. Let's get back to our car," Deryn grumbled.

"I take it you don't like him very much?" I asked softly.

"He's a good enough guy, just full of himself. Plus, everyone fawns over him like he's something special. I've beaten him before and so has Rhys. He's not perfect, like people think he is."

"Oh, did he steal a girlfriend from you too?" I teased him, trying to lighten his mood.

He rolled his eyes at me, but then his usual smile returned. "I actually stole one from him a few years ago."

"You're terrible," I said and shook my head. "I had no idea you were a thief."

"I stole your heart, didn't I?" he whispered huskily in my ear.

My hands gripped his shirt tighter and I tensed. "Don't. Tease. Me."

He chuckled and kissed my cheek lightly. "Sorry, baby."

The others came back, Thor with them, chatting and laughing like old friends.

"Thor, this is Jolie. Jolie, this is Thor," Nico introduced.

I stood up out of the seat I had been in beside Deryn and held out my hand. "Nice to meet you."

He took my hand, pulled me forward and hugged me, his nose tickling my neck as he inhaled deeply. "Hello, Jolie."

I heard three growls and two chuckles, one of which was mine. "Hello, Thor." I sniffed his neck and wondered what it was about his scent that smelled so familiar.

"Let her go," Deryn ordered him.

Thor released me with a smirk. "Don't worry, I was only saying hello."

"That's not how you say hello to someone you don't know," Deryn chastised him with a growl.

"It is if you're a werewolf," I said. "Especially a Northern Clan Werewolf."

That got everyone's attention.

"How do you know about that?" Thor asked suspiciously.

"Because that's what I am," Martin said.

Thor spun to face Martin. "I knew you smelled familiar!" He spun back to me. "You aren't a werewolf, though."

"No, but Martin and I dated in high school and I spent a lot of time with the pack," I admitted. I stared at Thor a minute longer and then gasped. "Tim!" I yelled at him.

"Tim?" Deryn asked.

Thor flinched. "Oh, wow. It's been years..." He froze and then pulled me forward to inhale the top of my head. He took a few big lungfuls and then he tilted my chin up with his finger to look into my eyes. "Jo?" he asked softly, recognition finally showing.

I nodded. "Yes, Tim."

"Holy wolf teats!" Martin yelled.

Thor smiled wide, dimples flashing, and he whispered, "Jo," before kissing me deeply.

I tried to push him back, but he was gone the next instant, Deryn having thrown him off of me and against the far wall of our car.

Thor wasn't even fazed. He was still smiling wide and tried to walk back towards me, but Deryn and Rhys blocked his path.

"Jo, how is it possible that you're even more beautiful now?" he asked me.

My cheeks were on fire. It had been a long time since I last saw him. Back then, he was Tim, not Thor, and he wasn't nearly as muscular.

"Don't touch her again," Deryn ordered him.

Martin pulled Thor into a bone crunching hug and Thor returned it. "I didn't even recognize your scent!" Martin exclaimed. "Your appearance and scent are so different!"

"Well, the last time I saw you two was graduation," Thor reminded us.

"You went to school with Jolie?" Rhys asked, for clarification.

Thor nodded. "She was my first love."

"Wasn't that Stacy H?" I asked with a teasing smirk. Stacy was the first girl he kissed and she had been head over heels for him.

"No, it was always you," he said seriously. He turned to Martin. "You let her get away? What the fuck is wrong with you?"

I flinched and Nico and Fox saw it, exchanging a look before turning back to Thor, who was still being blocked by Rhys and Deryn.

"It's a long and unpleasant story," Martin answered without looking at me.

"We've got hours left on this ride," Thor said. He looked at

Rhys and Deryn. "How long are you going to keep standing there?"

"As long as we think you might try to kiss her again," Deryn growled.

"Jo," Thor called, "come talk to me."

I squeezed between Rhys and Deryn to hug Thor, ignoring their growls again. "I can't believe it's you."

He chuckled. "I feel the same. They said your name, but I couldn't believe it was you. That you could be *the* Jolie."

We sat at the table and my guards took seats around me.

"You want to tell it?" Martin asked.

I shook my head, dreading this tale already. Thor held out his hand and despite the four males growling behind me, I set my hand in his. Thor could always tell when I was upset. He was very empathic.

"Jolie," Deryn growled softly.

Without looking at him, I reached back and held my other hand out to him. He linked our fingers and quieted.

"Remember how we kept seeing vampires in the area?" Martin asked Thor.

He nodded.

"There was a battle going on between the witches and vampires that we hadn't know about. Jo's dad was King of the Vampires and somehow the witches found out about Jo. We were out in Mrs. Lindstrom's field and they attacked us. It was just the two of us. I killed two of the witches, but another one grabbed Jo before I could stop her. She took Jo to the coven."

Thor's hand tightened around mine, but it was such a small movement, I wasn't certain he had done it consciously.

"Jo, tell your part," Martin said.

Thor turned toward me.

"Um, the witch took me to the coven. They had built a place on the other side of the river and cloaked the building so the wolves hadn't been able to see it. They, uh, they tied me to a post and tried to get information about my dad from me. I didn't know anything, though. They started torturing me to try to get me to break and…"

"We heard her screams," Martin continued for me. "We broke their illusions and I had to barter for her release."

A cost that I had been against and tried to convince him not to agree to.

"What was the cost?" Nico asked.

"That I separate from Jo and we never have a romantic relationship again. If we did, we would both become sterile."

For me, that wouldn't have mattered, but Martin had always wanted children. It was a definite deal breaker for him.

"So, you gave up your relationship to save her?" Deryn asked softly, his anger gone now.

Martin nodded. "But, they had already put a curse on her, two actually, that we hadn't known about."

"What happened?" Thor asked me.

"I was in a coma for a year until Grandma found someone who could break it. Then, just a few days ago, I had the final curse removed."

"And almost died," Deryn growled.

I jerked my hand away from his and stood up with fists clenched. "And I'd do it again," I growled at him. "Don't you get it? These witches put that curse on me when I was eighteen and I just now got it removed. I've been in danger and so has everyone else, because of it."

Deryn reached for me, but Thor pulled me forward so he could hug me. I hadn't even realized that he had stood up.

"What else happened, Jo? Why are you so angry?" he asked as he held me.

Like Fox, he had a soothing presence, and I relaxed into him. "A lot has happened," I whispered. "Some things I don't think I can even tell you about."

"No, she can't," Deryn growled.

"Deryn," Fox whispered, "calm down."

"Stop touching her," Deryn snarled.

"If she wanted me to release her, she'd pull back. You're not her mate. You may be prince, but you don't get to order me not to hug my friend and pack mate."

"She's not pack," Rhys pointed out.

"Semantics. I spent just as much time playing and hunting with her as I did the rest of my pack," Thor said.

He wasn't wrong. I had spent a lot of time with him.

"I'm his queen," I told Thor, looking up into his eyes. "Rhys, Deryn, Foxfire, and Nico are my guards. That's a secret by the way, so please don't tell anyone."

Thor chuckled. "Well, that explains their protectiveness. But, unless you're also sleeping with them, then…"

I glanced down and felt my cheeks heat up.

"Oh," Thor said. "Well, why didn't you say so?"

"Because it doesn't matter," I said and looked up at Thor. "You're my friend and they…" I jerked my thumb at the guys, "need to get used to seeing me hug my friends, no matter their gender."

"He kissed you," Deryn reminded me.

"Yes, before he knew anything," I countered. "I'm not marked, so he assumed I was unattached."

"I would have kissed you anyway," Thor said with a smirk.

I punched his arm and he released me and sat back down.

"Want to tell me the rest of the story?" he asked.

So, I did. I started from the end of the witch story and told him about almost everything that had happened to me and ended with coming on the train. I also made sure he knew to keep it secret.

"That's one crazy life," Thor said with a whistle.

"You never told us all of that," Fox whispered.

"Well, now everyone knows," I said and shrugged.

Deryn left, heading into the next train car with Nico following him.

A guy with tousled brown hair stuck his head into the car. "Thor? Alpha wants you."

Thor nodded, hugged me, and headed after him.

I got into my window seat and watched the scenery rolling by. Lush green hills made up the land we were traveling through with no building in sight. It was beautiful and peaceful.

Talking about all of the bad things that had happened to me had reopened emotions I didn't want to revisit, but was now forced to. After what had happened with Martin and the witches, I had distanced myself from people. I didn't want them involved or hurt, so I made myself a hermit. I made friends online in the gaming community and did my best to only let those relationships flourish. But, I had grown tired of being lonely. I needed physical companionship and not just sex, but the hugging and cuddling mainly. Growing up with werewolves had made me affectionate and going so long without touch had been driving me insane.

Deryn came back and plopped down in the seat next to me.

"I'm sorry," I whispered without looking at him. "I was being selfish again. I hadn't seen him in so long and the urge to touch him and-"

"No, I'm sorry," he interrupted. "You weren't doing anything wrong. And, I need to get over you removing the curse. You are here and fine, so it shouldn't matter."

"Why have you guys been so tense lately?" I asked him softly. "All of you have been worried about me, but I don't know why."

He held out his hand, but instead of taking it, I climbed into his lap and rested my head on his shoulder.

"You've been having nightmares. You cry out and sometimes call our names. You've even cried while dreaming, tears dripping down your cheeks and you'll be whimpering. It's been happening for weeks."

Shit. I hadn't realized they knew about my nightmares.

"Oh."

"What are your nightmares of?" he asked me softly, his voice gentle and his arms a secure band around my hips.

"Death," I replied softly.

"Whose?"

"All four of you."

He tensed beneath me. "What happens?"

"You're protecting me from something and one by one, you all die. I try to stop it, but I can't move. I just have to sit and watch as you're killed."

I was crying, evident by the wet spot on Deryn's shoulder. Deryn turned and licked my cheeks and eye, clearing away the tears.

"They're just dreams, baby. We are all here, safe and sound."

"What if it is a premonition?" I asked.

"We aren't going to die anytime soon," he assured me.

"You don't know that for sure," I argued.

"Do you really think they are premonitions?" he asked.

"No," I admitted, "but it won't stop happening. Almost every night."

"Perhaps it is your own fear getting the better of you," he suggested. "I know my biggest fear right now is losing you. I wouldn't be surprised if I had nightmares about it."

Part of me knew it was because whenever something good happened, something bad usually came next to counter it. I was trying really hard to just enjoy the happiness we had been having, but my subconscious was a jerk.

Now that I was surrounded by love and warmth, I didn't want to go back to being alone. I didn't want to be a hermit again.

"Hey," Deryn whispered and kissed my forehead. "What's going on in that head of yours?"

"Honestly?" I asked.

He nodded.

"After becoming used to being loved and touched again, I don't think I could handle going back to being a recluse. If I lose you, I won't be able to be alone."

"You won't be alone," he promised me. "You aren't going to lose us. I told you, no matter what happens, I will always be here for you."

"Even if I piss you off?" I asked softly.

"Always," he said adamantly, "and forever."

"I already used the lifetimes line," Fox called to him.

"Line?" I asked, feigning hurt. "So, it wasn't true? It was just a line you use on all the girls?"

Fox rolled his eyes at me. "You know it's not."

"Jolie, did you sleep with Thor?" Deryn asked in a whisper.

"No," I answered loudly. "Why would you think that?"

"He said you were his first love," Deryn reminded me.

"I was *his* first love. He wasn't mine. I only slept with Martin from that pack," I explained.

"So, he loved you and you loved Martin?"

I nodded.

"Wait, *that pack*? Were there other werewolves that you slept with from other packs?"

Oops. Spilled the beans. Shit.

"Um," I replied intelligently, totally ready for that question.

"How many other werewolves?" he asked.

"I don't ask you guys about who you slept with before," I countered.

"This is important," he said seriously.

"Why?"

"Because a representative from each of the packs will be at the Summit, so it is better if he is prepared ahead of time with knowing if any of them slept with you," Fox answered for him.

"Doesn't that mean I should let all four of you know if I have slept with others of your race?" I asked.

"Yes," Fox replied immediately.

"Do I have to give you names?"

"Yes," Deryn said.

Fuck.

"Yukio and Zelphar of the elves."

Fox's eyes widened and he blinked in silence.

"Declan and Kylan of the dragons," I said, looking at Rhys.

"Both?" he asked.

"Yes." They were twin brothers who I had dated one after the other.

"Werewolves?" Deryn prompted, growing impatient.

"Tobias, Ezio and..."

What was his name?

"Lorenzo," Martin answered for me.

I gaped at him. "How did you know that?"

"He called me to make sure we were actually over," he explained.

Wow.

"Anyone else fall in love with you? Like Thor?" Deryn asked with a scowl on his face and his body tense beneath me.

"I don't know," I snapped and stood up away from him. "You can't be mad at me about this. You knew I wasn't a virgin before we slept together. Plus, you're not a virgin either."

My anger was building, partly, okay mostly, due to my embarrassment. It wasn't fair for him to get mad at me for things that happened before we got together.

"No one likes hearing the list of prior conquests," Martin offered. "Not even me and we aren't together any longer."

"Or knowing you will see all of them at the Summit," Deryn growled.

"All of them?" I asked, my voice squeaking at the end.

"One big Jolie reunion," Deryn snarled.

I jerked back, feeling worse than if he had physically slapped me. Tears pricked at my eyes and I whispered, "Excuse me," before running out of the train car.

Rhys I might have expected a comment like that from, but not Deryn.

The train didn't have many places to escape to, but I knew towards the front was a car with glass ceilings and walls, so you could get a full view. I tripped over someone's foot and muttered an apology as I continued on.

Someone grabbed my arm and I turned, ready to attack, when through my teary-eyed sight, I recognized Dan.

"Alpha," I whispered, then sniveled.

"What's wrong?" he asked.

I shook my head. "I don't want to-"

Deryn entered the car, following me, and I pulled against Dan's hold.

"I don't want to talk to him," I begged him. "I just need some time."

He released me and nodded. "Go, I'll keep him."

I went through the next door and just as the door closed, I felt Dan use his power as he said, "Sit!" It was such a strong command that my knees wobbled.

I stumbled forward, right into Thor.

"Jo, what's wrong?" he asked, his eyes scanning my face and then behind me.

"Jus...need space," I said and hurried around him.

He let me go, but was scowling with furrowed brows as he watched me leave.

Finally, I made it to the car and found a seat. Surprisingly, there was no one else in the car. I curled my legs up, hugging my knees as I watched the hills go by.

There was something more going on with Deryn than he was telling me. He had been upset a lot recently. More than he should have been, even with me almost dying and my nightmares.

"The number one thing alphas hate, is not having control," Nico whispered from beside me.

"Nico," I sighed. "I want to be alone."

"No, you don't. Now, listen. alphas hate not having control. As prince, we have to operate knowing that for now, our fathers have control. And, we know there are some things we don't have control over and never will. Many alphas mate with a submissive because it ensures that we will have control."

"How loving," I scoffed.

"Shush," he ordered me.

"Fine," I mumbled and turned away from him.

"Deryn has always been in control of everything he possibly could be. Then, you fell into our lives."

"Is this the, Jolie fucked everything up, speech?" I asked with a snarl.

"You are incredibly unpredictable, wild, danger prone, and infuriating. You are emotional, independent, and happy to butt heads with anyone, even the kings."

"This is a fantastic pep talk," I grumbled. "Definitely making me feel better."

"On top of all of that, our lives drastically changed. We went from our happy and content foursome to our hectic fivesome."

I stood up and walked away from him. "Then, just fucking let me leave!"

He teleported in front of me and grabbed my shoulders, his eyes fell to the tears on my face and his scowl disappeared.

"Despite all of this, Deryn loves you more than anything else in the world. More than his own pack. Nothing regarding you is controllable. There is always something new for us to learn about you. We all figured we weren't the first Others you had had relationships with, but half of those wolves you slept with hate Deryn. They will use this opportunity to throw it in his face that they had you first. Since you aren't mated and our relationships aren't public knowledge, they can touch you if you allow it. He is once again not in control. You opted to put your life on the line and there was nothing he could do about it. You almost died and all we could do was pace and pray. He is stressed and hasn't been eating well because of it. He also hasn't shifted much lately. It is not an excuse for him saying such a cruel thing to you, but maybe you'll see things from his side if you know all of the facts."

My anger had dissipated, but I was still hurt.

Nico disappeared, leaving me alone with my thoughts.

What he said made sense. I could understand how infuriating someone like me would be to an alpha who liked to be in control of everything. I knew shifters preferred schedules and predictable events because chaos made them a little less in control of their beasts and an out of control werewolf was not something anyone wanted. For someone as powerful as a prince to lose control would be unthinkable. The fact that he hadn't shifted much recently was bothering me the most. I was a shitty girlfriend for not noticing he hadn't been shifting while we were together. He should have been spending at least half of our time together as a wolf.

I marched back to the car where Dan was sitting next to Deryn who was obviously frozen from his father's order.

"Shift," I ordered Deryn.

Dan said," You may go."

Deryn stood up and opened his mouth.

"Shift," I ordered him again before he could speak.

He scowled, but then did as I asked and shifted into his wolf form.

I held open the door for him. "Come on."

Deryn followed me on silent paws to the observation car. I lay on my back in the aisle, looking up at the sky. Deryn sat in front of me, slightly between my legs, head cocked, and looked at me.

I grabbed the fur on either side of his cheeks and gently tugged his head, so he lay down with his head on my chest, muzzle between my breasts. I pet his head with my eyes closed, inhaling his hot wolf breath and letting him breathe my scent in.

"What you said was rude and hurt me a lot," I whispered. He tried to lift his head, but I held him. I didn't continue until he had stilled. "It is not my fault that I didn't meet you until now. Yes, I have had a few sexual partners, but only one I had planned to mate with before you four. The way I see it, you have a few options. You can keep things as they are, withdraw your request to be my mate, but stay my guard, or you can completely cut ties with me. I love you so much, but I don't want to continue causing you misery."

And, I was crying again. Dammit.

His long wolf tongue licked up each cheek, then he shifted, laying atop me, but propped up on one arm so he wasn't squishing me.

"Baby, I'm sorry. I am a jealous asshole. It is not fair of me to take my frustration out on you. You aren't causing me misery."

"You were happy and smiling all the time, wanting to play and be carefree, but now you are mad all the time. That sounds pretty miserable. What's your decision?"

He kissed me deeply, his tongue sliding along mine in a slow caress as he gripped one of my hips, his thumb rubbing over my hip bone.

"I'm not going anywhere. Didn't we just talk about this? You are stuck with me for the rest of your life. I love you and I promise to work on my attitude and worrying. I want you to be safe and that has seemed impossible lately. I will do whatever I need to, to keep you safe, happy, and with me. I'm sorry for what I said. It wasn't fair of me."

"No, it wasn't," I agreed and sniffled.

He kissed each of my eyes, then my cheeks, neck, and my forehead. "I'm sorry." He sat up, pulling me with him, and hugged me tightly. "I'm sorry."

We sat like that for several minutes and then, I realized the train was heading toward the ocean.

"Does it turn ahead?" I asked, scanning the coast for the direction the train would turn.

"No," Deryn replied, but didn't elaborate.

Before I could ask where it went, I got my answer. We plunged straight into the sea, a shield of magic around us, keeping the water, as well as the creatures, away from the train.

I gasped and clung to him. More people filed into the car, stepping around us carefully as I took it all in, my mouth agape.

"You're beautiful," Deryn whispered. "I'm lucky to have you."

CHAPTER 6

The rest of the train ride was, thankfully, uneventful. We arrived at a land of swaying green grass and a huge castle, the largest I had ever seen.

A bus took us and two dozen other train riders to the castle. I sat between Deryn and Rhys, but kept standing up to lean over the top of the seat in front of me to talk to Dan.

"How old is it?" I asked him.

"One thousand years at least," he answered. "Over five hundred rooms, a huge ballroom, a courtroom, and three pools."

"I'm going to get lost," I whispered and Dan laughed.

Rhys pulled me down in to my seat. "You won't get lost because you will have a guard with you at all times."

"Is there indoor plumbing?" I asked softly.

All of them, including Dan and Thor who were sitting in front of me, laughed.

"Yes," Rhys promised.

"I'm hungry," I complained.

"There will be a huge feast when we arrive. We actually will only have time to change and then head to the throne room to eat," Dan told us.

"I have to wear a dress, don't I?" I asked with a resigned sigh.

"Yes, but don't worry, the dresses will all be in styles you like," Fox said behind me.

"That's reassuring," I whispered.

"Who is guarding her while you are in meetings?" Thor asked.

"Me," Martin answered. "That's why I'm here."

"If you need me, just howl," Thor told him. "I know she's quite a handful."

"Rude," I growled at him, but couldn't deny he was right.

Deryn squeezed the hand he was holding, having grabbed it at some point, though I wasn't certain when.

"Is there anything I should know before we get there?" I asked Dan.

"Yes," he nodded, "but I don't have the time to teach you everything right now. Just be on your most polite behavior and bow to everyone to be on the safe side."

"Right, being overly respectful is better than being disrespectful, even if I'm ignorant to who is actually important or not," I agreed.

"Right," Dan said.

"My clan kept our relationship a secret, so we are basically at square one. You're just our friend and here at Dan's invitation as Princess of the Four Clans. They will probably want to talk to you or at least say something to you, but I wouldn't worry about it too much," Rhys told me.

"So, no holding hands or anything?" I asked softly, feeling a bit of pressure in the center of my chest knowing I wouldn't be able to be affectionate with them in public.

Deryn squeezed my hand. "No, we won't be able to hold hands once we are there," he whispered.

"We should have had a cuddle puddle on the train before we departed," I mumbled.

"We can do that once we are in the rooms," Nico offered.

"Are we all staying near each other?" I asked, hopefully.

They all nodded.

"We wanted to make sure that you were safe, and that you wouldn't get yourself into trouble," Nico explained.

"I never get myself into trouble," I grumbled. "It finds me."

"One last thing," Dan whispered.

I leaned forward, so I could hear him through the crack in the seats.

"If anyone gives you trouble or threatens you, you tell one of us immediately. There will be a lot of things going on politically, and if they can find a way to use you for their own agendas, they will take it. They will make up a ton of lies about you, if it furthers their cause. So, let us know if anyone says anything that you think is weird or might have been a threat. It most likely will be one."

"Super positive pep talk there, Dad," I teased.

"Dad?" he whispered.

"Oh, uh, I just meant...you know the pep talk...it's like when a dad-"

"I like the sound of that," he said and turned his head to look over the seat at Deryn. "Someday, I would like that to be official."

"Don't look at me," he mumbled. "That's her decision. You know how I feel about it."

"Hm, yes. It's giving me one less chip to bargain with at the table," Dan said. He looked at Rhys. "Did you say the same to your father?"

"What?" Rhys asked, not having been paying attention to us.

"About not taking a mate for political purposes?" Dan said cryptically, so no one would know that we were actually talking about them not wanting anyone, but me, as a mate.

"Yes," Rhys said with a nod. "Father knows that is my feeling as well. He said that once he saw us together, at the Den, that he knew he wouldn't be able to separate us anyway, even if she never takes me for a mate."

"Hm, well, Daughter, I think you and I need to have a talk soon," Dan told me.

"I don't like the sound of that," I grumbled. "Dad-talks never went well for me. They usually ended with me being thrown into a closet."

"Dad won't throw you into a closet," Deryn promised me. "And if he did, I would just rip the door off for you again anyway."

"My hero," I whispered and batted my eyelashes at him dramatically.

"You should call me that more often," he whispered and kissed my cheek.

"And you said *I* have a big ego," Thor scoffed.

"You do. You refer to yourself as a god, Tim," Deryn growled.

"Don't call me that," Thor growled back.

"Boys," Dan chastised them. "No growling at each other. We're on the same side, remember?"

"No, we're not," Thor argued. "We both love her and both want her."

"You can't have her," Rhys growled at him.

"That's her decision," Thor whispered.

"Thor, knock it off," I growled at him. "If you want to spend any time with me, you have to drop the façade of trying to win me."

"I still love you," he whispered.

"As a pack mate," I reminded him. "You don't know me anymore. I'm much different than I was at eighteen."

"Pack mate?" Dan asked. "You were part of the pack Jolie grew up with?"

Thor nodded. "Yes."

"Did you really let her go on hunts with you?" Dan asked.

Thor nodded. "She would ride on Martin's back, or mine, and we would chase after animals. Normally, if we had her on our back, we would hunt rabbits instead of the deer that the rest of the pack was hunting. Sometimes, we set her down and joined in, but normally we were content to chase rabbits."

"And none of your pack tried to harm her during the hunts?" Dan asked.

Thor shook his head. "Of course not! She's pack."

"But she wasn't marked," Dan pointed out.

"She didn't need to be. We all knew her scent. She played with us and went to school with us. You have to remember that our town had only about six hundred people in the total population. Everyone knew everyone."

"Most of the town was the pack," I explained. "There were very few people living there who weren't pack."

"Your family being one of them," Dan added.

I nodded.

"I'm surprised your dad stayed in that town, with him becoming a vampire and all," he commented.

"Me too," I said honestly. I still wasn't sure why he had stayed when he knew the werewolves would be able to tell he was a vampire. It didn't really make sense, but then again, my dad hadn't made much sense to me, ever.

"Jo, what was the name of that girl that you punched?" Thor asked.

"Jolie punched someone?" Deryn asked, shocked.

"Anna Smith. She was talking bad about Others, werewolves especially, and none of them could do anything, but since I was human, like her, I could. So, I walked up to her and punched her right in her raised nose. She cried like a baby."

"Didn't you get in trouble?" Thor asked.

I nodded. "Alpha made me stay away from the pack for a week."

"He made you stay away? Why?" Dan asked.

"Because he knew that I hated being away from them. I grew up like a shifter, craving affection and touch. Being away for a week meant I didn't get any touch, since my mom was dead and my dad was psychotic."

"That's a really harsh punishment," Rhys said with a frown.

"He was trying to teach her not to fight people, like we are always taught," Martin explained. "Plus, I snuck over after a few days to ensure she didn't go crazy."

"That's why you're so affectionate," Dan whispered. "You're basically a werewolf who can't shift."

"I guess so," I whispered.

"Would you have gone crazy?" Rhys asked.

I nodded and looked at Deryn. "I told you that I wouldn't be able to go back to being alone again."

He pulled me into a tight hug and said, "You won't ever be alone, Jolie."

"No, you won't," Thor promised.

The castle was larger than a few college campuses I had been to. Sticking to my spot in the center of my guards, we walked down the hallway to our rooms. My room was in the center of theirs, giving me added protection. In the closet was a month's worth of dresses in various colors and styles. I opted for a silver dress with a snug bodice, but flowing skirt.

Someone knocked on my door.

"Just a minute!" I called as I put on all of the jewelry the guys had given me.

"You look stunning," Deryn said from behind me.

I spun around, my heart pounding in my chest. "Mage's mana! You scared me!"

His smile let me know that he didn't feel bad at all. "Are you ready?"

Now that I wasn't hyperventilating, I looked at him. He had black slacks, a white button up shirt, and black tie and jacket.

"You look hot," I said, stepping forward and resting my hands on his chest.

"Stop looking at me like that or we won't make it to the feast," he whispered and kissed me.

"We could have our own feast here," I tempted.

"You need to eat," Deryn said. "I can hear your stomach growling."

"Sounds like she's thirsty," Fox said with a wink as he, Rhys, and Nico walked in.

"You present me with a gift and then get mad when I want to unwrap it. It's not fair," I fake pouted.

"You can unwrap all four of us later," Nico promised. "First, we need to get some food."

"Wait," I ordered them. "Before we go and I can't touch you all." I grabbed Deryn, since he was closest and pulled him into a deep kiss, and did the same with all of the others.

"Maybe we could be late," Nico rumbled and pulled me back for another kiss.

I pushed him away with a wide smile, glad that I still had that effect on them. "No. No. We need food, remember?" I said to Nico as I walked away.

Rhys opened the door, preventing us from continuing the teasing, and we all filed out. The guys took their positions around me and walked down the hallway confidently, making turns, and arriving without asking for directions.

"How many times have you been here?" I asked.

"Every year since we were five," Fox answered.

"Well, I'm glad you guys know your way around. I'd be completely lost right now other—"

"Jo?" a male voice asked.

I stopped and turned toward the speaker. It was actually two of them, both dragons with identical faces and smiles.

"Declan and Kylan!" I called happily, stepping out of the protection of my guards to hug the twins. "You guys haven't changed at all."

Declan kissed my cheek. "You look gorgeous, like always."

Kylan nodded and kissed my other cheek. "I'm so happy to see you. We were just talking about you the other day."

"Good things, I hope," I said with a smile, squeezing their hands, each holding one of mine.

"Of course," Declan assured me.

"Declan. Kylan. Nice to see you both," Rhys greeted them.

They bowed to Rhys, but hadn't let go of my hand. "Prince," they said in unison.

Kylan turned back to me. "Are you going to the feast? You should sit with us."

"Sorry guys, but I'm sitting with my friends already," I said and indicated my group.

"Well you have to visit with us and catch up," Declan begged.

"I will definitely try," I promised, unsure how Rhys would react to their proposal.

They kissed my cheeks again and headed off.

"You sure you're not a witch?" Nico asked.

"What? Why?"

"They never touch anyone, unless it is to hurt them," Rhys told me.

"What? That's crazy! They're super sweet and really affectionate."

The guys exchanged glances and then we headed back down the hallway. I hated their shared glances, since I couldn't figure out what they were communicating.

The ballroom was ginormous. It reminded me of a warehouse due to its size, but surprisingly, it was warm and inviting. Currently, it was filled with tables and people milling about, talking to each other.

As soon as the guys entered, a group of females rushed over to fawn all over them. More than a few snuck touches in, and some gave brazen offers to visit their rooms later.

"Jolie?" a soft voice asked behind me.

I turned and smiled up at Tobias. "Hey!"

He pulled me forward and rubbed his cheek along mine. "It is you."

He looked and smelled the same. Light stubble on his cheeks, deep brown eyes, and dark brown hair accented his medium-brown skin. Tobias had been the first male I had slept with after Martin. It had taken me a while to take that step and he had been a patient hunter and gentleman the whole time. I had started to fall for him and when I realized that, I had broken it off and left.

"You look great," I offered and kissed his cheek.

"Tonight, I need to talk to you privately," he said urgently.

"About what?" I asked.

"Tobias, good to see you," Deryn greeted him stiffly.

Tobias tensed and bowed slightly. "Prince Deryn."

"Jolie, do you know-" Tobias started, but Deryn draped his arm across my shoulders.

"Jolie and I are friends," Deryn said, his eyes sparking with gold.

Tobias nodded then looked at me. "Promise?"

I nodded. "Promise."

He left and Deryn pulled away from me before he asked, "What did you promise him?"

"To come talk to him tonight," I answered, not wanting to keep anything from him.

"About what?"

"I don't know," I admitted.

Something was up, though. He had seemed nervous, almost scared. Tobias was never scared. And why talk to me? Why not Dan or Deryn?

"Come on, let's go sit down," he said, starting to reach for me, but dropped his hand and instead waved in the direction of the guys. They had escaped the herd of females and now sat at a table with three open seats. Deryn sat beside Rhys, quickly whispering to him, and I sat between the empty chair and Martin.

"You look beautiful," he whispered and rubbed his cheek along mine.

"Thanks," I whispered, rubbing his cheek back for comfort.

Someone slid into the seat next to me and I turned, expecting to find Dan or Thor, but instead found Ezio.

He was one of the most handsome males I had ever seen, even more attractive than my guards. Copper hair, sapphire eyes, and a smile that had me clenching my thighs together to hide my arousal, was coupled with the body of a god.

He waited for me to stop ogling him and leaned his face forward, waiting.

I met him, sliding my cheek along his silky soft skin and practically purred at his cologne-like scent. "Ezio," I whispered.

He pressed our foreheads together and whispered, "Jolie, my love. I've missed you."

Deryn and someone else growled, but neither of us moved.

"I'm sorry," I whispered and pulled back, not clarifying if I was apologizing to my guards or Ezio for prior transgressions. Honestly, it was a bit of both.

Ezio looked at the four scowling faces of the princes. "What's wrong?" he asked them.

Ignoring them, I pushed up Ezio's tuxedo jacket sleeve, so I could see the small scar on his wrist. I flinched at the sight of it, hoping it would have disappeared by now.

Ezio took the hand on his wrist and raised it to kiss my knuckles. "Leave the past in the past, love. I am perfectly fine and healthy."

"A story you didn't share?" Deryn asked me.

"No, I try very hard not to recall that night," I admitted while staring into Ezio's eyes. "The night I almost lost you."

"That's an exaggeration," he said with a smirk.

"Hardly," I countered and looked away from him, the image of the blood-soaked ground coming to my mind.

"Care to share?" Deryn asked.

"No, this is a private event between us," Ezio told him, turning to give him a glare before looking back at me. "Why aren't you mated yet?"

"I'm working on it," I said, trying really hard not to glance at my guards.

"The sooner you have a mate, the sooner you will be safe. My offer is still open."

"Please," I begged him, "let's not open old wounds."

"What do you think happened as soon as I saw you," he whispered into my ear. He kissed my cheek and vacated the chair beside me. I watched him leave, going to a table with Thor, Tobias, Lorenzo, and a few others I did not know.

"What was that about?" Deryn asked.

I looked at him and was shocked to see that he wasn't mad, but curious.

"Nothing," I whispered and clutched at my chest. Ezio had been the best friend I needed after Martin. We would have mated, but I wasn't ready at the time. Plus, he had gotten hurt protecting me and I had left before he was killed.

I tugged on each of our four bonds, reassuring myself with their metaphysical presences since we couldn't touch.

They relaxed a bit and we all turned to watch the kings and elders walk in. There were a few other older males I did not recognize with them, and all eleven took seats at the long head table.

Dan's eyes roved across the attendees before stopping on me, a smile replacing his scowl.

The older male in the center stood and the room silenced.

"That's Amos," Deryn whispered. "He's the Leader of the Summit."

"Welcome to the Summit. Thank you, representatives, for attending. This year marks our two thousand five hundredth Summit!" Amos announced.

Everyone clapped.

"We will convene on business for the first three days, then we will hold our tournament. This year, the prize is extremely valuable, one that I know our strongest will be fighting for. However, I won't announce the prize until the first day of the tournament. Now, let the feast begin!"

Servants brought out silver platters of food and set them in front of us, making us wait a beat before they lifted the lid and showed us our meals. Prime rib, cheesy mashed potatoes, broccoli, and pesto pasta.

"It smells amazing," I drooled, and ripped a piece of meat off, tossing it in my mouth. "It tastes amazing."

We didn't talk as we ate, and I surprised the guys by asking for seconds when they ordered theirs. Not only did I order seconds, but I finished them.

Dessert came and I enjoyed my chocolate pudding slowly, letting it melt in my mouth.

"This is the longest she's ever been quiet," Nico said with a playful smile.

I continued my quietness until I finished my dessert. All I wanted was to curl up and take a nap now. However, I didn't get that option since it was now time to dance.

The tables disappeared and before they could discuss who was dancing with me first, Martin pulled me out onto the dance floor.

"When was the last time we danced?" he asked me.

"Senior prom," I answered with a smirk as I recalled that night.

His smile slipped and he whispered, "You know that I only agreed to the witches' cost to save you, right? That I loved you-"

I put my finger over his lips. "I know. And I'm happy for you and Sharla. Plus, I love them," I said, knowing he would understand that I meant the princes.

"I can tell," he said, pulling my hand away from his face.

We spun around the dance floor, two friends enjoying each other's company and having a wonderful time.

"My turn," Nico said, grabbed my hand, and spun me away.

"Hello, sparkles," I said with a wide smile.

He shook his head. "If you weren't so pretty, I might get offended."

"My looks have nothing to do with it."

"Rhys had to leave to cool down," he whispered.

"Why? What happened?" I asked, worried about my dragon.

"He couldn't handle how Ezio and you interacted. Deryn left too. The love in his eyes...it is hard to see our most feared and violent fighters fawning over you and professing their love."

"I-"

"You haven't done anything wrong. Though, perhaps next time you should let us know the extent of your previous relationships."

"Jo," Yukio gasped, releasing the hand of the female elf he had been dancing with to grab mine and pull me away from Nico. "Jo, is it really you?"

"Hey, Yukio. It is me," I said and hugged him.

"Who is this human?" the female elf asked, annoyance obvious.

"Princess Jolie of the Four Clans," I said in introduction with a smirk.

"Oh, now you use the title," Nico mumbled behind me.

"Dance with me," Yukio ordered, pulling us into the flow of dancers without waiting for my agreement.

"You look well," he commented.

"As do you."

"Become my mate," he said, making me stumble.

"What? This is the first time that I have seen you in a decade."

"Does it feel like we have been apart that long?"

No.

"I can't. I-"

"You aren't worthy of her," Zelphar hissed, stopping us in the middle of the dance floor.

"Zelphar!" I gasped.

"You think you are worthy of being her mate?" Yukio scoffed.

"Neither of you is taking her as a mate," Ezio growled, abandoning his dancing partner to join the argument.

"Neither are you," Deryn growled. Rhys, Nico, and Fox stood right behind him. When had Deryn and Rhys come back?

They started closing in on each other, fists clenched, tension thick.

"Guys!" I yelled, getting all of their attentions'. "Stop this right now. You know I hate this shit. I'm not a commodity and I make my own decisions."

All looked cowed, thankfully.

"Martin!" I called. "Thor!"

Both appeared next to me.

"Yes, Princess?" Martin asked.

"Thor, keep them from fighting over me."

"As you wish, Princess," he said and bowed to me.

"Martin, take me to my room."

He held out a bent arm and I put my arm through it.

"Good night, gentlemen," I said and marched out of the ballroom with my head held high.

Once we stepped out into the hall I whispered, "I need to get word to Tobias to come to my room to talk to me. He seemed really nervous and like it was important."

"You sure about that?" Martin asked.

"Why wouldn't I be?" I asked.

"He's one of the craziest fighters I know. He's known for his viciousness."

"He won't ever hurt me. Plus, he asked to talk to me and I promised I would talk to him," I explained.

"Fine, I'll have someone find him and send word to come see you. I'm not leaving the room with him there, unless one of the princes comes," he told me with a tone that held no room for bartering.

"Fine."

Once in my room, I changed quickly into comfortable pajamas and put some socks on to keep my feet warm. Martin sent word via a servant and then we waited in the room together.

"You sure caused quite the raucous. I don't think I've ever seen fighting at the feast before."

"I didn't do anything. Those idiots did it by trying to stake a claim to me when they didn't have one," I grumbled.

"We don't have one?" Rhys asked from the doorway.

I sighed loudly. "I wasn't talking about you four and you know it."

They could be so frustrating sometimes. Obviously, they knew I wasn't talking about them. Plus, we had to keep our relationship a secret, or this would have been easily fixed.

"What are you doing?" Deryn asked me, stopping in front of my chair.

"Waiting for Tobias to come. He wanted to talk to me," I explained.

"And you don't know what he wanted to talk to you about?" Deryn asked.

"No. He just made me promise to talk to him tonight."

"You seem worried," Fox commented.

"He was acting scared or nervous. Tobias never acts like that," I explained.

"She's right about that," Deryn agreed.

"How did you tame the twins?" Rhys asked.

"I didn't tame anyone," I snapped.

"You had our most terrifying males ready to fight over you," Fox said.

"That's because they are stupid and as stubborn as you all," I argued.

"I'm going to find Tobias," Martin said, leaving quickly.

"They are all in love with you, still," Deryn said.

"I made it clear when I left them, that it was over."

"What offer was Ezio talking about?" Nico asked.

"That's personal."

"You are supposed to be open and honest with us," Fox reminded me.

"You want to be open and honest? Fine, I want names of every female you have been with, especially if they are here," I ordered them.

That shut them up.

"You've got my list, so give me yours."

"Do you really want that?" Rhys asked.

"Yes, I want to know which of those females you've slept with so when they touch you, I can plan their slow and painful death."

My teeth had changed, my canines lengthening and thickening.

"Easy," Deryn whispered to me.

"You think I am," I snapped, my anger continuing to grow out of control.

"Jolie," Fox whispered, using his power on me.

Why was I so mad? Sure, the situation was irritating, but I was pissed, way beyond what I should have been.

"None of us is mad, right?" Deryn asked the guys, who all just looked shocked. "Didn't think so."

I paced across the room, trying to calm down. Rhys reached out for me, but I jerked away from him. "Don't touch me right now."

Thor knocked and then walked in, his eyes focused on me. "Jo."

"What?" I growled, facing him.

He shifted and rubbed against my legs like a cat.

"No," I snarled, pushing him away.

He tackled me to the ground and licked my face. I growled at first, but as he continued doing it, something in my chest loosened. I relaxed beneath him with a sigh.

He lay down on me, pinning me with his body and huffed loudly.

"Sorry," I whispered.

"What was that?" Deryn asked.

Thor looked up at him and communicated with him through their pack bond.

I ran my fingers through his fur as he talked, content to relax now.

"How often do you have these anger episodes?" Deryn asked.

"Once a year," I admitted.

"What did you do when you didn't have a werewolf with you?"

"I just need an alpha of any race, or a werewolf. If I don't, I just let the anger out until I pass out."

"When did this start?" Rhys asked.

"She's always had it," Martin said as he came in. "Those from my pack are more attuned to it because we had to help her often."

"Where's Tobias?" I asked, pushing Thor off of me to sit up.

"He's sick," Martin said with furrowed brows.

"What? He's a werewolf. You don't get sick."

"They quarantined him because of it," Martin said. "I talked to him though and he said he wanted to warn you about the tournament prize."

"What about it?" Rhys asked.

"He got sick, throwing up, before he could tell me and they ordered me to leave."

"What could make a werewolf sick?" I asked aloud.

No one answered, which was answer enough. There wasn't anything that should be able to make a werewolf sick, except a curse of some kind.

And why was he trying to warn me about the tournament

prize? I wasn't participating. It didn't matter to me what the winner got.

"Are you guys participating in the tournament?" I asked them.

"Yes."

"It's mandatory."

"We always do."

"Why wouldn't we?"

"What's the prize usually?" I asked. Maybe we could figure out what this year's would be.

"It varies every year," Rhys said. "Last year it was cash. The year before it was a house."

"A house? Someone won a house?" I asked.

"I did," Fox said. "It's here, in the center of downtown. We could visit it, if you want," he suggested.

"You own a house here?"

"We can come back for a vacation sometime," Fox promised.

"So, what could this year's prize be that Tobias would need to warn me about?" I asked them.

"No idea," Deryn said with a shrug.

CHAPTER 7

Martin and I spent the next day playing card games and cuddling together while he was in wolf form. He was really drowsy, abnormally so, and when the guys came back, he rushed off to the bathroom.

"Oh no," I whispered and started to move towards the bathroom, but Fox grabbed me and stopped my progression.

"Get the healers," Fox said.

Someone left, but I didn't see who.

"Let me go," I ordered Fox.

"No, I can't let you get near him and catch what he has," Fox told me, pulling me farther away from the bathroom.

"I was already touching him, all day," I reminded him.

"Hush," he ordered me.

A stranger came in, I assumed the healer, and he took Martin away.

"Is he going to be okay?" I asked, trying to follow them, but not getting anywhere because Fox still held me.

"We'll make sure he has the best healers on him," Fox promised me.

This was not good. I couldn't let anything happen to him. If something happened to him, Sharla and the girls would never forgive me. I would never forgive me.

"What am I going to do now? I don't have a guard," I whispered, leaning back into Fox.

"We'll figure it out," he whispered and kissed my cheek, his power soothing me.

"Fox, come outside," Rhys ordered them. "Jolie, stay inside please."

"No secrets!" I growled.

"We'll be back," Rhys said and shut the door behind him, shutting me inside.

"Rude!" I yelled.

They came back an hour later, but thankfully they brought food with them.

"So?" I asked as I ate.

"Thor is going to guard you," Deryn told me.

"Really? You're going to let Thor guard me?" I asked him with folded arms.

"Yes. We need you protected tomorrow and while we are in the tournament," Rhys said. "Thor is one of the strongest werewolves and one of the few who knows the truth about our relationship, so he won't actually try to mate with you."

"The others wouldn't either," I muttered. "They'd try, but stop when I said no," I told them.

"He'll be here tomorrow morning to guard you," Deryn said. "And we are going to finish as fast as possible so we can get back to you."

At the end of the day, I was beyond bored. Thor had finally agreed to take me out of the room and on a tour of the castle. The castle was simply amazing. There was so much to see.

I waited outside of a bathroom for Thor to come out, when I heard King Johann talking to someone. Slowly, and quietly, I walked around to the entrance of a small courtyard. The courtyard had a single tree in the center with a circular bench around it. Sitting on the bench was King Johann, King of the Mages and Nico's dad.

What shocked me most, was the person he was talking to. Justina. Justina was a dhampir who had been my coworker for a bit before she joined my father and helped him use me to make the guys attack the President. Thankfully, they had overcome it without actually killing the President. Justina hadn't been with my father at the final battle, the one where he was killed. I hadn't really thought much about what had happened to her, but now I was very curious about what she was doing with the Mage King.

"Will you agree to my deal or not?" Justina asked him.

"You aren't giving me much negotiating power," he scoffed.

The stone I was leaning on moved, making my presence known to them both, so I walked in confidently, like I hadn't been snooping.

"What the fuck are you doing here?" I demanded of Justina.

She hissed at me and then ran off, leaving me with King Johann.

"You won't tell anyone about this," King Johann told me. "Do you understand? If you tell anyone about this meeting, I will make you regret it."

He was threatening me! Wow. That was not something I expected.

"What were you trying to make a deal with her about?" I asked him. "What could she possibly have for you?"

"That's none of your concern. You would do well to learn to stay out of things that aren't your business and keep your mouth shut. Now, you get out of here before one of your guards comes in," he ordered me.

Asshole. I obeyed, though, knowing I needed to get back to Thor. I stepped out of the courtyard and Deryn and Thor stood there, scowling at me.

"What?" I asked softly, walking by them toward our rooms.

"We heard," Deryn told me. "We heard everything he said."

"If you say anything…" I started, not sure what the Mage King would do. Would he have me killed?

"Don't worry about it," Deryn said and pulled me into his side with an arm around my shoulders. "I'll take care of it."

Thor didn't say anything, just walked on my right side with a scowl on his face. He looked ready to punch someone.

"Why are you mad?" I asked Thor.

"He threatened you," Thor snarled. "That fucking asshole threatened you."

Yeah. He had. I was shocked too.

Deryn's grip on me tightened and he didn't let up until we were in my room.

"Nico," Deryn growled. "We need to talk. Now."

"I didn't do it," Nico said, but when Thor, Deryn, and I didn't crack a smile, he walked out with Deryn.

"What happened?" Rhys asked.

"If he tries to touch you, I'll fucking kill him. I don't care if he is a king or not," Thor told me. "I'll tear his fucking head off."

"That's enough," I ordered him. "Be quiet."

"What happened?" Rhys asked again, his pupils changing to slits as they changed to his dragon eyes.

"Go talk to Deryn," I told him, feeling tired and unsure of what to think.

What could Justina have that King Johann would want? He said she wasn't giving him much negotiating power, which meant she had the power in the exchange. What? What the hell could she have?

"More shifters are sick," Fox told me. "The healers still don't have any idea what is causing it, but they are keeping everyone comfortable. Tobias and Martin are doing okay. They're still throwing up and sick, but they aren't dying."

"Thanks for updating me," I said and walked into his arms, letting him hold me and try to ease my stress and worry.

"Jolie," Nico whispered from behind me.

I turned around to face him, unsure what he was going to say or how he would react.

"You're my queen, so no matter what he says, or what orders he tries to give me, if they are to harm you, I will not follow them. I will continue to protect you. You are my top priority."

"So, we're okay?" I asked.

He pulled me into a hug and said, "We're great. I love you. I'm sorry my father did something so crass. I can't believe he threatened you. I mean, I believe he threatened you because Deryn witnessed it, and I would have believed it if you had said it. I just don't understand why he did it."

"Me neither," I admitted and tried to burrow into him, getting as close as I could. "Tomorrow is the tournament, right?" I asked. "What happens?"

"We all go to the tournament grounds and they explain the rules, the prize, and what is going to happen in the events. Sometimes we all have to be in there at the same time, so we are going to have you stay with Dan," Nico said. "We know he won't hurt you and he'll protect you from my asshole father if he needs to."

❀

AFTER AN EXTENSIVE CUDDLING EPISODE, THE GUYS ESCORTED ME to the tournament stands. The "stands" turned out to be a coliseum made of stones likely as old as the castle. The coliseum was oval shaped with a set of box seats on one end where the kings and other summit members sat. There was a magic spell in front of their view that magnified the arena, so that even though they were far away, they could see everything clearly.

King Katar of the Elves and King Emrys of the Dragons both hugged me. King Johann nodded once at me with thinly veiled anger. Shit. I swallowed nervously, but then Dan grabbed me in one of his infamous bear hugs and led me to the seat between his and King Emrys's.

"How are you?" Dan asked.

"Worried about Tobias and Martin," I whispered back.

He patted my hand. "The best healers in the world are with them. They'll figure out what is wrong."

The stands were filled with attendees from various races. I scanned the crowd and Gavin waved at me with a wide smile.

"Your family is here?" I asked Emrys, seeing the other siblings and Adelaide.

Andras winked at me and I gave him a small wave.

"Yes, everyone's families are here, but they aren't allowed to sit up here with us," Emrys answered.

"Then why am I here?" I asked.

Amos stood, getting everyone's attention. "Welcome to the Summit Tournament!"

Everyone cheered loudly.

"Today, our strongest and most talented warriors will be put to the test to see who is the best. As I announced at the feast, this year's prize is the best yet!"

The anticipation was palpable, everyone sat on the edge of their seats. Everyone, but my four princes who stood next to the arena with bored expressions on their faces.

Amos motioned at me to come forward. I looked at Dan, but he just shrugged and pushed me to obey. I walked to stand beside Amos, my heart beating faster than a hummingbird's. Why was I up here?

"This year, the winner will obtain the honor of becoming the mate of Jolie, Princess of the Four Clans!" Amos announced.

Now, the princes weren't bored, their expressions ranging from shock to murder.

"Excuse me!" I demanded. "What?"

"Didn't anyone tell you, dear?" he asked. "You're our Princess and unmated, so it is the logical prize. You're a bit old to be unmated still and it's really us doing you a favor."

"I'm not-"

Dan pulled me to my seat and fixed his glare on Amos. "Who made this decision?" he demanded.

"Me," Amos said with a smirk. "Unless you have a reason we shouldn't offer her?"

They knew! That asshole knew I had guards. Somehow, someone had spilled the beans to him.

"The Summit doesn't take kindly to lies and deceit," Amos whispered to me and Dan.

"Fuck y-"

Emrys put a hand over my mouth, stopping me from finishing. "Quiet," he ordered me. "This is a test."

I hated tests. "I didn't agree to this," I whisper hissed to him.

"As princess, you don't have a choice. I'm sorry. I didn't think something like this would happen or we wouldn't have named you princess."

"I know this isn't your fault, King Emrys," I whispered while glaring at Amos.

I looked back down at my guards and they all bowed to me.

"That's them promising to win," Dan whispered to me.

Ezio bowed to me before he hopped into the coliseum's sandy arena.

"Apparently, Ezio too," Dan mumbled.

Declan and Kylan bowed to me next and I let out a loud groan. "Dammit."

"Why are my dragon twins bowing to you?" King Emrys asked.

"Because they are stubborn assholes," I growled.

Then, to my amazement, Thor bowed to me and leapt in. What was wrong with these males!

"Thor?" Dan asked.

"I'm his one true love, if you ask him," I growled. "He and I never dated or anything, but we grew up together and he always wanted me." I growled again. "Those fucking assholes are going to regret this if they hurt my-"

Emrys & Dan both put hands over my mouth.

"Just be quiet," Dan said with a chuckle

I folded my arms over my chest, pouting and angry at the same time.

"So, Princess, do you have a favorite?" Amos asked.

"No, I don't have *one* favorite," I answered honestly.

I have four.

Fifteen males of various races faced off with each other, but thankfully my four stayed side by side.

"No shifting," Amos ordered them. "No killing. Maiming is fine as long as it is not life threatening. Magic is permitted, but no deadly force. Last five standing will move on to the next round."

What would happen if one of my guys didn't make it?

Dan set his hand on my knee, which had been bouncing quickly. "It'll work out," he said, but I could tell he was worried too.

Ezio faced Deryn, a feral smile on his lips. "You aren't worthy of her."

Deryn smiled, looking completely calm and relaxed. Like he wasn't about to fight for my hand. "She'll be mine," he told Ezio. "She'll be mine and you can take whatever that offer was and shove it."

Oh boy.

"She didn't tell you what it was, did she?" Ezio asked with a smirk. He looked up at me and raised his right hand, now holding a sword. "I'll prove I'm strong enough to be your mate."

"Dumbass," I muttered.

"You and Ezio-" Emrys asked.

"We were together a little over a year," I confirmed. "I broke it off so he wouldn't get hurt again."

"Again?" Dan asked.

"The one scar on his entire body," I whispered, "was gained by protecting me."

"Oh, boy," Dan sighed. "He told me about you. He hasn't stopped loving you."

"I know," I muttered.

An idea popped into my head and before Amos could start the event, I shouted, "I won't have children!"

That got everyone's attention, even my guards.

"What?" Amos demanded.

"I refuse to bear children," I told him.

Two males left the ring, giving up.

"You can't-" Amos sputtered.

"She can," Dan growled.

I had already chosen this course, when I officially decided to take my four as my mates.

"I already have the surgery scheduled to tie my tubes," I told everyone, blushing slightly since I was airing my business with hundreds of strangers.

"Were you going to tell-" Rhys asked.

"Yes," I said before he could finish that sentence with "us."

"When?" Nico asked.

"After I claimed who I was going to mate with."

All four blinked in silence, my declaration sinking in. I had planned to claim them as my mates. I saw the moment they all understood. Their faces grew serious and they all pulled weapons out.

"Let's go!" Rhys growled, swords in his hands. "Start this tournament, now!"

"Begin!" Amos ordered.

Rhys bellowed and in two movements had sliced off an arm from two males I didn't know.

"I've never seen him so aggressive in the tournament," Emrys said. "What did your statement just now mean to them?"

"It's personal," I said softly, blushing.

"You turned them feral," Dan said, eyes fixed on Deryn.

Deryn was fighting against Ezio, their blades making a

shower of sparks, arc around them with each hit. Both wore feral snarls as they fought.

Fox had his hands full, fighting Yukio and Zelphar. Both were attacking him in earnest and his eyes glowed as he fought them, not backing down and it looked like he was winning.

Nico was fighting another mage, keeping that mage from attacking my other guards. In seconds, the mage was unconscious and he was moving to his next victim.

The pool went from thirteen down to nine. Thor was unconscious behind Deryn now, though I hadn't seen how it had happened.

Deryn and Ezio were still battling, Rhys was fighting Declan and Kylan. Fox was fighting Yukio, and Nico fought Zelphar.

Dan grabbed my hand, stopping me as I moved forward unknowingly. Declan had cut Rhys's arm and Rhys was now bleeding.

"Emrys," Dan snapped.

Emrys blocked my view, jerking my chin up so I had to meet his eyes. "Calm down!" he ordered me, pouring his power as alpha into me.

The dragon inside of me had been rushing to the surface and I hadn't known until he said something. I shoved the dragon back down, but it was hard. We wanted to protect Rhys. We wanted to hurt the one who had hurt our guard.

"He's not going to die," Emrys assured me.

"He's bleeding," I growled, my voice much deeper than usual.

"It's fine. I promise that I won't let them hurt Rhys enough to put his life in danger or cause permanent damage. Now, calm down and put her to sleep or everything will be ruined," Emrys whispered in my ear.

He was right. I needed to get a handle on myself. Taking a deep breath of Emrys's scent, I rested my forehead for a brief moment on his chest and let his power help me put the dragon completely to sleep.

"Good," he praised me and we took our seats again. Thankfully, Amos had been too engulfed in the battle to pay attention to me.

Yukio and Zelphar were out, unconscious on the ground, and now Fox was helping Rhys fight the dragon twins.

"Sir," a human male whispered to Amos and handed him an envelope.

Amos took the envelope, reading it quickly so he could look back at the fight. He finished reading it and handed it to Johann. Johann read it and chuckled darkly. "Fitting," he whispered.

"What is it?" Dan demanded.

Johann gave him the letter and as soon as he read it, Dan growled and said, "No. Absolutely not."

"It's her decision," Johann said.

"Oh, this is her decision, but who she mates with isn't?" Emrys snarled after reading the letter.

Clearly, this was about me.

"What is it?" I asked.

"The illness that is affecting the shifters is a poison. There is an antidote, but the price they are asking-" Emrys shook his head. "We can't."

"What is it?" I asked, dreading where this was headed.

"You. We hand you over and they give us the antidote," Johann said.

"There has to be something else that they want," Dan said.

"Seems pretty clear that they only want her," Johann said.

"Why are you being such a dick?" Emrys asked, his eyes glowing.

"Say that again," Johann threatened him, standing up to face him.

"I'll do it," I whispered.

"You fucking heard me," Emrys snarled at Johann.

"I'll do it!" I yelled at them.

"Do what?" Rhys asked from the arena.

Shit, I hadn't realized that I had been *that* loud.

The fighting had stopped, the remaining five males looking up at us.

"The five have made it through!" Amos announced. "Rhys, Deryn, Nico, Foxfire, and Ezio will continue on to the second round."

The ones who had been knocked out were now sitting up, rubbing their heads.

"Thor. Ezio. Declan. Kylan. Yukio and Zelphar," I called down to them.

"Yes, Princess," they called back.

"Restrain the princes," I ordered them.

"What are you doing?" Dan demanded.

The six males followed my orders, grabbing the princes before they knew what was going on.

"What's this?" Deryn demanded.

"I'm saving my best friend," I told them. "I won't let his children grow up without a father."

"Jolie!" Rhys roared.

"Let's go," I told Johann.

Johann nodded and led the way.

"Father!" Nico yelled. "Don't let her do this! Please!"

Johann paused a moment at the anguish in Nico's voice, but it was just a brief pause before he resumed walking.

Sounds of fighting broke out and I knew my guards were fighting my exes to get free. Johann placed a hand on my shoulder and teleported us out of the coliseum and to the center of the downtown area.

"This way," he told me, walking towards a bakery.

While we walked, I touched each of my guards through our bond and then built solid walls of impenetrable metal so they wouldn't be able to locate me. They would barely be able to feel me now, which was for the best.

Johann walked into the bakery, straight through the back, and up a set of stairs to a second floor that was empty, save for one person.

"You have the antidote?" Johann asked.

Justina stepped forward and held out a vile of green liquid. "One drop for each victim," she ordered him.

"Thank you," he said and bowed, backing away from me. He paused and asked, "What will you do with her?"

"That's none of your concern," she told him sweetly, twirling my hair around one of her fingers.

He nodded once, bowed to me, and then disappeared.

Justina walked around me, looking at my dress and said, "It's a shame that something as beautiful as this will get ruined."

Her hand wrapped around my throat and she threw me up against the wall, choking me. "You. You ruined everything."

"Boo. Hoo," I gasped out with a snarl.

She chuckled. "I forgot how much I liked you. Well, it sucks for you, because no matter how much I liked you, your father's death has cured me of the weaknesses I had left in me."

Revenge? This was for revenge because of my father's death?

"You're pathetic," I snarled.

She snapped her fingers and chains slid out of the walls, wrapped around my arms and legs, and secured me to the wall. She pulled out a silver knife and sliced it down my arm slowly, making me scream loudly.

"Your physical pain isn't going to cut it," she told me. "No pun intended. I need emotional pain from you. And, I know just the thing."

I watched in shock as the bonds between me and my guards became visible. She stroked her finger down Deryn's, making me shiver in revulsion.

"Don't touch that!" I snarled and thrashed against the chains.

"I lost the one male who viewed me as more than a female. The first who viewed me as an equal," she told me with a sigh. "This one, this one views you as his equal. No, as more than his equal. He views you as his queen." She took her silver knife and ran her finger along its hilt. Symbols down the blade began to glow and she used it to slice through Deryn and my bond.

It felt like my heart had been stabbed. I screamed loudly, my body shuddering against the wall as I lost my connection to Deryn.

"No!" I screamed. "Stop!"

She grabbed Nico's bond, squeezing it tightly in her hand. "Now, you will all experience the pain I felt. The loss of the one you love."

The knife sliced through Nico and my bond, and I felt energy leave me, his magic disappearing with the bond.

I tried to shift into a dragon. I still had Rhys, so I just needed to shift.

My scales started to form, but she wasn't cutting my skin. She was somehow cutting through our magical bonds.

"Stop!" I begged. "Please!"

"No!" she screamed at me and cut Rhys's bond, the dragon left me in an instant, leaving me feeling cold and helpless.

Three of them were gone. Their absence a hole in my chest. An aching and bleeding hole I couldn't repair. Fox was the only one left. I opened our bond and tried my hardest to send him all the love that I felt. I still couldn't use the bond as well as they could, but I could convey feelings, so I sent him as much love and gratitude as I could. I felt his fear. I felt his anger. I felt his love and it was enough. Knowing they loved me was enough.

"Did you know that Foxfire never knelt to anyone, not even his own father, and yet he has knelt for you numerous times, in front of numerous witnesses. He loves you and everyone can see it. Why you? What makes you so special?"

The knife severed our bond and I wailed in sorrow. Fox, my happy and kind Fox, was gone.

They were all gone. All four of my guards were gone. I was

alone in my body for the first time in nearly a year. It had been ten months ago that I met them and we developed these bonds.

"Fuck you, you piece of shit," I snarled at her weakly, my body hanging in the chains. "You're just a jealous child who can't handle the fact that the evil asshole who was manipulating her was killed. He never loved you. He was just using you. You were a means to an end. Nothing more."

She wrapped her hand around my throat and squeezed tightly, cutting off my air supply.

Yes. This is what I wanted. Without them, I wasn't powerful. Without them, I couldn't do anything.

"Why give yourself up?" she asked me. "Did you think they would save you?"

"Save. Martin," I gasped out.

"Martin? Martin got affected by the virus? Poor bastard," she said. "Well, at least that antidote will save him. You. You won't be saved."

Now, it didn't matter what happened at the tournament. Now, it didn't matter if I thought I was good enough or not. Now, they would find new mates. They would go back to their normal lives.

"Your torture isn't over yet," she told me with a wicked smile. "No, this is just the beginning." Her hand wrapped around my face and then, I fell into a dark tunnel, spinning and swirling with black mist. There was no down. No up. Nothing, but darkness and cold air.

CHAPTER 8

"How do you feel today?" Justina asked me, her smile happy and warm, like it had been when we'd worked together.

I had no idea how long I'd been here and I didn't really care.

"Were you ever my friend?" I asked. "Or was it all a ruse?"

"Do you care?" she snapped. "You should be more worried about the fact that your wound never stopped bleeding."

That explained my lightheadedness and the weakness throughout my entire body.

"Did you find me because of my father? Or was it just a coincidence?" I really did want to know.

"Coincidence," she said. "How I wish I hadn't gotten to know you, though."

"Just kill me already," I begged her. "You took them away from me. What more can you do?"

"Well, your dad did tell me that torture never worked well on you. So, I suppose I should just put you out of your misery."

Finally. Death was better than this hollow shell I was now. I hadn't realized how much they had filled me until now. How could I live like this?

I couldn't. This emptiness would eat me up.

What must they be going through?

Well, it likely wasn't as bad as I was dealing with, since they still had each other and their warrior's bond.

"I'm going to let you bleed out," she said. "I think it's a fitting death for the person who took a vampire from me." She sliced my other arm open and waved as she left.

"Bitch!" I called after her.

I faded in and out of consciousness, my arms went numb and my body followed that numbness. Soon, I knew I would be dead. Part of me wanted to fight. Part of me wanted to live. But, that part of me was buried beneath the pain and the loss.

There was no one to blame. I had given myself up, knowing full well that I was likely going to die. And, I would do it again. My death for Tobias's and Martin's lives was a small price to pay. They would be furious with me, but I didn't care. They deserved to live. They deserved to continue on in life.

I had never done anything worthwhile. The Others thought I was a hero for bringing them their necklace, but that was purely coincidence. Had I not stumbled into that park, drunk, I would still have that necklace. I wouldn't be here either. I wouldn't have had the four princes bind themselves to me. I wouldn't have seen my ex-boyfriends again. I wouldn't have been the reason that Rhys and the others fought so hard in the tournament.

I was a walking curse. My death would save the princes. My death would save them all.

"Jo!" someone yelled.

It sounded like Martin, but I wasn't sure. My eyes were too heavy. The room stank of my blood and I couldn't move.

"Jo, hang in there," Martin said, his voice far away.

Hang in there? I was hanging in chains and he said, hang in there? I snorted softly at the pun.

The last thing I heard before I died *would* be a pun.

"Stand back," someone ordered Martin.

There was movement all around me and I was pretty sure they had taken me out of the chains, but I was too cold and numb to feel anything for certain.

"Don't die on me," Martin ordered me. "Do you hear me, Jolie? Don't you dare die on me!"

"Too late," I whispered.

"No, it's not," he growled. "You have four princes losing their shit and they need you to come back. I need you. My daughters need you. How are they going to take the news that their favorite aunt died trying to save me?"

"I'm their only aunt," I grunted.

"Stop talking," the other person, male it sounded like, ordered me. I didn't recognize the voice at all, so it must have been a healer.

"I love you," I whispered to Martin.

"No!" he yelled. "Don't give up! Jolie. Please! Don't give up!"

He was safe. That was what mattered. The princes would learn to live without me again. It might take time to adjust, but they would do it.

"She's lost so much blood," the healer told Martin.

"What do you need?" Martin asked.

"We need to find someone who has the same blood type as her," he explained.

"I'm the same," Thor said.

"Thor," I whispered. "Why are you here?"

"Shut up," Martin snarled at me.

"We've been searching the entire city for you," he told me. "Martin found you and we let everyone know. They're on their way."

"Why? Just let me sleep," I requested.

"Hook me up," Thor ordered the healer.

Something stabbed my arm, but I barely felt it.

"Remember when we went skinny dipping in the lake?" Martin asked me. "You were terrified that Mr. Smiton would come out of his house and find us. But, we did it anyway. We were having a great time and then the entire pack showed up to drink from the lake."

I did remember. I was mortified. I had become used to them being naked, but not them seeing *me* naked.

"You were blushing so much, that alpha was worried you were going to faint," Thor chuckled. "You were redder than a tomato."

"If that water hadn't been so clear, it wouldn't have been an issue," Martin said and laughed.

"Remember when I first met you?" Thor asked me.

Oh, I remembered. He had been terrified of me. It had hurt my feelings and I had stayed away from the pack for an entire week because of it.

"You smelled so good and so weird at the same time."

Oh, gee, thanks.

"I didn't understand what the smell meant until I was older, but it was Martin who convinced me that you were good and to give you another try. I'm glad he did. Every time we were together, it was one of the happiest days of my life. You always made me smile and you made sure that I never felt like a third wheel, even after you and Martin had started dating."

"Remember that time that Delphine stole her clothes from the PE locker?" Thor asked Martin.

"Oh, yeah!" Martin said. "She sent me a text message asking for help and when I came to the door of the locker room, she practically tore my shirt off of me."

"Where is she?" Dan boomed, his feet thundering across the wooden floor.

"She's alive," the healer informed Dan. "Just barely, though."

"What do you need?" Dan asked him.

"We need to take her back to the castle, but I'm afraid moving her will reopen the wounds and-"

"I'll teleport her," Johann said.

Before I could voice my protests, someone picked me up and then set me down on a cold, metal cot.

"I'm sorry," Johann whispered to me. "I'm sorry this happened to you. My son may never forgive me."

I didn't care if his son forgave him or not. He made his bed. He could have teleported me away too, but he hadn't. He had left me because he was still furious that I'd interrupted him and Justina's deal.

"I was trying to work out the deal with her when you interrupted."

"Why didn't you tell them where I was?" I asked, remembering that they had said they were searching the entire city.

"Because I'm an old fool who can't get over his own ego," he whispered.

"Get away from her!" Nico growled, his voice shaking everything around us. I still hadn't opened my eyes and now that I knew he was here, I was glad that they were still closed. I couldn't look at him. I couldn't see him knowing we weren't bound.

"I'm leaving," Johann said.

"Jolie," Nico whispered from nearby. "Jolie, say something."

"Go, away," I begged, my throat constricting as I tried to keep from crying.

"What happened?" he asked. "What cut the bonds?"

"Justina did," I whispered.

"Stop talking," the healer ordered me. "If your presence is going to upset her, then you need to leave."

"Jolie," Nico whispered. "Please, look at me."

"No, it hurts too much," I sobbed.

"What does?"

"The emptiness."

"Leave," the healer ordered him. "You can see her when she's healed."

"No," I told him. "Stop healing me."

"Sorry, that's not something I can do," he whispered. "We need to find another blood donor for you."

"It doesn't matter. Nothing matters," I whispered. "Just let me go."

"No," he said adamantly. "You're in pain, yes, but you aren't going to die. Now, shut up and lie there while I heal you."

I obeyed, mainly because I didn't have the energy to fight. Talking to Nico had reopened the emotional wounds inside of my heart and I couldn't breathe well.

"I'm going to knock you out," the healer said. "It will speed up your healing."

He wasn't asking my permission. He just knocked me out.

When I came back to, my arms were healed and I could not only open my eyes, but sit up. The room was empty and I looked down at my arms, two giant scars ran down the center of my forearms.

That bitch.

"You're awake," the healer said happily.

I nodded.

"Are you up for visitors?" he asked.

"Can I travel yet?" I asked instead of answering.

"Yes," he replied nervously.

"Who do I talk to about traveling back to Jinla?" I asked, wanting to get away from the princes as soon as possible.

"Me," Dan said as he walked in.

I looked away from him. "I want to go home."

"I thought your home was with my son and his friends," he whispered.

I shook my head and tears began to fall. "Not any longer."

"Hope isn't lost," he whispered and pulled me into a hug. "They still love you."

"They're gone," I gasped. "They're gone! My soul, my heart is empty. They're gone and I can't get them back."

It had been what the Elders had told us, that once I removed the warrior's bond, I couldn't get it back.

"The warrior's bond is gone, but you can still become their queen. You can still become their mate," Dan informed me.

"Only the one who wins her hand in the tournament can claim her as their mate," Amos said.

"Leave us," Dan ordered him.

"You don't order me around, King of the Werewolves," Amos reminded him.

"I'm talking with her. This is a private conversation. You can come see her later when I'm done," Dan told him, his body tightening around mine.

"The second round has yet to happen, so you cannot leave for Jinla. You have to wait until your mate is chosen. Once that happens, I will book you on the first train ride out," Amos said to me.

"Fuck you," I grumbled into Dan's chest.

"What?" Amos asked.

I pulled back to face Amos and said, "Fuck. You."

His shock turned into anger and he reached towards me, but Dan stepped between us.

"You will not lay a fucking finger on her. She's my princess. She's my daughter. You will leave now, or I will rip your fucking head off and explain to everyone that you were trying to kill the princess."

Dan was pissed. I felt his body shaking with anger where it still touched me.

"She is not your daughter," Amos spat. "She's hardly even a princess."

"Get out!" Dan bellowed, the room shaking with his voice.

I heard Amos's footsteps retreating and a door close.

"He's right," I whispered.

"Stop. That's enough," Dan ordered me. "You have to come with me to the coliseum. If you don't want to talk to your guar…

the princes, then I will keep them away from you for now. They have to finish the tournament, though."

"Why? I'm not their queen any longer. I'm just-"

"Their friend," Dan finished for me. "Their lover. Their love. They will continue to fight for you."

"There are four of them," I reminded him. "They can't all win me."

"Let's go get you a change of clothes," he said, picking me up and carrying me. "And some food, because I'm sure you're hungry."

"I'm not," I whispered. The emptiness in me was so big, that food would just make me sick.

"Let's get you changed. We'll focus on one thing at a time," Dan whispered.

My room was empty of princes when we arrived, thankfully, so I took my time bathing and getting into another one of the dresses that was in the closet. Dan carried me again, this time taking me to the coliseum.

Ezio and Deryn were fighting, while Rhys, Nico, and Fox stood off to the side just watching. The idiots must have decided it was Deryn's job to fight Ezio, since he was a werewolf.

"Jolie," Emrys breathed as Dan set me in the chair between them again. "How are you feeling?"

"Cold," I whispered, pulling my legs up on the chair beneath the long skirt of my dress.

Emrys blew a ring of fire around me and it sat even with my chest, without moving, the flames warmed me.

"Thanks," I whispered, trying to look away from the arena, but unable to do so.

Fox looked up at me and his eyes widened. He took a few steps towards me, as if he would come to the box, but Nico grabbed his arm and stopped him, shaking his head.

They were keeping him away from me. I knew it. I knew they would feel different once the bond was gone.

"The princess is back," someone in the crowd called and that sentence was repeated over and over again by others until the fighting stopped.

"Jo," Ezio called. "Are you alright?"

"I'm alive," I whispered, not sure if he could even hear me, and looked away, glancing down at the flames around me.

"Jolie," Fox called in a rasping voice.

"Finish your fight!" Amos ordered them. "The three of you should be fighting each other while Deryn fights Ezio!"

"I concede," Ezio said, jumping out of the arena. He ran up the stairs until he reached me, kneeling before me. "Jo, say something."

I shook my head, tears welling up. "Please, go."

He rested his hand on my foot a moment and then bowed and left.

"Four left!" Amos announced to the crowd, as though it were exciting.

"We are done," Rhys called up. "We four claim her."

"You can't do that," Amos snapped. "Only one of you will win."

"Shouldn't it be her decision?" Dan asked Amos.

"Nothing has been my decision," I snapped, leaping up and somehow avoiding the circle of flames still around me.

Emrys extinguished them and stood up next to me. "It's alright," he whispered.

"No, it's not!" I turned to Amos and said, "I'm not a god damn pawn for you to use! I'm not someone you can treat like a trophy. I'm a living, breathing, person! I deserve to choose my own mate."

"Then choose," he said and waved at the princes. "Choose one to be your mate."

"No," I growled and looked away from them. "No. I won't choose one."

"Are they not good enough? Do you think you're too good for the princes?" Amos asked.

"Shut up!" Rhys roared at Amos. "Don't you dare talk to her like that!"

"Silence!" Amos ordered him. "At this Summit, I am the head. I am the ruler. I make the decisions."

"Not about my life," I told him. I turned away and walked back towards the castle and my room.

The crowd erupted into shocked chatter and I ignored all of Amos's demands for me to return. I was done. I was done with all of this.

"It's alright, Jo," Martin whispered beside me. "Everything will be alright."

"Please, don't touch me yet," I begged him as he moved closer.

He kept his distance and nodded. "Okay."

"I want to go home," I sobbed. "Now."

"Okay," he agreed. "I'll help you pack."

In my room, he locked the door behind us and started packing my bag. I tried to help, but it was hard to see anything with the tears flowing down my face.

I was pissed at Amos. I was pissed at Johann. I was pissed at Justina. Most of all, I was pissed at myself.

"Jolie," Rhys called through my door. "Please, let us in."

"No," I whispered, packing faster.

"I love you," he yelled. "I don't care who hears it. I don't care who knows. I love you, Jolie. Please, don't shut me out. Don't shut us out!"

"It's over!" I yelled. "The bond is gone! She severed them. She severed them all!"

"Oh, fuck," Martin whispered. "I didn't know. Jolie, I-"

"We love you. We want you to be our mate. We want you to be our queen," Deryn said.

"I'm a fucking curse. I've always been a curse. Justina came here because of my dad being killed. She hurt me because of that. If you'd never gotten involved with me, none of this shit would have happened. Please, just...stay away."

There was silence on the other side of the door, so I assumed they had listened. Finished packing, Martin grabbed our two bags and put his arm around my waist. "Ready?" he asked.

I nodded.

Yes, I was ready to go home. I was ready to go back to Jinla to start over.

Martin opened the door and unsurprisingly, four princes stood in the hallway. Before I could move away, all four dropped to their knees before me.

"Oh, shit," Martin whispered and backed away.

"Stop," I whispered, tears in my ears. "Stand up."

"Jolie Bernardo, will you become our queen?" Rhys asked me. He pulled out a small black box from his pocket and opened it, revealing a diamond ring. It was a human engagement ring.

"I thought I couldn't become your queen," I whispered. "That's why I joined the warrior's bond, because I'm human."

My voice came out steady, which shocked the hell out of me, since I felt like crying and screaming at the same time.

"That only happened because of how we added you. There is a different set of procedures for you to become our queen," Nico said. "And we can do that still."

"You're finally free," I whispered, looking at each of them in turn. "Why bind yourselves to me again?"

"We love you, you idiot," Deryn said with a soft smile, his words soft instead of harsh. "We want to spend the rest of our lives with you."

Could I do this? Could I become their queen? What would it feel like if I was removed from the bond as their queen?

"It would most likely kill you," Nico said.

Apparently, I'd said that last part out loud instead of in my head.

"Do you want to be with us?" Fox asked.

More than anything.

"More than anything," I said, sniffling as tears built in my eyes and my throat grew tight.

"Say what you want," Rhys whispered.

"I want to be your queen and your mate," I whispered back, the tears spilling over. "But, I don't want to hurt you anymore. I don't want to cause you pain. I don't want you to get hurt because of me."

I was trying to leave to avoid this. I was trying to leave so they could move on. They were so stubborn. And, I loved them so much.

"Kitten," Rhys whispered, "that's what it means to be together. We get hurt protecting what and who we love. We were getting injured in the tournament long before we met you. We'll get hurt in the tournament next year and the year after, no matter what the prize is."

"You are the only one we will bow to," Fox said. "You are our equal. You are the most important thing in our lives. More important than each other."

The other three nodded in agreement.

"You're sure?" I asked softly. "You're sure that you want me? This is a lifelong commitment. This is something we can't go back on. If you decide to do this now, you are going to be rescuing me and getting hurt and who knows what else until I die!"

"We're sure," they all said in unison.

"Jo, come on, just give them your answer," Martin groaned.

"What about Amos?" I asked.

"Let me handle Amos," Dan said from behind me, making me jump and spin around.

"For such a large man, you're too damn quiet!" I snapped at him. Then, realized that Emrys and Katar were with him as well. "Oh, hi."

They waved at me, but then looked at their sons.

"They won't even bow to me," Katar grumbled.

"Jolie," Deryn rumbled.

I turned back to them and said, "I have one condition."

"What condition?" Rhys asked.

"If I become your queen, you have to become my mates," I said. "That way, even if someone breaks one of our bonds, we'll have another one available."

All four surged to their feet and surrounded me with hugs. Their towering figures made for a wall of protection and I felt safe again. Rhys slipped the ring on my finger while hugging me and I sobbed softly.

"It hurt so much," I whispered. "To feel you each taken from me, from my heart. It's so cold. I feel so empty."

"So do we," Fox whispered.

"But you have each other," I reminded them. "I have no one. I'm alone and hollow."

"We're still there, in your heart," Rhys whispered. "But, you don't need to worry. We'll make our vows to you and you'll be bonded with us once again."

"We'll wait on the mating bonds until we get home," Deryn said. "We don't need to rush to make those while we are here."

"Finally!" Dan bellowed and pushed aside Deryn and Rhys to pull me away from them. He looked down at me and said, "Welcome to the pack, Jolie. Welcome to my family."

"Guys," Thor called as he walked towards us with what looked like a newspaper. "This was published today."

Dan took the paper and sighed. "Well, looks like you won't need to make an announcement." He handed me the paper and I read the headline.

Princess of the Four Clans bonded with the Four Princes.

"How did they find out?" Fox asked, taking the paper from me.

"Justina," I whispered. "She probably did it to try to hurt me more. Everyone being told that I was bound to you when she'd just severed those ties *is* pretty fucking painful."

Fox handed the paper to Nico and then pulled me into his arms. "We're here. We'll make our connection again tonight."

"Are you still going back home?" Deryn asked.

For once, he wasn't ordering me around. He was asking what I was going to do. Maybe, our painful experience had done something good.

"I'll stay with you four," I whispered and kissed Fox's neck. "I don't want to be alone right now."

"Good," Deryn said and pulled me away from Fox so that he could hug me. "I don't want to be away from you."

"How do you want to handle this?" Rhys asked.

"We can make an official announcement when we return home that we are her guards and she is our mate," Nico said, hugging me from behind. I turned and wrapped my arms around his neck. "I'm sorry," he whispered to me. "I'm sorry for everything my asshole father did."

"Not your fault," I whispered back, kissing his cheek and inhaling his scent. I wanted to burrow into him so that his scent completely surrounded me.

I pulled away from him and looked at my ring. "So, what's special about this ring?"

All four chuckled.

"Yes, it was expensive," Rhys answered my unspoken question. "It's magically enhanced so that it will expand when you shift forms."

"Will I be able to shift forms as your queen?" I asked, my chest aching as I thought of the dragon being torn away from me.

Warm hands wrapped around mine, stopping me from rubbing my chest. "Yes," Rhys said, taking his turn to hug me. "You'll get your dragon back."

"I was mid-shift and she stole the dragon," I whined. "She

took the dragon and all of my heat vanished. I've been so cold since then."

Rhys's body warmed, heat surrounding me. "I'm sorry," he whispered, rubbing my back. "It wasn't a picnic for us either."

"What did it feel like for you?" I asked, my voice muffled as I buried my face in his shirt.

"Like my heart had been ripped into two, and half of it vanished," Rhys said.

"Like the sun was destroyed and our lives were thrown into darkness," Fox said.

"It was as though half of my body was destroyed," Nico said.

"It felt like someone stuck their claws into my chest and shredded me from the inside out," Deryn said.

"They flipped out," Emrys told me. "When the first of them, Deryn, felt your connection snap, he began tearing out of the building, trying to rush to you. But, as each one was cut, they fell from the pain. They were all crawling toward the city on their hands and knees, snarling and cussing. Then they started going berserk."

"It was excruciating," Rhys snarled into my hair.

"Come, let's get into the room so we can talk," Katar ordered us.

Rhys picked me up before I could even take a step and carried me into my room.

"I love you," he whispered softly into my ear. "When our fathers are done, we are cuddling the shit out of you to try to cope with what happened. Okay?"

"Okay," I whispered back. I wrapped my arms around his neck and nuzzled my nose into his neck. "I love you, too."

"So, we came to let you know that Justina escaped," Dan told us.

"Not surprising," I whispered. "She's a crafty bitch."

Rhys sat on the end of the bed with me in his lap, my arms still around his neck.

"How did she sever your bonds?" Katar asked.

"She had a silver knife that she cut them with."

"Did it have any designs on it?" Johann asked.

I hadn't seen him come in and I had no idea when he had shown up.

"It had strange symbols. I didn't recognize them, but I could draw them for you," I offered.

"Please," he requested.

Nico handed me paper and a pen and I turned around in Rhys's lap, using a book as a hard surface to draw on. I tried to draw the knife and the symbols like I remembered, but it wasn't exact.

"I was a bit preoccupied with pain at the time, so these aren't accurate," I mumbled as I drew. After finishing, I handed it to Nico who cussed and held it up for everyone else to see.

"The Blade of Tate," Dan growled. "I had a feeling it was that cursed blade."

"That blade can cut anything," Johann told me. "It can even cut through mating bonds."

"So, what you're saying is that I'm still not safe? That she could cut our new bonds when we make them?" I asked softly, fear sliding up my back and making me shiver.

Rhys wrapped his arms around me and increased his heat once again. "We won't let that happen," he assured me. "We won't let you be taken again. *We* value your life." The last sentence was said with such venom, that it made me flinch, even though I knew he was directing it at Johann.

"What's the plan for tomorrow?" I asked. "Aren't you supposed to finish the Tournament?"

"We will. We will announce that you are their queen, and as such, we aren't going to make you choose a single mate. We will announce that we are leaving you to make your choice for mate at a later date and not force you to make it now," Emrys said.

"Amos-"

"Amos isn't as powerful as he thinks," Johann said. "He's old and has let the power go to his head. It is time we reminded him that he may be there for the reason of keeping us in line, but this is an instance where *he* needs to be put back in line."

"Seems a few of us need that reminder," Nico grunted.

"She needs to eat," Dan told them. "She hasn't eaten since yesterday and she's refusing to."

"I'm not hungry," I whispered and looked at the floor in front of me. Even though they were going to make me their queen, and they were going to become my mates, I was still empty - hollow.

"You have to eat," Rhys growled at my back.

"Martin, can you get some food for her?" Deryn asked him.

"Certainly," Martin said and set my bag on the ground before leaving.

"You were really going to leave us?" Nico asked.

"Yes," I said, not feeling remorseful at all. "I was going to go back to the apartment and try to figure out what I was going to do to with the rest of my life, without you in it."

"You're so damn stubborn," Deryn growled at me.

"Ditto," I replied with a smirk.

Fox sat in front of me, leaning his body against Rhys's legs so that his head could lean into my lap. "We would have followed you," he told me.

I ran my fingers through his hair and said, "I figured you would try, but I was hoping my exes would keep you busy." I froze a moment, my hand buried in his hair and asked, "Did you guys hurt them?"

"Who?" Deryn asked.

"Ezio, Thor, Declan, Kylan-"

"Oh, you mean when you ordered them to hold us so you could run off and sacrifice yourself?" Rhys growled at my back.

"Yeah, then."

"No one was killed or seriously wounded. They got a few

heavy hits from us and scratches, but we couldn't punish them when they were following your orders," Fox said.

"Next time you pull something like that, I'm going to tie you up for an entire week," Deryn threatened me.

I winked at him and said, "Promises, promises."

Dan burst into loud laughter and stood up. "I love you, Jolie. You're the only female I've ever seen who keeps my boy on his toes."

I smiled back at him while Deryn scowled at us.

I climbed away from Rhys and Fox to wrap my arms around Deryn's neck and lean into him. "Are you still mad at me?"

"No," he admitted, wrapping his arms around me and burying his head into my neck while my arm covered him. "Having you here, alive, has made my anger vanish."

"Good," I whispered.

"I'd recommend staying in here the rest of the night," Emrys said. "Nico, put up wards."

Nico nodded. "I will as soon as Martin returns with her food."

Emrys nodded and they all left, leaving me and the guys alone in the room. Deryn's mouth crashed into mine, need and worry spurring on his movements. I kissed him back, glad for the physical touch. I tugged at his shirt and he ripped it in half, so we didn't have to break our kiss. My hands splayed across his chest and I moaned at the heat he was giving off.

"No shirts," I gasped, pulling back long enough to order the other princes.

They all removed their shirts and I followed my own order, removing mine as well, but leaving my bra on. Four male chests pressed against me from all sides and I sighed.

"She's so cold," Nico whispered worriedly.

"I told you I was," I reminded them.

"When are we making the bond?" Deryn asked Rhys.

"After she eats," Rhys said. He blew air against my skin and it was so hot that it burned me a moment.

"Ouch!" I gasped and jerked away from him.

"What?" he asked.

"That burned," I told him and turned around.

"Shit, Rhys. You burned her," Deryn said and touched the top of my back.

"I didn't use fire. I just warmed my breath," Rhys told us. He cupped my cheek. "It shouldn't have hurt you at all."

Fox set his hand over the burn and I felt his magic pulse into me, cooling the burn and then giving me relief.

"Thanks, Fox," I whispered and leaned my forehead against Rhys's chest.

"I'm sorry," Rhys said. "I don't know why that burned you."

"She's fully human right now," Nico reminded him. "Without the bond, she's not enhanced by our powers. I think we all got used to her being tougher than a regular human."

"So, we need to be extra careful with her," Deryn said. "Which means, no rough sex."

"Boo!" I yelled, which earned me four rumbling male chests against my body as they laughed. "Seriously? Where's the fun in that?" I grumbled.

"Uh," Martin said from the doorway.

"We're not naked," I assured him, since he couldn't see me surrounded by the princes.

"You need to eat," Rhys ordered me, stepping away to get the platter of food Martin had brought with him.

Martin handed it over and asked, "Do you need anything else?"

"No, you can go," Rhys said.

"We're good," I assured Martin.

He nodded and then left, shutting the door behind him. Nico went to the door, swiped his hand across the doorway, and a silver line stretched from the doorway, all the way around the room, creating the ward.

"Eat," Rhys snarled at me.

"I'm not hungry," I groaned, but sat down at the table where the food sat. Meats, cheeses, fruits, vegetables, and various dips rested on the large platter. None of it looked good.

"Please," Fox begged me, sitting down cross-legged beside me. "We need you to eat and get more strength back or we can't do the binding ceremony."

"Can't we just do it tomorrow?" I asked as I pushed around some of the fruit with my finger.

"You'll be even weaker tomorrow if you don't eat," he reminded me.

"None of this looks good," I complained.

"What do you want?" Nico asked. "I'll go have the chef make whatever you want."

I was being a spoiled brat. Shit.

"No, this is fine," I said with a sigh and chewed on a carrot.

"Seriously, we can go get you something else to eat. The chefs here are top notch and can make you whatever your heart desires," Fox said.

What did I want?

"Nothing sounds good," I admitted after a moment. None of my favorite foods sounded good. Not even dessert sounded good.

"We could get you a protein shake," Deryn offered.

"No," I almost gagged. "There's no way I could drink the entire thing. I'd end up getting sick before I finished it."

"Are you ill?" Fox asked and put his forehead against mine. "No fever."

"My insides are scrambled," I told them. "Did you guys eat?"

They all frowned and looked at each other.

"No, I guess we didn't," Rhys admitted.

"See!" I said victoriously. "It's not just me."

"We need to eat," Deryn said and grabbed a piece of meat. He looked at it and then sighed. "I don't want to eat this. Shit. What's wrong with us?"

"Maybe we need more skin to skin time," I suggested. "Then we can try to eat afterward."

"She might be right," Rhys admitted. "We all lost something and it hasn't really settled into our minds, and souls, that we have it back."

"Can we do the binding now?" I asked. "Without eating?"

"If we use the extra power that's in the necklace," Nico said and pointed at my necklace, the gift I had received from the kings for ending the war.

"Okay, let's do this," Rhys said and held his hand out to me. I took it and let him pull me to my feet.

CHAPTER 9

They said that normally, the queen would take the guards one by one, but since we wanted to conserve magical power and energy, we were going to do it for everyone at once. All four faced me, on one of their knees, and had their heads bowed. I touched each of their heads and then touched the necklace. The necklace glowed, and the magic began to flow into me.

"Will you, Rhys, Nico, Deryn, and Foxfire, become my guards, my protectors, and keep my life safe even if it means giving up your own?" I asked, my voice sounding louder and otherworldly.

"Yes," they replied in unison.

"Will you protect me above everyone else, even above your king, your mate, and your family?"

"Yes."

"Will you promise to love me until our last breaths?" I asked. I had added this part in, going off script.

"Yes," they replied without hesitation.

"I bind you, Rhys, Nico, Deryn, and Foxfire, to me, Jolie, as my guards, as your queen, until our last breaths."

All four looked up at me. "Yes, my queen," they replied.

From my chest, four strands grew, like tentacles, and continued to grow until they connected with each one of the princes. The instant the strands attached to them, energy surged into my body and my back arched as I gasped in pleasure.

Their echoing gasps led me to believe they had felt it as well.

"I am your guard. You are my queen. My sword is yours. My fangs and claws are yours. I will protect you until my final breath," all four said and stood.

"You are my guard. I am your queen," I replied.

The spell ended and the power disappeared, leaving me weak. I dropped to my knees in front of the princes. They reached out their hands and I flopped onto my side on the ground, so they could all touch my body as I tried to catch my breath.

"The necklace will need to be recharged, my queen," Nico whispered.

I nodded in understanding, rolling my head to the side so that I could look at them. "Now, you are all stuck with me."

"Pretty sure it is the other way around, my queen," Nico chuckled and stroked his hand down my cheek.

"I love you four. More than anything," I told them.

Their hands tightened on me. "I love you, too, my queen," they said.

"Is that going to be a common thing now?" I asked.

"Yes, my queen," Deryn said. "It's pretty much programmed into us that we are supposed to refer to you by that title."

"Can't I order you not to call me it?" I asked. If I was their queen, I should be able to order them to stop doing things.

"No, my queen," Rhys said and smirked. "Nice try, though."

"What do I call you?" I asked.

"Guard," Rhys said. "Though, you can still call us prince if you want to."

"So, I can yell, 'Guards, fetch me my crown!'?"

Rhys smirked and said, "Yes."

"Really? Do I get a crown?" Not that I wanted one.

"We can get you one, if you want," Deryn offered.

"A really shiny one with lots of diamonds and jewels," Fox agreed.

"Has to be *super* expensive," Rhys added.

"At least half a million dollars," Nico agreed.

"Whoa," I ordered them.

"We definitely need to have it enchanted, which will double its price easily," Rhys said.

"I should really learn how to enchant things," Nico said and rubbed his chin. "I wonder how long it would take me to learn?"

"I'm honestly surprised you don't already know how to do that," I admitted to him.

"I started to learn, but it was boring and I wanted to focus more on combative spells," Nico told me.

"Maybe I should learn how to do it," I said. "It could be a second income for me."

"I really wish you would just let us provide for you," Rhys muttered and folded his arms across his chest. "We make more than enough money individually to provide for you."

"I have to make my own money. I have to contribute in some way. I don't want to freeload off of you guys."

"You could play video games all day," Deryn tempted me.

"That is *really* tempting, but I wouldn't feel right. I would feel like a gold digger or something."

"Remember her face when she figured out you were a prince?" Nico asked Rhys.

Rhys nodded. "I was terrified she was going to freak out and never talk to me again."

"I considered it," I teased him.

"No, you didn't," he said.

"Maybe," I shrugged.

"She was going to faint at first," Rhys told the others. "I thought I was going to have to catch her."

"Whatever," I said and rolled my eyes at him.

They laughed and I sighed happily as I felt their love and happiness through our bonds. *Yes!* Once again, I was full and warm. I finally had them inside of me and filling me up. I didn't believe in fate, but I truly believed they were meant to be part of me. Without them, I had felt too empty.

"Cuddle puddle?" Fox asked.

I nodded. "Yes."

Everyone changed into pajamas and then we got into the massive bed, Rhys lying above my head, Nico on my right, Deryn on my left, and Fox at my feet. Fox hugged my feet to his chest and said, "If you told me that I would be cuddling a female's feet, I would have told you that you were insane. Yet, here I am, cuddling your feet and happier than a wolf with a bone."

"I know what you mean," Rhys agreed.

"If you had told me that I would be in love with four males at once, especially four Other princes, I would have laughed in your face," I told them.

"I still can't believe you turned your ex-boyfriends on us," Deryn grumbled.

"I knew they would do what I asked," I said. "Plus, they're probably the only ones, aside from your father's, who are capable of holding you back for at least a few moments."

"I can't believe Ezio withdrew from the Tournament," Deryn whispered. "He was so set on winning you for a mate and proving himself."

"He could tell that I love you," I said. "He doesn't want to take me as a mate if I won't love him."

"You do care for him, though," Deryn said.

"I'll always care about him, but we aren't meant to be together. I tried to explain that to him when I left, but he was as obstinate as you four are. He was adamant that what happened wasn't that bad and—"

"What did happen?" Deryn asked.

Crap. I'd opened the door for that question.

"We were out on a date," I told them. "He was taking me to dinner at a nice restaurant, but on the way there, an ogre attacked us. He killed the ogre pretty quickly, but it turned out to be a herd of ogres rampaging through the city. When they heard their companion's death yell, they rushed us. Ezio would have been fine, but he was trying to keep me safe. One of the ogres got close to me and he had to try to help, which left him open and the damn ogre drew a dagger and nearly cut his hand off. There was so much blood and his hand was barely hanging on by a thread. Ezio acted like it was a fucking flesh wound and continued fighting, putting his arm into his jacket to keep his hand from completely falling off. I threw up all over and was a mess when he finally defeated them all."

"How many were there?" Rhys asked.

"A dozen at least," I whispered. "I remember counting eleven severed heads as we walked away from the bodies. He had killed a few more without decapitating them though, so I'm not positive how many there were."

"Dan said you got really angry when you saw Rhys hurt in the Tournament," Fox commented.

I nodded. "I was about to shift into a dragon and beat some sense into Ezio. Emrys forced me to calm down, but it wasn't easy."

Rhys slipped his fingers through my hair and said, "I appreciate your concern, but that really was just a flesh wound."

"Maybe you guys just bleed way too much," I commented.

"There was *a lot* of blood at the place Justina tortured you," Nico whispered.

"You went there?" I asked in disbelief. *Why would he go there?*

"Yes," he nodded. "I wanted to see what had almost traumatized Martin.

"What do you mean?"

"He kept saying that he didn't know how you could survive when you had lost so much blood."

"Thor gave me some of his blood," I told them. "The healer hooked him up to me somehow, my eyes were closed so I couldn't see, but he let me take some of Thor's blood to keep me from dying."

"I hope we find her soon," Rhys growled. "I'm going to show her the true meaning of torture."

"You say the sweetest things," I whispered with a chuckle and reached up to link our fingers together. "I don't want you guys going anywhere near her."

"Too bad," Rhys growled.

"I order you not to seek her out," I snapped. Something sharp and cold zipped down our bonds and the guys hissed. "Uh, what happened?"

"You gave us a direct order," Rhys said.

"Now, we can't disobey or it will physically hurt us," Nico told me.

"I'm sorry!" I yelled and sat up. "I didn't know. I didn't mean to. I mean, I did, but not like that. Can I take it back? What can I do—"

"It's alright," Fox assured me, grabbing my hand in his. "You meant the order, or it wouldn't have been issued like that. We will abide by your order and not seek her out. However, if we see her, or if someone else finds her, we will still get our revenge."

"Don't forget," Nico said, "she hurt us too. You weren't the only one affected by her severing the bonds."

"We want our pound of salt too," Rhys said adamantly.

I collapsed back down on the bed. "Are there any other important things I should know about being your queen now?"

"Even if you order us to, we cannot hurt you," Fox told me.

"Like, even spankings?"

That got all four of them laughing again.

"As long as we aren't actually *hurting* you, we can enjoy whatever rough sexual fun you want. But, if it hurts you, we won't be able to do it," Rhys explained.

"What about choking?" I asked.

Nico let out a bark of laughter and shook his head. "Since when do you want that?"

I shrugged. "I didn't say I did, but I like having options. Choking might be fun every once in a while."

"Oh, boy," Fox exhaled. "I feel like she just became an even bigger handful. How is that even possible?"

"We should all know by now not to underestimate Jolie," Rhys teased.

"Ha. Ha," I muttered.

"Go to sleep, my queen. Tomorrow will be a busy day," Nico said and scooted closer to me, resting his head on my shoulder.

"Can't we just run away?" I whined. "We could elope! You know, run off without telling anyone to become mates! It's super romantic and I'm sure the kings would forgive us."

"No," they all said at the same time.

"So, unromantic," I sighed. "For princes, you aren't very fairy-tale like. You're supposed to be super sweet and romantic. You're supposed to sweep me off my feet."

"We do that on a daily basis," Rhys rumbled, his voice heavy with sleep.

I always envied how quickly he fell asleep.

"We can sweep you off your feet tomorrow," Fox said around a yawn.

"Fine," I agreed, feeling my eyes growing heavier as well.

It seemed like seconds had passed by, but when I awoke screaming and crying, the clock showed it had been five hours.

"What?" Deryn asked, growling and throwing his arms around me.

"Sorry," I sobbed and leaned into his touch. "Nightmare."

He pulled my head to his chest and rubbed my back. Nico rubbed my lower back, where Deryn couldn't reach. Fox ran his hand up and down one of my legs and Rhys pet my hair.

"What happened?" Nico asked.

"Memory, not nightmare," I whispered.

"Losing us?" Deryn guessed.

I nodded. All four moved closer to me, projecting their feelings of love down our bond, and soon, my body relaxed and I fell asleep again.

☙❧

MARTIN WAITED IN THE HALLWAY WHEN WE CAME OUT AND WALKED next to me to go get breakfast. "How are you feeling?" he asked.

"Pretty well," I admitted and looked at my arms. "I feel stronger today than I did yesterday."

"Good," he said with a sigh. "I was really worried about you."

I hugged him and pecked him on his cheek. "Thank you."

We entered the dining hall to chaos. Hundreds of reporters swarmed around the front half of the dining hall, bombarding Amos with questions so fast, he couldn't even answer them.

"There she is now," Amos declared, a predatory smirk on his face. "You are free to ask her questions."

"Asshole," I muttered.

The princes stepped in front of me, but that didn't deter the media.

"Jolie! Is it true that you bound the four princes to you?"

"Why?"

"What are you after?"

"I'm after some food!" I growled.

"Come," Ezio said behind me. I turned and he linked our fingers together, pulling me away from my guards, and towards a table where my other exes sat.

"Hey," I said and waved at them.

Declan stood to pull my chair out for me and then pushed it in for me as well. He kissed my cheek and returned to his seat. Ezio sat next to me after kissing my other cheek.

"Thank you, for holding the princes back the other day," I

said. I opened my napkin and put it on my lap, knowing I was likely to spill on myself since I was wearing a light blue dress that would easily stain.

"Orange juice?" Kylan asked.

"Yes, please," I replied and pushed my glass towards him.

"You are welcome," Ezio said and then leaned closer to me. "But, if you ever order us to do something that results in your near death again, I will steal you away and lock you up in a tower where no one will find us."

He wasn't joking. Ezio's eyes were dead serious.

I swallowed and then nodded, unsure if my voice would work properly if I tried to use it.

"Yeah," Yukio said, "that was really awful. We felt responsible for your pain."

"Is it true that they're your guards?" Zelphar asked.

I nodded. "Yes, they are."

"I heard your kidnapper cut your bonds though," Thor whispered.

"She did, but those were bonds that added me to their warrior's bond. They accepted me as their queen last night," I explained. It was nice to get to tell people the truth. I really preferred this to keeping secrets.

"Are you going to take them as mates?" Ezio asked, a strange fire in his eyes that I couldn't place. Was it jealousy? Anger?

"I don't know," I lied.

"Liar," he accused.

"I haven't taken them as mates," I said.

"Thor said you were cursed," Ezio commented.

I nodded. "I was."

"So, you weren't wrong when you told me you needed to leave because you were cursed," he said softly.

"I didn't know I had it then. I just assumed I did because of all of the bad shit that kept happening to me," I admitted to him.

"Still," he whispered, "to know that you actually were cursed back then. I feel like an ass."

"You were a bit of an ass," I teased, "but, you also nearly lost your hand to keep me alive."

"I'd lose my head if I needed to," he told me.

"She's got enough guards," Deryn growled.

"The offer is open still," Ezio said with a smirk and winked at me.

"I am not rising to your bait this time," Deryn said, setting his hands on my shoulders.

Everyone at the table zeroed in on his hands.

"Guys," I growled.

Their eyes moved to my face. "He's one of my guards, remember? He's allowed to touch me. Plus, I'm *not* with any of you any longer. We broke up years ago."

"It still bothers us," Ezio said. "We all love you, haven't stopped loving you, and you've been through a lot. We are all worried about you."

"You don't need to worry about her any longer," Rhys said, coming to stand on my left side. "We'll protect her."

"You'd better," Ezio snarled. "If she gets hurt, or killed, I'm coming after all four of your asses. Princes or not, I don't give a shit. You protect her or I'll kill you myself."

"We'll die before we let her die," Fox promised.

"Good," Ezio said and returned to eating.

I sipped on my orange juice and sighed. Males were so territorial and aggressive.

"What would you like to eat?" Nico asked, squatting down on my right side.

"Waffles, eggs, and bacon!" I ordered, suddenly feeling ravenous.

"Scrambled eggs?" he asked.

I nodded. "Yes, please."

"Anything else?" he asked.

"A kiss?" I whispered.

He smiled and brushed his lips across mine. They barely touched before he was gone, off to order my food.

"What happened with the media?" I asked.

"We gave them what they wanted. We admitted that you are our queen. We told them that we were the ones who asked you, since that is true. We told them that we in no way regret this decision and plan to try to earn your love to become your mates, but that we may not be worthy of being your mates," Rhys said.

"Ain't that the truth," Ezio scoffed.

I smacked his arm. "Hey."

He smiled, but didn't say anything else.

"Is there a shopping area nearby?" I asked Fox, since he had a house in downtown.

"Yes."

"I need to do some shopping."

"For what?" Deryn asked.

"My final Christmas presents," I told them. "I still have a couple I need to get."

"If you know what they are, you can just tell us and we can have a servant go get them for you," Kylan told me.

"I have to get them myself. That's the whole point of Christmas shopping, you buy presents for your loved ones. I only have a couple of things left to get, so it shouldn't take me too long to buy them."

"We can go with you, to provide additional back up, if you want?" Yukio offered.

"That would be most appreciated," Rhys said before I could decline.

"Seriously?" I asked him.

"You have a knack for getting into trouble. Taking you to an area that is open to the public will be a huge safety risk, plus, the media is bound to be there, and fans who will pester us," Nico said.

"Can't you just do your final shopping at the dragon's den? I know you saw a few things you wanted, but didn't buy there," Rhys said.

"No, they didn't have the last few items I need," I admitted.

"Food," Nico said and set a plate of food in front of me.

"Did you cook this?" I asked him.

He nodded.

"You cooked for a female?" Zelphar asked, his jaw hanging slightly open.

"Not just a female," Nico reminded him. "I cooked for my queen."

"Thank you," I said and dug in, moaning as the waffle melted in my mouth. It was super buttery and he had already poured syrup on it. The eggs were also really fluffy and light, just the way I liked them.

"You're the best," I mumbled around the food in my mouth.

"I think so," he said with a proud smirk. Everyone else rolled their eyes.

"Aren't you guys going to eat?" I asked Nico.

"Once you're done eating, we will," he told me.

"Why? Please tell me it's not going to be like this all the time? I don't want to eat while you guys just sit and watch me. That's totally creepy!"

Everyone chuckled.

"No, it won't be a normal occurrence," Fox promised. "For today it is, but we will eat together like we normally do."

"What are we having for Christmas dinner?" I asked.

"Oven roasted goose, mashed potatoes, gravy, brussel sprouts, ham, oven roasted turkey, sweet potatoes, yams, green bean casserole, chocolate mousse pie, and some appetizers," Nico announced.

"Can we come too?" Kylan asked with a laugh.

I actually liked the sound of that. It made me smile to think of having everyone together to eat and exchange gifts. But, I knew my guards wouldn't appreciate having my ex-boyfriends there. Especially, since we were supposed to mate that week. I knew that males got super possessive the week after they mated. I didn't want them getting into fights and hurting each other. Maybe next year we could, though.

"You guys should all come next year," I said and looked at everyone at the table. "This year is going to be a bit crazy, but next year should be fine."

"We'd be honored to," Ezio said and bowed his head to me.

"Don't start bowing to me," I whispered and went back to eating my food. "I don't like it."

"Well, you do outrank me now," he reminded me. "You're the princess."

"Still," I whispered.

I finished eating and as one, the guys sitting in chairs stood up and the princes took the seats. My exes took turns kissing my cheeks before dismissing themselves. Servants brought out food for the princes and I took my time to admire them.

They all had dark bags beneath their eyes, something highly unusual in Others. It told me more than they were telling me. They were still feeling the aftereffects of the bonds being removed. Were they also weighed down by our new bond? Did it cause them problems?

"You are scowling awfully hard over there," Deryn commented. "What's wrong, baby?"

"Does the new bond cause additional issues for you? Or added weight?" I asked, since he had opened the door for me to ask.

"No, why?" Fox asked.

"You all have bags beneath your eyes."

"That's because we didn't get enough sleep last night and the day before was very taxing on us," Nico explained. "We'll take a nap today and everything will be back to normal."

"Swear?" I asked.

He nodded. "I swear, my queen."

"You were free of her and then you made her your queen again, why?" Rhian, Rhys's youngest sister, asked.

"Because I love her, baby sister. You are young yet, so you likely won't understand for a few more years at the very least," Rhys replied to her.

"Many years at the very least," Emrys said from behind me.

"*Dad*," Rhian complained with a whine.

"You guys are needed in the coliseum," Emrys informed us.

"Do I have to go?" I asked with a pout.

Emrys walked around my side and into my range of view and smiled. "While your pout is adorable, it won't get you out of this."

"Pouting never works on dad," Rhian told me.

"It works on Rhys just fine," I told her.

"Really?" she asked, her mouth gaping a second. "I could never get it to work on him."

"You've got to look as pathetic as possible. You probably just focused on looking cute, but that won't cut it when it comes to Rhys. You have to look pathetic and vulnerable," I explained.

"Hey!" Rhys yelled. "Don't give her pointers on my weaknesses."

"You've really got to stick the lip out too," I advised her, completely ignoring Rhys. "As far out as possible and give him the big puppy dog eyes."

"I'll work on it," she assured me and smiled at Rhys. "Love you."

"Love you, too," he muttered and shoveled food into his mouth.

"I'll see you at the coliseum," Emrys told me. "You'll sit in the same spot you have been."

"Okay."

"I've got to keep her away from my family," Fox whispered. "She'll tell them all of my weaknesses and they will exploit them!"

"You could always bribe me," I offered.

"With what?" he asked.

I smirked. "I'm sure you could come up with something."

"Choking?" he asked.

That had everyone laughing and made Deryn choke on the food that had been in his mouth.

"You all seem happy today?" Dan said as he gripped the back of my chair.

"Hello, Father," I said and smiled up at him.

"Daughter," he replied in greeting, a huge smile splitting his face.

"You sure I can't feign sickness to get out of going to the coliseum?" I asked.

"Sorry, not today," he told me, pulling my chair out and helping me to my feet. The boys stood as well, their plates cleaned, and we made our way to the coliseum.

Dan escorted me to our seats, ignoring the looks we received from Amos, who scowled heavily.

"Today is the end of the Tournament," Amos told me.

"Really?" I asked, sarcasm dripping form my tone. I hated that asshole.

"A choice has to be made," he snapped.

"It has been," I snapped back.

The four princes jumped down into the arena to cheers from the stands. They were well-loved by their people, which was something I wanted to learn more about. I knew they were good people, but what had they done to earn their peoples' respect?

"Will you four battle for victory?" Amos asked them.

"No," all four said at the same time.

"We all claim her," Rhys said.

"Let it be known that Jolie Bernardo is Queen of the Four Princes," Foxfire announced loudly.

The crowd was split between cheering and murmuring. I could understand how they felt, even though I knew what they were going to say. Even though I knew we were now connected.

It still felt surreal that I was their queen, completely, now. And, soon, I would become their mate.

"Jolie," Dan said to get my attention. "Go down to them."

I walked to the edge of the platform and smiled down at my guards. Wings popped out of Rhys's back and he propelled himself upward, flying straight up in front of me, snatching me into his arms as he went, and then turned and floated down to the others.

I stood before them, my heart full with their love, as felt through the bond.

"This concludes the Tournament," Amos snapped, his anger carrying his words sharply across the coliseum.

"Now we can go shopping?" I asked Rhys.

"Yes, now we can go shopping," he agreed.

CHAPTER 10

Yukio, Zelphar, Ezio, Thor, Martin, Declan, and Kylan joined my four guards and me for my shopping trip. Our huge group made quite the scene as we walked around to the different vendors.

The town was old and the buildings were beautiful with ancient styles I knew Rhys enjoyed seeing, with his architect experience. The buildings looked to be made out of a stone, but the stone was in colors I had never seen before. I thought it might be painted, but Rhys confirmed the stone was naturally those colors.

I had had a pre-shopping meeting with my exes, getting them to agree to keep my guards away from me, so I could buy their presents without them seeing the gifts. And, to pay attention to see if they were eyeing any gifts. I was blessed to have these males in my life, continuing to be my friends despite our romantic relationships ending.

"What are you smiling about?" Ezio asked me. He wore a pair of sweatpants and a tank top, showing off his muscular arms. I found it a bit hard to keep from staring, but I was trying my hardest!

"Just thinking how lucky I am to have you and the others in my life. A lot of females wouldn't have their ex-boyfriends helping them shop for their current boyfriends," I replied.

"There's always been something about you. Something magnetic," he said. "You make me happy just by being near me. You're easy to be around and my wolf is always calm when I'm with you. Well, except for when I'm having to save you."

"A few shifters have said that to me," I mumbled. Did it mean something? Was there something unique or different about me that called to shifters?

"It's not just shifters," Yukio said from my other side. He held a pendant in his hand that was shaped like the moon and sun together. "You have always made me feel calm and relaxed as well."

"I wonder if it effects humans as well?" Ezio asked Yukio.

"I don't know. I never spent time with her and other humans," Yukio replied.

The jeweler we were standing in front of had many beautiful items, but the one thing I needed, I didn't see.

"Excuse me?" I asked the seller.

"Yes, dear?" she asked. She was an older female with gorgeous grey hair that flowed down to her butt.

"Do you have any, um…" I leaned forward so I could whisper without anyone else hearing, "bloodstones?"

"Sorry, no. I would try Klinton. He has a stall about halfway down the alley here, selling potions. He should have some," she said apologetically.

"Thank you, so much!" I said quickly. I didn't want to leave without getting something from here, so I purchased the pendant Yukio had been eyeing, tucking my new purchase into my large backpack I was wearing.

"I can carry your backpack for you," Ezio offered for the fifth time.

"No, I want to carry it," I told him. Plus, one of his presents was inside the bag.

"What did you ask her about?" Yukio asked, coming back to us. He'd gone to talk to Zelphar and Nico when I had started talking to the seller.

"I need a specific item, but it turns out she doesn't have it. She did tell me one of the other vendors here has some. So, on we go!"

Fox caught up to me and asked, "Are you sure you don't want me to give you-"

"Foxfire, I already told you, no." I told him. "No."

"You've spent quite a lot and I know you don't make *that* much at your job. I just don't want you spending a bunch of money on us because of what you think we are going to spend on you. You don't need to match our prices."

"Go back with Zelphar," I ordered him. "You're going to see me get a gift for you and it will ruin the surprise."

"Yes, my queen," he whispered, bowed, and stopped to let me continue on without him and let Zelphar catch up to him.

"You've always been stubborn about taking money from others," Ezio commented.

"It's not my money. Plus, it doesn't really make it a gift from me if I am using their money to buy it." And, if they didn't like it, I would feel even worse, because then I had wasted their money on something they didn't want. No, I would use my money. Even though it meant dipping into my savings a bit. They were worth it.

I bought a few more items from the vendors, but I was truly looking for Klinton's stand. I finally found it, and ordered Ezio to keep everyone far enough away that they wouldn't be able to hear me and the seller speaking. He stood ten feet away from me, his arms crossed, and refused to let anyone approach.

"How can I help you?" Klinton asked.

"I need bloodstones and I was told you might have some," I informed him.

"I do," he said with a smile. "How many do you need?"

"Five," I said and pulled out my wallet. "How much?"

"Five hundred," he said, bent over as he grabbed something from beneath his stand. "Do you need boxes?"

"Yes, please."

"I charge ten for each box," he explained.

"That's fine."

He set five black boxes on the flat surface of his stall and slid a clear crystal the size of a grain of rice into each one, into a pocket designed to hold them securely. I was so excited to have finally found them, that I was practically dancing in front of his stand.

"I'm so glad I was able to find some," I told him and held out my money.

"These are actually the last five that I have, so you definitely came at just the right time."

"Why are they so hard to find?" I asked. Bloodstones were very popular, used by mates of every race.

"This time of year, a lot of new matings happen and so, the demand for the crystals is high. I usually have a large enough supply, but I miscalculated and ran out. Hopefully, I will have another shipment coming soon," he explained.

"That makes sense," I whispered.

"Is there anything else?" he asked.

"Oh, can I have two healing potions?" They were expensive, but they would give you double your stamina for ten minutes.

"Sure. They are one hundred each," he said, grabbed two glass bottles with heart shaped stoppers with pink liquid in them, and added them to my bag.

I gave him the additional money and put the items into my bag. "Thank you, so much."

"Happy Holidays," he said and waved.

"Ezio!" I called. "I'm done!"

Ezio nodded and jogged over to walk beside me. "Find what you need?"

I nodded happily. "I did! I think my shopping is actually complete."

"Jo!" Martin called. "Let's get some food!"

"Food sounds great!" I called back, turning to go back to the others.

"I love seeing you happy and smiling like this," Rhys whispered into my ear.

I squeaked, shocked because I hadn't seen him approach. "You scared me!" I snapped.

He kissed my cheek and said, "Do you think Ezio would let some stranger get this close to you?"

"No," I said and glanced at Ezio who rolled his eyes at me. "Your voice still startled me."

"Well, that squeak was awfully adorable, so I won't apologize for it," Rhys told me and wrapped his arms around my waist as he walked behind me. I had no idea how he was able to walk so well with me, considering our height difference, but he didn't even stumble as we went.

"Rhys," Nico called. The rest of our group stood in front of us, blocking my view of whatever had caused them to stop. Rhys kissed my head and then walked through the rest of them.

"What's going on?" I asked Ezio, who had moved closer and stood behind me, so my back was protected. He was tall enough, that he could likely see what was going on.

"Media," he growled. "They're harassing them to get interviews."

"They sure are persistent," I sighed. "And now I'm royally exposed, everyone knows I'm part of the Other royalty now."

Soon, they would know I was even more entangled than before. Once we announced being mated, I would be hounded just like they were.

"Rhys is handling it," Ezio assured me. "As much as I hate

seeing you with someone else, they do love you and are doing everything in their powers to keep you safe."

"Oh, my gosh. Was that a compliment? Did you just give another male a compliment? I didn't even bring my jacket," I said and rubbed at my arms and tilted my head back so I could look up at him.

"What? It's warm," he said with a frown.

"Yeah, but clearly hell has frozen over, so the snow and ice are bound to descend upon us any moment."

"Ha. Ha," he replied, his eyes fixed ahead.

"Why haven't you taken a mate yet?" I asked him. "And don't even try to say it is because of me. Yes, I know you still love me, but that's not the reason. You knew we were over when I left."

"I had some hope that you might come back to me," he whispered. "At first, but you're right. I just couldn't find anyone who could match your perfection."

"Flatterer," I whispered and turned my face down to hide my blush.

"Do you know how hard it is to find someone who doesn't care that you shift into a wolf and that you spend a lot of time playing video games? Girls generally hate playing games and that their guys ignore them to play games."

I hated that. I wished girls would just get online and play the games with their guys. If he spends a lot of time on a game, talk to him about you joining him online. There was always room for a healer on the team.

"Maybe you set your bar too high," I said, but didn't really mean it. Ezio was amazing and any girl would be lucky to have him.

"Thank you," he said and hugged me. "Hearing you say that means a lot to me."

"Say what?" I asked.

"That anyone would be lucky to have me," he chuckled. "You didn't mean to say that out loud, did you?"

"No," I mumbled, but leaned back into his hold. "But, I meant it. Anyone would be lucky to have you as a mate. You're handsome, kind, and a fierce protector. Though, you are a shitty tank."

"Hey! I had just learned to play the game that week. I was a newbie."

"Still are," I teased.

He growled in my ear, but didn't say anything else.

"How long are we going to be stuck here?" I asked with a sigh. "I'm hungry."

"Rhys!" Ezio called. "Wrap it up, yeah?"

Rhys put an arm behind his back to flip Ezio off and I burst out into a fit of laughter. Rhys looked like the prim and proper prince he was, but behind his back he had his middle finger up to Ezio to tell him to shove it. It was hilarious.

"Is that the princess?" someone asked.

"Princess Jolie!" someone else called.

"Crap," I snapped and sat on my butt behind Martin's legs so they couldn't see me.

"You've never been good at hiding," Martin whispered to me. "Somehow you always ended up making noise and would get caught."

"Shut up," I growled. "I'm not ten anymore."

"You sure about that?" he asked and chuckled.

"We have answered your questions," Rhys said. "So, please let us pass and continue on with our day."

Nico took my hand and pulled me up to stand. "I'm going to make you invisible."

"Why?" I asked.

"Because if they see you, they're going to follow us and yell questions at you," he explained. A sphere wrapped around us and I couldn't see him anymore.

"Nico?" I asked.

He grabbed my hand and said, "It's okay. I'm here. We're both invisible to everyone else now. Just follow the others."

"You still there?" Ezio asked. "I can smell you, but I want to make sure that it's not a lingering scent and you've been kidnapped again."

"You're so rude," I grumbled.

"She's here," Nico assured Ezio with a chuckle.

Ezio nodded and followed just behind us, giving us enough space that he wouldn't step on our heels, but also kept the media from following us too closely. Rhys walked into a building that had delicious scents wafting from it.

"Meat," I whispered and followed everyone inside.

Thankfully, there was a huge table available, one that could seat us all. Nico released his spell and pulled out a chair for me, to sit beside him. I sat down and Deryn sat on my other side, leaning over to rub his cheek against mine.

I kissed his cheek and rubbed mine against his. "Hello."

"Hello, beautiful," he whispered. "Did you get all of your presents?"

I nodded and set my backpack on the ground between my legs, under the table. "Yep! Now, I just need to get them all wrapped and ready to give you guys when we get back."

"Where are you living these days?" Yukio asked.

"With us," Fox answered. "She has an apartment in our building."

"You let her sleep in a separate apartment?" Declan asked. "I would have assumed you all kept her in your apartments."

"We usually stay in the same apartment together, but it varies which one we stay in," Rhys told them.

"And, we give her her space when she wants it. As long as she's in the building with us, we're fine," Deryn said.

"Except when she sneaks out to get donuts," Rhys growled.

"They were a gift for you guys, remember?" I said and scowled at them.

"You went out, unprotected, to get them donuts and coffee?"

Ezio asked. "I'm not surprised in the least, to be honest. That sounds like something you would do."

"Yes, I would do something nice like that," I said and picked up my menu. The menu was huge and I couldn't even begin to make a decision.

"Deryn," I said to get his attention.

He just nodded and said, "I'll order something for you, baby."

I set my menu down and leaned my head on his shoulder. "You're awesome."

"Don't forget it," he whispered and then chuckled. "What do you want to drink?" he asked.

"Strawberry daiquiri, please."

"Okay," he agreed and returned to looking at the menu.

It was weird to think about the fact that I had just been on my first date with Deryn less than a year ago. Things had moved so quickly between us all, but I didn't regret it.

"So, what did you get me?" Fox asked, sitting across the table from me.

"I'm not telling you," I scoffed.

"It was worth a try, right?" he asked and laughed, his infectious smile spreading to my face immediately.

"Jo," Thor called, "did you get the items you were searching for?"

I nodded. "The last vendor had them. So, my shopping is done."

"Great, then after we eat, why don't we go back to the coliseum for some fun?" Ezio asked.

"Sparring?" Deryn asked, obviously intrigued by that prospect.

Ezio nodded. "No weapons or shifting. Just some hand to hand fun."

"Sounds great," Rhys said with a wide smile.

"When do we return home again?" I asked, a bit anxious to get back.

"Next week. We've only been here, what, less than a week?" Rhys said.

Everyone nodded.

"It feels like it's been an eternity," I mumbled.

The waiter brought out bread and took our orders. I ate a piece of the bread, which was unlike anything we had in Jinla, loving the strange, but delicious taste.

"Don't you just love watching her enjoying foods?" Ezio asked everyone.

"She gets such enjoyment out of good tasting food," Deryn agreed.

"Her blissful expression makes you feel happy, even if you weren't the one to make it," Nico said.

Everyone nodded.

I was blushing, bright as a tomato, I was sure. "You guys," I whispered.

"You ever see her eat beef bone broth soup?" Declan asked.

Everyone smiled.

"She sips it with her eyes closed, a small smile on her face, in supreme contentment," Fox said. "It's glorious."

"I like food," I said and shrugged. "I can't help it."

"We enjoy watching you eat," Nico said and patted my leg. "It's one of the few moments where you will drop your guard completely and you're just you."

"I don't wear masks," I argued. "I'm me all the time."

"Most of the time," Deryn corrected me. "There are often times where you put a mask on. Mostly in public places, especially if they are crowded."

"I don't like crowds," I said. "So, what?"

"No one is saying it's a problem, Jo," Martin said. "They're just telling you that in situations you are uncomfortable with, you wear a mask. But, when you're eating yummy food, you are completely defenseless. It's refreshing to see."

Males were so weird.

"Whatever," I mumbled and then smiled happily at the waiter as he set my drink down. "Thank you," I said to him and took a big drink. Strawberries and rum, a wonderful combination.

"Euphoria, that's what that face is," Ezio said. "I don't think I've ever experienced something like that, especially not with something as trivial as food and drink."

"I need to make her open the bond next time she is about to experience something like that," Rhys said. "Then, I'll know what she's feeling and get to experience it myself."

"Wait until you get a mating bond with her," Martin said. "It's ten times better!"

"Are you mating with them?" Ezio asked, a slight frown marking his handsome face.

"No serious talk," I whispered, closed my eyes, and took another drink. Paradise! Give me non-stop daiquiris, the males in swimsuits, warm sun, and cool water, and I would be set.

"What are you thinking about?" Deryn purred into my ear.

"We should go on a beach vacation this summer," I whispered, feeling my lips tug up in a smirk.

"Oh, are you thinking about me in a banana hammock?" Deryn whispered even quieter.

I burst into laughter, setting down my drink as I bent over and clutched my stomach. "Now I am!" I shouted over my laughter.

"I look good in one," he said and folded his arms across his chest.

"I'm sure you do." I gasped as I tried to calm back down and wiped my teary eyes.

"Your salad," the waiter said, drawing my attention. I was sitting forward, so he couldn't set my salad down.

"Sorry," I said and leaned back. Everyone at the table apparently ordered salad, which I found strange. Most of the time, the shifters didn't eat salads.

"They're part of the meals," Martin said and smiled at me.

"What?" Deryn asked him.

"She was shocked to see shifters eating salads," Martin explained. "So, I explained that they are part of the meal, which is why we are eating them."

"How'd you know that's what she was thinking?" Deryn asked.

"Was that what you were thinking?" Nico asked me.

"I've known her a long time," Martin reminded them. "She learned about shifters from me and my pack. So, I can read her pretty easily."

"Yes, that was what I was thinking," I told Nico. "I know shifters eat healthy, but normally, they don't eat salads. They'll eat a vegetable with their steak dinner, but not a salad."

"Sometimes we eat salads," Rhys countered.

"Yeah, if they are full of meat or other protein like eggs," I replied.

"She does know an awful lot about shifters," Yukio commented.

"Yes, I do. I grew up with them. I did a lot of research and asked a lot of questions. Even after Martin and I broke up, I still studied as much as I could."

"Why?" Declan asked.

"I wanted to know as much as I could about them. I wanted to make sure that when I interacted with them I didn't do anything offensive on accident. I wanted to make sure I was as respectful as possible. I really wanted to make sure if I touched a male, in front of his female, I didn't do anything to make her want to rip out my throat," I explained.

"She wouldn't have ripped out your throat," Martin said and rolled his eyes. "It was my fault for letting you come over during the mating week. She apologized to you and you are best friends now, so it's old history."

"She still tried," I reminded him. "And, I wanted to make sure nothing like that happened again. I didn't want it to be my own fault that a shifter lost control."

"That's not just because of Sharla, is it?" Rhys asked.

I blushed and shoveled a huge bite of salad into my mouth, giving him a small shake of my head.

"That's my fault," Ezio said.

"What?" Deryn asked.

"I lost control one night. She blames herself for it. No matter how many times I tell her it was completely my fault, that a shifter should be able to control their beast no matter what, she still won't forgive herself," Ezio explained.

"They were going to kill you," I snapped, slamming my fork down. "You were almost killed by them because of me."

"Whoa," Deryn said and rested his hand around the back of my neck. "Calm down, baby."

"I think we should hear this story," Rhys said softly, then looked at Ezio. "If, you're willing to share it? We can discuss it privately later, if you wish."

Ezio waved his hand. "It's fine. I was young and violent. It is something I've made certain can never happen again."

"Only because I'm not there to provoke you," I muttered, feeling as small as a mouse.

"About a week into our dating, during, um, fun time, she went for my neck," Ezio explained, fumbling over his words as he looked at Rhys and Deryn. "I hadn't had a female do that before. I overreacted, tossing her off of me and immediately shifted. She'd told me she had been with werewolves before, but I didn't realize she wouldn't know that for how early we were in our relationship, she couldn't do something like that. I was out of control, but to make matters worse, someone had called the cops on us because they'd heard her screaming. Pleasure screams are apparently the same to whoever called. So, the cops burst into the room."

"They saw her naked and terrified on the floor and you, in wolf form, on the bed and flipped?" Deryn guessed.

"Bingo," Ezio said. "They moved towards her and that made me more protective, I deemed them a threat and charged to attack them. Several drew their guns immediately."

"So, who died?" Fox asked.

"No one. She leapt between me and the officer I had charged at, and stood, buck-ass naked, arms spread wide, in front of me so the officers who had drawn their guns couldn't shoot me. They were yelling at her to get down and she refused, telling them to get out and taking steps towards them."

"What did you do?" Deryn asked.

"Nothing. I sat there and stared at her in disbelief. I'd hurt her, growled at her, tossed her off the bed, and she'd thrown herself in front of the humans to protect me without a second's hesitation," Ezio said. He looked over at me and smiled. "That was the night I fell in love with her."

I'd been terrified of Ezio in that moment. I had never had a wolf growl at me so viciously before and he was a huge wolf when shifted. But, I couldn't let him get hurt because of a misunderstanding. Those cops would have killed him first and asked questions later. I could see that Ezio had wanted to protect me when the cops moved towards me and I did the only thing I could think of. I stood up to protect him. In his wolf form, he couldn't communicate with them. He had no way of telling them to back off, except to snap his teeth at them. Had I known that putting my mouth over his neck so early in relationship would make him react that way, I would never have done it. I hadn't realized he would think I was being aggressive towards him or trying to hurt him. I was ignorant and there was no reason for it. So, I started researching their behaviors and laws.

"Is that why you only date alphas?" Zelphar asked. "Because you know we have the highest levels of control?"

Shit.

"Maybe," I mumbled, shoveling more salad into my mouth.

"It's also because she has an alpha personality," Martin said. "She doesn't see it, but I'm sure you all do."

Everyone nodded.

"What?" I asked.

"You're essentially, a human alpha," Rhys said. "You may let others take charge in certain situations, but you are an alpha, through and through."

I didn't believe that for a moment. I was terrified and indecisive a lot of the time. I had panic and anxiety attacks. I was not alpha material, at all.

"She hasn't realized that eventually, she's going to be Queen of the Four Clans, has she?" Kylan asked softly.

Fucking casuals! He was right! Oh, god. Oh, goddess. No. No. No.

"She's freaking out," Nico whispered.

Queen of the Four Clans. Queen of the Dragons. Queen of the Mages. Queen of the Werewolves. Queen of the Elves. I wasn't any of those things. I was human! I wasn't capable of being queen to one of the clans, let alone all four.

"Baby, come back to us," Deryn whispered from what sounded like far away.

"Someone cradle her in your lap and hold her tightly," Martin snapped. It sounded like he was underwater. Wasn't he just across the table from me?

Wouldn't it be better if they had queens of their races? The werewolves didn't have a queen, but only because she had died a few years ago. I couldn't hold a candle to someone like Adelaide. She could rule with fangs and claws. I could shift, thanks to being Rhys's queen, but I wasn't vicious. I wasn't a ruler.

Warmth surrounded me. My cold, numb body slowly came back into feeling and heat radiated from my side. What was the warmth coming from?

"It's working," Martin said, still under water.

There wasn't warmth from one spot. No, there was warmth

from my side, my cheek, my neck, and my legs. Four places. Four. That was the number of my guards. Four. Four males. Four princes.

"We're here, my queen," Deryn whispered in my ear. "We've got you. You're safe. You're fine. Come back to us."

Back? From where? Where was I? Hadn't we just been at the restaurant? The restaurant. Yes. Then, someone had said something and I spaced out. Right. Attack. This was a panic attack. Okay.

"One. Two. Three. Four. Five. Six. Seven. Eight. Nine. Ten."

"Why is she counting?" someone asked from the same under water place Martin was.

"Shush," Rhys ordered them. His voice sounded closer.

I was alive. I was not hurt. I was not bleeding. I was protected. I was free.

The feeling, sounds, and surroundings came rushing back at once and I buried my face into Deryn's neck, the source of the heat on my side.

"You okay, baby?" Deryn asked.

I nodded. "Sorry."

"Don't apologize. You have no reason to apologize," Fox told me, his hand running up and down my leg.

"Sorry," Kylan said.

"What are your plans for Christmas?" Thor asked Martin loudly, drawing everyone's attention.

"We'll be getting a tree when I get back, it's a family tradition. Then, Sharla will cook a huge meal, which we will eat while the children open their presents," Martin said. "What about you, Thor?"

"I'll be going home this year. I haven't seen my parents in a couple of years," Thor answered. "What about you, Ezio?"

He was changing the topic so we could move on. I loved them, so much.

"Your meals," the waiter said as he, and a few others, brought out trays with plates of food on them.

Deryn set me back in my seat and Rhys and Fox returned to their seats as well.

"Thanks," I whispered.

"Anytime," Nico whispered back and kissed me lightly on the lips.

I didn't even know what Deryn had ordered for me. I was pleasantly surprised to find sushi rolls.

"Sushi!" I exclaimed.

"You weren't paying attention when I ordered?" Deryn asked me with a smile.

I shook my head. "No, but this is wonderful. It's been a long time since I last had sushi."

"Didn't we just have sushi like a week or two ago?" Nico asked.

"Yeah, a long time ago," I said, picking up the chopsticks they had provided and quickly ate a piece of the first roll. Crab mix, avocado, and cucumber inside. Fresh salmon, avocado smear, masago, two types of sauce, and green onions on the top. It was my favorite type of roll. "So good," I moaned. The other roll had barbecued eel on the top with a dark sauce. I grabbed a piece of it next and popped it into my mouth. "Paradise," I said.

After finishing my sushi rolls, I returned to sipping on my strawberry daiquiri and looking at the males around me. They were all smiling and talking to each other like old friends. Something that, just a few days earlier, had seemed impossible. Now, the strongest of the races were friends instead of rivals. Was this what they meant about me being an alpha? This was definitely what the kings meant when they questioned whether I was a witch.

A smile spread across my mouth as I surveyed my unintentional work. Maybe my life and death situations were meant to provide something good. They provided an opportunity for males who usually fought to get along. To find a common goal.

"Time to spar!" Fox exclaimed.

"**G**o Rhys! Go Ezio!" I cheered from the stands of the coliseum. The coliseum was completely empty, save for my entourage and myself.

"You can't root for both of them," Fox chastised me.

"Yes, I can."

"Who are you going to fight?" Thor asked Fox.

Fox shrugged. "Whoever wants to challenge me."

"What's your favorite weapon?" Thor asked him.

"Swords, but I do love playing with throwing axes," Fox said.

"Throwing axes sound fun," I said.

"No," Fox said immediately. "You will somehow end up injured if you participate."

"I'm not a klutz," I growled.

Rhys and Ezio were dancing around on the balls of their feet, fists raised in front of their faces. They looked like boxers. They exchanged a few tentative hits from each other and then, they were moving so fast, that I could not track their movements. Their arms moved so fast, that they were just a blur to me.

"Who's winning?" I asked Fox. "I can't see their punches."

"It's pretty evenly matched right now," Fox said. "Rhys may be testing him to see what his style is or trying to find any breaks in his defense."

"Ezio's defense is pretty damn solid," Thor commented.

"Jojo," Declan called in a sing-song voice.

"What's up Declan?" I asked without turning towards him.

"Nothing, just wanted to come sit by you," he said and plopped down onto the seat next to me. "Who do you think will win?"

"I honestly don't know," I admitted.

"You're supposed to say Rhys," Fox mumbled.

"I would, but you forget that I've seen Ezio in full attack mode. With one hand, he destroyed a dozen ogres. I'm not saying Rhys couldn't do that too. I just haven't seen him in a fight like that." And hopefully, I never would. I didn't fancy the idea of my guards getting hurt.

"She's so honest," Declan chuckled.

"Who are you going to fight?" I asked Declan. I still couldn't see their movements, but it looked like they were starting to use kicks as well, since their bodies would drop lower sometimes.

"Deryn," Declan said. "I've wanted to spar with him for a long time, but never had an opportunity."

"Me?" Deryn asked. "Really?"

Declan nodded.

"Well, no matter who any of you fight, I know they are going to be good fights. I'm honestly surprised that you've never sparred with each other before," I said.

"They are going to have to call a draw," Fox whispered. "They're just too evenly matched. This could go on for days."

"You think they'll call a draw?" I asked. They were both so damn stubborn, I couldn't imagine them calling a draw.

"Yes. This isn't a typical fight. If this was part of the tournament, neither would back down, fighting until they passed out or were too injured to protect themselves," Deryn answered.

"Declan," I said quickly, spinning to look at him. "I almost forgot!" I reached down into my bag and grabbed one of the packages. "Here," I said with a smile. "Merry Christmas."

"For me?" Declan asked, his eyes wide and mouth slightly parted. "This is a gift for me?"

I nodded.

"Do I open it now? Or wait until Christmas?" he asked.

"It's up to you," I said with a smile and kissed his cheek. "I don't care either way."

"I'm going to wait," he said with a nod of finality. "That way, I will think of you on Christmas and have a piece of you with me."

I had zero idea what to say to that. It warmed me and I found tears in my eyes. "You're so sweet," I finally whispered and hugged him.

"Draw!" Rhys and Ezio called at the same time.

Both were drenched in sweat, breathing heavily, but I didn't see any blood.

"Next," Rhys called and hopped up into the stands.

"Deryn?" Declan asked.

Deryn nodded. "Sure."

Declan set his gift next to me. "I'll get it after my match. I don't want to lose it or have it smooshed if it's in my pocket."

"Okay," I said with a nod. "I'll keep it safe until you return."

Rhys plopped down in front of me and leaned back, so his upper back leaned against my legs. "Hey, beautiful," he said with a wide smile.

"Hello, handsome. Did you have fun?" I asked, giving him a light kiss on his lips, having to lean around him to do so.

"Yes, I did," Rhys answered. "I'm glad we got to do this."

"Me too," Ezio said from behind me,

I tipped my head back to look at him. "You had fun too?"

"Yes," he said with a nod. "It has been a long time since I've been matched so well with someone in a fight. I miss matches like this."

"Well, you shouldn't have gotten so strong," I teased.

He chuckled, but didn't say anything.

"Their fight is starting," Rhys said, getting my attention. He sat forward, his arms on his legs as he focused intently on the fighters.

"Who do you think will win?" I asked Fox.

"Deryn," he said immediately.

"I don't know," Rhys said. "Declan is pretty quick."

"Yes, but so is Deryn when he's focused. I think he might let some of his true skill shine," Fox said.

"Deryn is a bit lazy," Rhys chuckled. "Maybe Jolie will finally get to see some of his true skills."

Deryn and Declan faced each other and then bowed. Once they straightened, all humor left their faces as they focused, but I was glad to see that there wasn't any hostility.

Honestly, seeing them getting along so well despite knowing I'd been with the others, made me really happy. They were all incredibly dominant, each definitely alpha material. Maybe that was what I saw in them. Maybe I was drawn to the dominant males because I knew they would be the most able to protect me.

Deryn darted left and I was blown away by how fast he moved. I knew he could move quickly, he was a werewolf after all, but I had never seen him move *that* fast before.

"You weren't joking," I whispered to Rhys and Fox.

"I didn't know he was that fast," Ezio said.

"I'm surprised you didn't want to fight him," I told Ezio.

"I was worried he might hold some animosity towards me. I figured Rhys was the better option. Plus, I always wanted to fight him," Ezio explained.

"Seems that all of you wanted to fight each other," I chuckled.

Deryn was suddenly still and Declan was on his back in the arena.

I stood up in shock, worried that he had hurt Declan.

Declan laughed and then leapt to his feet. "Nice job," Declan told Deryn and shook hands with him. "I didn't even see that hit coming."

"What happened?" I asked as I sat down again. Maybe it wasn't a good idea for me to watch them. My heart was pounding hard.

"Deryn broke his defense and landed a hit right to his jaw," Rhys told me. "That was a really nice punch."

"Thank you," Deryn said, sitting next to Fox again. He took his shirt off and wiped the sweat from his forehead. My eyes were glued to him, admiring his exposed muscular body.

"Hey," Fox snapped, putting himself in my line of sight. "Stop drooling."

"I'm allowed to look and admire my guards," I said and folded my arms across my chest.

"Who's next?" Deryn asked.

"Me," Fox said. "Who wants to challenge me?"

"Me," Zelphar said and leapt into the arena.

"Alright." Fox smiled happily as he joined Zelphar in the arena.

"Who will win this one?" Ezio asked, grinning.

"Fox," Deryn and Rhys answered at the same time.

"He's pretty amazing in battle," I whispered, leaning my elbows on my knees and my chin in my hands. I had gotten to watch him battle enemies in the park and at the party when my father and his minions had attacked.

"Oh, so Fox is your favorite?" Ezio asked.

"What?" Deryn asked, turning his eyes toward me.

"She couldn't pick a winner from any of the other fights and didn't praise any of you. Yet, she swoons over Fox," Ezio said.

Fox removed his shirt and looked up at me. "See, plenty of muscles to look at here."

Fox was the most muscular, shorter than the others, but buffer. Somehow though, his bulk didn't hinder his movements and he was very lithe. I supposed, that could be due to his being an elf.

"I'm not going to be able to see anything, am I?" I asked Deryn.

"You mean because they're moving too fast?" he asked me.

I nodded.

"Most likely," Deryn said.

"Shouldn't she be able to tap into your powers to see better?" Ezio asked.

"We've tried it before and it didn't work. You might try now, since you're officially our queen," Rhys suggested.

"Okay." It was worth a shot. I closed my eyes and focused on our bonds, being sure not to touch Fox's, since he would need all of his focus on the fight. I opened my eyes and everything was brighter, clearer, and I could see so many things I had missed before. I could see a single gray hair on Declan's head. They started fighting and I was finally able to watch it.

Fox was fast, his fists punching and blocking as Declan returned his aggression. There wasn't one on defense while the other was on offense. They were both being offensive and defensive at the same time. The movements were so fast, I supposed that was probably the easiest thing for them. If you were on defense too much, you might get backed into a corner.

"Shit," Ezio whispered. "I've never seen an elf fight before. That's insane."

"Declan's holding his own," Rhys commented.

"Not much longer," I whispered. I could see it, the small faltering movements Declan made. I was certain Fox saw them as well.

"She's right," Deryn whispered in shock. "Wow."

Declan held up his hand and Fox stopped, mid-punch. "I give," Declan said. "I can't keep up with your speed."

Fox bowed to him and they headed up to us again. I released

the connections, letting my normal eyesight return. Everything seemed so dull and bland now.

"I'm hungry," I announced. "Can we get some food?"

"You're always hungry," Martin chuckled.

"We need to get a bigger refrigerator for all the food she eats now," Deryn said and draped his arm around my shoulders. "Maybe a deep freezer."

"As if you four don't eat a ton too," I said with a roll of my eyes.

"We should get a deep freezer," Rhys agreed. "We could store a ton of frozen meats for cooking meals."

"So you can stop eating so much fast food and takeout?" I guessed. Honestly, it surprised me how much our interactions revolved around food. It seemed strange to humans how much Others ate.

"I love pizza," Deryn complained. "I don't want to eat healthy all the time."

"I never said all the time," Rhys countered. "I'm still going to eat pizza."

"As long as the pizza guy doesn't kidnap me again," I said and laughed at the memory. Now that I was able to laugh at it.

"What?" Ezio asked. "A pizza guy kidnapped you?"

"Yes," I said. "Then a dragoness took me from him and delivered me to my father."

Ezio reached out and took my hand in his. "Did he hurt you again?"

I squeezed his hand and smiled. He remembered! I'd told him about my father when we were dating. "He's dead now. The guys killed him. So, I don't have to worry about him any longer."

No, now I just had to worry about his ex-lover and my ex-friend, Justina. Would she try to come after me again? Would she want to hurt me once she found out that I was their queen once more and their mate? I was betting so. If I was her, I might.

"You're scowling now," Deryn whispered.

"Thinking about Justina," I whispered.

"We'll keep you protected," Deryn promised.

"Is it wrong that I feel bad for her? I mean, she tortured me and tried to kill me, but she's trying to deal with her sorrow."

"You're too nice," Ezio chastised me. "She tortured you and severed your connections with the princes. What if it had been permanent? What if she had severed them and there was no way to get them back?"

He was right...I knew. And, had that been the case, I would still feel numb and hollow, which would probably be driving me insane. Yet, we had been friends. She didn't stop being my friend because she hated me. She stopped because my lovers killed her lover. It was an age-old story that happened again and again.

"We'll kill her if we see her. You know that, right?" Deryn asked.

"I know." I sighed. "I know."

"I have some errands to take care of," Ezio said as he stood.

"Wait!" I ordered him. Reaching deep down into my bag, I grabbed his present and handed it to him. Then, I handed Kylan, Thor, Martin, Yukio, and Zelphar theirs as well.

"You got us all presents?" Yukio asked.

"Yes. I wanted to get you something to thank you."

"Thank us for what?" Ezio asked.

"Being part of my life, protecting me when you had to, loving me, and helping me this week," I said. "You're all part of me, even if we aren't a couple any longer. I still cherish your friendships."

"Friend-zoned!" Thor gasped and clutched at his heart. "No!"

I smacked his arm and he smiled at me. "Knock it off."

"Thank you," Thor said and kissed my cheek. "I appreciate it. It means a lot to me that you would think of me and buy a gift."

"I'm going to wait to open mine, like Declan," Yukio told me. "Can I call you after I open it, to thank you?"

"Of course, you can," I said and hugged him.

Yukio looked over my head and asked, "Prince?"

"You are all welcome to contact Jolie," Fox said. "Just remember that she's ours and everything will be fine."

"And that we'll kill you if you touch her inappropriately," Rhys said with a bright and warm smile.

The death threat and smile were in such contrast, that I found myself unable to say anything.

"Understood," all of my exes said.

"Hugs," I ordered them.

Each took a turn giving me a hug and Ezio and Declan gave me kisses on the cheek.

"She's like an omega," Deryn said. "She's so calm and happy to see everyone, that we are all relaxed. She's the reason so many dominates were able to get along just now."

"I thought you said I was an alpha?" I asked, feeling confused.

"You're a human alpha, but somehow you've turned yourself into a wolf omega. So much time in the werewolf pack gave you the ability to have the dual personalities," Deryn explained.

I supposed what he said made sense. I still didn't see myself as an alpha personality as a human, but they would be the better judges on that anyway. Maybe I would ask Dan what he thought.

I realized that I hadn't spoken to Nico much that afternoon. I turned and held my arms out to him. He wrapped me up in a warm hug and then slung one arm beneath my knees to pick me up.

"Hello," Nico said with a smile. "What's up?"

"Nothing. Just wanted some Nico time," I told him and leaned my face into his neck. "Mm, you smell good. Like cologne."

"No cologne on," he told me.

"I know. It's just your scent. I love it."

"What did you buy from that mage merchant?" he asked me softly.

"I'm not telling you," I said quickly, jerking my head back to look at him.

"If it's something dangerous or something you could-"

"Nico, I'm not stupid. I promise to be careful with my purchases. I'm actually planning on talking with King Katar about it."

"My dad?" Fox asked. "Why?"

"I need help with something magic related," I explained. "And I can't ask you guys. And, I don't really want to use your dad," I whispered to Nico.

"Understandable," he nodded.

"So, I figured King Katar was my next best option. Plus, I haven't really gotten to spend much time with him."

"Why can't you tell us?" Nico asked, frowning.

"Because I can't."

If I told them what I was doing, it would ruin the surprise! The whole point of having my exes with me today was to keep my guards away, so they wouldn't see what I purchased. If I asked for their help in finishing it, they'd know what it was. Why didn't they get that?

"We just don't want you hurt or doing something you could be hurt with. Magic is dangerous," Nico said.

"I'm sure King Katar will keep me safe," I told him and rolled my eyes. "He likes me, remember?"

"Yes, he does," Fox agreed. "He likes your omega, but alpha personality. It intrigues him."

"Oh, so now I'm like a weird science experiment?" I asked, defensively.

Did they think of me as some weird human that needed to be observed? Were the kings really nice to me because they liked me being around to see what I might do? I was a bit strange, yeah, I knew that, but I wasn't completely weird.

"That's not what I meant," Fox said. "I meant that it's unique to have a female like you. You're not weird or a freak. You're refreshing. It's nice to have a female who likes the same things that we do. Do you know how hard it is to find a female who plays video games more than we do? Most get upset if we're playing for more than an hour. You'll play even after we go to bed."

"Yes, I'm a video game addict. I know."

"We love it," Nico whispered and kissed my cheek. "It's one of the great things about you."

"We need to play more games," I grumbled. "I haven't played much lately. My clan has started to tease me and is calling me Jolie's ghost. I've been dead to them for months."

"We will," Nico promised.

※

"THIS SEEMS PRETTY EASY FOR SOMETHING THAT'S SO IMPORTANT," I told King Katar. I was facing him, sitting at a table in his house, with the bloodstones on the table between us.

"It is easy, but that's because it is something that we wanted to be sure almost anyone could do. Now, take the crystal in your hand, fill it with your energy, and then put a drop of your blood on it. It will soak up the blood and seal it inside," he instructed me.

It was simple and wouldn't take long, but I would have to do the process four times. I didn't like knowing I would have to cut myself four different times.

It was worth it though. I was really looking forward to seeing the guys' reactions when they opened this gift. I knew without a doubt, that it would be the best present I would ever give them.

The bloodstones were small, the size of a grain of rice, and their purpose was to embed them in your skin, to add a piece of your mate to your body, so they would permanently be part of you. Most put the crystal on their wrists, so it was visible, but not in a way that drew your eye. I had seen some people put them on their chests and behind their ears. I wasn't sure where the guys would put theirs, but I was anxious to find out.

The crystal was warm in my hand and it warmed even more

as I filled it with my energy. Since I didn't have my own magic, I had to use my energy. Once it was full, I used the needle Katar had given me, and smeared blood onto the crystal. As he had said, the crystal absorbed the blood and turned red. I put the crystal into a small black box, similar to a ring box, but with a groove made specifically for the crystal.

"Doing it one time is no problem," I muttered. "Most are lucky to have just one mate."

Katar chuckled softly. "I think you're pretty lucky."

"I didn't mean it like that," I said, blushing. I was the luckiest female on the planet. Four hot males, who were princes, and loved me more than anything else. I couldn't ask for more.

"Round two," I said with a sigh, grabbing another crystal and putting it in my hand.

When I was finally done, I let my head fall onto my arms on the table. "Done!" I exclaimed.

Katar patted my arm. "Well done."

"Thanks."

"Are you ready for Christmas now?" he asked as he packed up the things on the table and wiped it down, even though none of my blood had spilled.

"Yes. Now, I just have to wait to give them their gifts," I said. "I need to hide these somewhere so they won't find them. If they see the boxes, they'll know right away what their gifts are."

"Would you like me to put a cloaking spell on them?" Katar asked.

"You can do that?" I asked him in shock. "It would stay even after I leave?"

He nodded. "I can make the bag you put them in look like a present box, and you can put it under your tree. Even if they touch it, they won't know the truth. It will last until you take the boxes out of the bag."

"That's amazing!" I exclaimed.

He smiled. "I enjoy talking with you. You let your emotions

out, which is refreshing since Others hide their emotions all the time."

"Rhys said I need to learn to use a court face, to hide my emotions when I don't want people to know what I'm thinking or feeling," I said. "But, it's really hard!"

"They're taught how to do it from a very young age," Katar said. "It is not something you will pick up after a month or two. You will have to continue practicing the rest of your life. You are such an emotional creature, that I'm not sure if you will ever be able to do it."

"Thanks for the pep talk," I mumbled.

He laughed and wrapped me up in a hug. "It gets better."

"I hope so. I'm really far behind the curve."

"Let me spell your bag and then I can go fetch Foxfire. I'm sure he's paced a moat around the house by now."

I put all of the boxes into a single black, drawstring bag and handed the bag to Katar. He held it in his flattened palms and whispered some words I didn't understand. Then, the bag disappeared and a beautiful green Christmas box with a red bow appeared in its place.

"So, I just open the drawstring, pull out the boxes, and the illusion will disappear?"

He nodded.

"You're amazing!" I exclaimed and hugged him.

"Don't start that," Kara said with a sigh. "It will go to his already big head."

Kara was Fox's mother and Katar's queen and mate. She was tall, slim, and had gorgeous silver hair that flowed tangle free down her back. I envied her hair and her beauty, mostly because she was also super sweet.

"Hello, Kara," I bowed my head in greeting.

She pulled me into a hug and kissed my cheek. "Hello, Daughter."

This was a new thing that I was not used to yet. Deryn, Rhys, and Fox's parents had all begun calling me their daughter. It was a high honor that I didn't feel comfortable having.

"Is Foxfire still pacing?" Katar asked Kara.

She nodded. "He's convinced something is going to go wrong."

"They're so rude," I grumbled.

"They just don't like not being involved," Kara said. "They want to keep you safe, but when you're away from them, holed up with their father, they have no way to help you."

"I'm certain if I screamed, he would come running," I said.

"Try it," Katar said with a smirk.

"Really?" I asked him.

He nodded. "I want to see what his reaction will be. He knows I'm here and that I'm helping you. I wonder how quickly he will run here."

"He's out front, right?" I said.

Kara nodded.

I took a deep breath and then screamed loudly. Fox was there the next instant and had me in his arms before I could even suck in a new breath.

"What is it?" he asked, scanning the room.

"So little trust," Katar said with a sigh. "I'm hurt, Foxfire."

"What?" Fox asked, looking from me to his parents.

"Nothing's wrong," I assured him. "Katar wanted to see how fast you would come here if you heard me scream, even though I'm in his protection."

"It has nothing to do with you, Father," Fox argued.

"Are you ever going to call me, 'Father'?" Katar asked me.

"Sorry," I whispered. "I'm just not used to it yet."

"It's what you call Dan," Kara pointed out.

"I'm used to assembling myself into a werewolf pack. I'm trying," I said. "Maybe it will come easier once Fox and I are mated."

"Did you give her the present?" Kara asked Katar.

He shook his head. "I figured you would want to."

"It's not Christmas yet," I said.

"We're just very excited to give it to you," she said. "I suppose I can wait until Christmas to give it to you. You are coming the morning of Christmas, right?"

"Yes, Mother," Fox said. "We will come here no later than nine o'clock."

"But, we can only stay for a couple hours because we have to go visit the other clans as well," I reminded them.

"Nine to eleven with the elves. Eleven to one with the dragons. One to three with the mages. Three to five with the werewolves. Then, home to do our presents," Fox explained.

"That's a lot of parties and food," Kara said. "Are you going to survive?"

"Hopefully," I laughed. "I'll just make sure to eat small amounts at each place."

"I'll make sure to package you the best foods to take home with you," Kara said.

"Make sure you pack the fudge!" Fox said. "She has to be able to eat your fudge."

"I'll make her her own special batch," Kara promised.

"You're the best," I told her, tapping Fox to put me down so I could hug her.

She hugged me and kissed my cheek as she pulled back. "I'll see you tomorrow."

"Yes," I agreed, hugged Katar, and then picked up the present and smiled at Fox.

"What is that?" he asked me.

"A gift," I answered.

"But they said they didn't give it to you yet," he said.

"It's one she cannot open until you guys are opening presents," Katar covered for me. "Don't even think of trying to open it," he threatened Fox.

Fox led me out with our hands linked and kept looking at the present. Was the illusion faulty? Could he see through it?

"What?" I asked.

"I'm just trying to guess what they got you that is that size," he said.

I hid it from his view and said, "No! Don't spoil my surprise! I don't want you to know until I open it."

"Okay. Okay," he said.

Martin waved from the side of the SUV. "All done?"

"Sorry I kept you waiting so long," I apologized.

"No sweat," he said.

"We better hurry home or there won't be any food left," Fox told me.

"Aren't they wrapping presents still?" I asked him.

"They're done. I made sure they were just now," he said and held up his phone.

"You can give me some hints about what the guys are getting me," I said with a smile.

He laughed and shook his head. "Nope. You can wait for their surprise, just like you're waiting for my parents'."

"Rude," I grumbled, but wasn't serious. I was glad to wait for their gifts. It was something I was really looking forward to.

"Buckled up?" Martin asked.

"Yes, *Dad*," I said in a childish voice.

"Don't make me turn this car around," he threatened.

"We haven't even left yet. How could you turn it around?" I asked with a laugh.

"He could turn it around literally, so it is facing the other way," Fox said.

"That's just preposterous."

"Sharla said to tell you that when you come to the werewolf den, you better come see us," Martin told me.

"Of course I'm going to come see you! I have to give my nieces their presents," I said. "They're going to love them! I'm the best auntie ever!"

"And totally not full of herself," Martin chuckled.

We drove through town, headed towards the apartment building. It was strange, I had been in this town awhile now, but I hadn't really explored it. I'd driven from one place to the next, but never spent time in the places in between. I would have to fix that! The guys and I could start going on walking trips around town to see what stores and restaurants there were.

There I was, focused on food again. It had been increasingly worse since they made me their queen. I was constantly hungry and ate way more than a normal human should.

CHAPTER 12

I awoke to the first Christmas morning with excitement coursing through my veins, but as I woke up, surrounded by four princes, I knew I already had everything that I could ever want. Or need.

"Morning, beautiful," Deryn grumbled in a gravely morning voice.

I rolled over to face him, a smile on my face before I even saw his smile. "Hello, handsome."

He pulled me closer, kissing my forehead gently. "Did you sleep well?"

I nodded.

"Cold," Fox whispered and rolled closer to me. "Why'd you move away?" he asked, pressing his back against mine.

"Where are the blankets?" I asked.

"I threw them off," Rhys said and yawned, stretching his arms and sitting up so that I could see him without moving.

"Hello, Puff," I teased and held out my hand.

He pulled me up with it and gave me a deep, passionate kiss. My body became an inferno and I wrapped my arms around his neck, trying to climb into his lap.

His lips were gone as was his body and I groaned, draping my arm over the edge of the bed where he had abandoned me. "My guard has abandoned me!" I moaned as though terribly upset.

"Either I abandon you, or pee on you," he called from the bathroom.

"We need to get ready," Nico said. "We've only got an hour before our first Christmas."

"Elven Christmas!" I yelled, leapt to my feet, and rushed to take a quick shower. "I can't miss this!"

My shower was shockingly solo, for the first time in months. Taking advantage of the time I had been given, I shaved all my parts, and thoroughly washed and rinsed my hair. After putting my silver and blue dress on, I styled my hair into a braid over my left shoulder and put on some neutral colored eyeshadow and black eyeliner. Satisfied, I walked out of the room to find the guys all sitting on the floor by the tree, staring at the gift I had placed there.

"What, are you *doing?*" I demanded with my hands on my hips.

They leapt away from the tree, guilty expressions on their faces.

"It's only half a day," I growled at them.

"We're sorry," they all said at the same time.

"I can't believe you guys," I grumbled, stomping over to slide my low heels on.

"Everyone ready?" Fox asked.

"Yes."

"Yeah."

"Where's my coffee?"

The last had come from Rhys, no doubt.

"We will pick some up on the way," Fox promised.

"Ready, my queen?" Nico asked.

I looked up from the small handbag I was inspecting and took his offered hand. "Yes, my guard."

We walked out of the apartment building's front doors into a crush of media. They shouted questions, but with so many different voices shouting so many questions, I couldn't understand them. My guards put me in the center of the group and pushed their way through, to the SUV that waited for us. This time, it was a werewolf I did not know driving. Martin must have been home with Sharla and the girls.

I heard rapid gunfire and immediately ducked down and covered myself in dragon scales. The media members screamed and scattered like cockroaches when the light turned on. The guys spun around to face outward, all of them except Rhys, who was looking at his hand, which was coated in red.

"Rhys!" I screamed and spun him towards me, now up on my feet and still covered in scales. The shoulder of his white shirt had a hole through it and a blood stain spread out slowly. "Rhys, talk to me," I whispered.

"My fucking scales didn't automatically cover me," he whispered in disbelief, still staring at his bloody hand. "Ow."

I glanced up, glad to see a shield around us. "Thanks, Nico," I whispered.

"Getting shot hurts," Rhys growled and looked at me. "Seriously, ow."

"You okay?" I asked, opening his shirt buttons so I could move it aside to inspect him.

"Yeah, I'm fine. The bullet went clean through," he said. "It's been awhile since I've had anything pierce my skin."

"My teeth don't count?" I asked with a smirk, trying to get him to snap out of the weird mood that clouded his face.

He chuckled and dropped his hand, the mood gone. "No, those don't count."

"Get in the damn car," Deryn growled at me.

"Nico put up a shield," I said, "and I'm covered in scales."

"Now," Deryn growled louder.

I obeyed, climbing in and tugged on Rhys to come in with me. "Why didn't your scales cover you?" I asked him.

"I'm not sure," he admitted. "I haven't been practicing lately, so maybe I've gotten lazy."

I poked his rock-hard abs and said, "You are getting pudgy."

He laughed, grabbed my hand, and pulled it up to his mouth, kissing my fingertips. "I guess we'll just have to increase our physical activity to combat that."

"Tease," I hissed at him.

Everyone got into the car and we drove away.

"What? No cops?" I asked. "No one is going to go after the shooter?"

"I got him already," Nico said with a smirk. "You okay, Rhys?"

Rhys nodded. "Yeah, but that hurt."

"You're such a baby," I said and rolled my eyes, only teasing him since I was certain it had to have hurt.

"Good thing we're going to the dragon's den today, so you can talk to your dad," Fox said.

"Yeah," Rhys agreed.

"Who was the shooter?" I asked.

"Human," Nico answered as though that explained everything.

"And he's dead?"

"No, he's in police custody," he told me.

"Oh. Okay."

"No, we did not kill someone and just leave their body on the roof of a building," Nico said with an eye roll.

"I don't know!" I snapped. "Every time we've been shot at before, we've just run off."

"No, you've been taken away. One of us has always stayed and taken care of the person or their body," Rhys explained quietly to me.

"Are you still bleeding?" I asked.

"No," he shook his head.

"Good."

"I need coffee," he told the driver. "Please."

"You got it, boss," the driver said, switching lanes as he changed course.

"What is our first meal going to be?" I asked Fox.

"I'm not ruining it. You'll just have to wait to see," he said.

"I'm getting fudge though, right?" I asked.

He laughed. "I'm sure my mother did as she said and made a special batch of fudge just for you."

"She's getting her own fudge?" Deryn asked with an open mouth. "Your mom never gave me my own fudge."

"You aren't her son's future mate," I reminded him.

"Oh, say that again," Fox said, moving his head next to mine. "Say it again, please."

"Future mate," I whispered into his ear.

His body shuddered and he moaned. "Yes."

We went through a drive thru for Rhys's coffee and then continued on our way to visit the elves. My nerves were frayed, not only was I spending my first Christmas with the guys, but with each of their families. It was so much at once. So many new experiences for one day.

Rhys found a spare shirt in the SUV and changed into it, grumbling about guns and scales incoherently. Once he had the shirt on, he linked our fingers together, scooted closer so that our arms were touching, and whispered, "You're going to be fine. One of us will be with you at all times, no matter where we are. If you need to step out and get some air, just tell us."

His words were reassuring and I calmed a bit, not completely, but a bit.

Katar and Kara were waiting on the porch when we arrived. Both had pleasant smiles on, though Kara looked a bit worn.

"She spends all night working on food preparation and then wakes up very early to get the meal ready. She's tired, but she enjoys it. This is her favorite time of year," Fox whispered in my ear.

Our group stepped out of the SUV, Fox in the lead with me right behind him, and the others following lazily behind.

Katar patted his son on the back and pulled me into a hug. "Everything working?"

"I caught them all staring at it this morning," I whispered.

He chuckled. "Fox has always had an insatiable curiosity."

"You're hogging her again," Kara whispered. "Let me get my hug."

"Sorry, dear," Katar said, giving me a wink before letting me go.

Kara instantly pulled me into a hug.

"Can I have my queen back now?" Fox asked, his voice held nothing, but affection for his mother.

"Fine, Son," she said and let me go. "It's time to eat, anyway."

"Food," Rhys grumbled, a growl in his chest.

Everyone turned to face him.

"Rhys?" I asked softly.

"Sorry," he said and wiped a hand down his face. "I'm really hungry."

"We didn't eat breakfast," I explained to Kara.

"Let's get inside and get you some food," she told Rhys, setting her hand on his shoulder and guiding him inside.

"Is he okay?" I asked Fox softly.

He nodded. "We didn't eat yet and he got shot, so his body needs food. He's fine. As soon as he gets food in his belly, he'll be back to his normal self."

Linking our arms, he pulled me inside and then pulled out a chair for me. I sat and my eyes widened in surprised to find my plate already filled with food. Everyone ate in silence, our appetites too ravenous for courtesies. Kara and Katar didn't seem to mind, smiling at each other occasionally as they ate.

"Where is Silverowl?" Nico asked Fox, breaking the silence.

Fox finished chewing the food in his mouth and answered, "He's on an errand. He should be back soon."

"The meal was delicious," Rhys complimented Kara.

"I'm glad you enjoyed it. Do you need any healing?"

I had forgotten that Fox said his mother was the best healer out of them.

"Can you at least give him a check?" I asked before Rhys could decline her offer.

"Jolie," Rhys sighed.

"No back talk," I ordered him.

Kara rested her hand on Rhys's hand and closed her eyes. Light shimmered from her fingers, spreading from Rhys's hand up his arm, and covered his entire body.

Rhys's shoulders lowered, his face relaxed, tension leaving it that I had not even noticed. "Thank you," he whispered.

"Next time, you tell your queen that you are injured," she ordered him, pulling her hand away and the light with her.

"Yes, Kara," he said with a resigned head bow.

"Thank you," I said to her. "Sometimes, they're a bit-"

"Defiant. Stubborn. Headstrong. Bullheaded," Kara supplied.

I laughed while all of the princes scowled at her words.

"Who is ready for dessert?" Kara asked.

"Me!" I said eagerly.

I had not been prepared for the dessert course. Pies, fudge, cookies, and even a cake were laid out on a table in the living room.

"No fudge for you," Fox said, grabbing the piece from my hand before I could pop it into my mouth.

"What?" I gasped.

"You have to wait until we get home and you eat a piece of the fudge she made for you," he explained.

"Fox," I pouted, sticking my lip out and giving him my best puppy dog eyes. "Just one little piece," I begged, ran my hands up his chest, and leaned into him.

His eyes heated and he pressed himself closer to me. His lips brushed against mine as he whispered, "No."

"Gah!" I yelled and smacked Fox on the chest, pushing him away from me.

"Here, baby," Deryn said, holding out a slice of pie with a ton of whipped cream on top.

"At least someone loves me," I said with a glare at Fox before taking the offered pie.

Deryn kissed me softly and gave Fox a cheeky grin.

"Suck-up," Fox growled at him.

I scooped whipped cream off the top of the pie with one finger and licked it off slowly, drawing the attention of four princes.

"Do that again," Fox threatened, "and you won't get *any* fudge."

"Foxfire," Kara growled, "don't you dare use my treats as part of your threats."

"Sorry," he mumbled.

"Busted!" I laughed at him.

Everyone laughed, including Fox.

❦

ANDRAS AND EMRYS STOOD AT THE STEPS TO THEIR HOUSE, waiting for us to exit the cars. Rhys tried to hold my hand, but I quickened my step to hug Emrys and kiss his cheek. "Hello, Father."

He kissed my cheek and smiled, warmth filling his eyes. "Daughter, you look well."

Leaning close with my hands on his shoulders to keep my balance, I whispered into his ear, "Take Rhys away and speak to him. Something happened."

His shoulders tensed beneath my hands and he nodded.

I turned to Andras and opened my arms. "Brother."

He snickered. "That is not what I'd like to hear you call me, but I suppose that is the best I will get."

My arms started to drop, disappointment stinging in my chest and my expression tightening.

Andras rushed forward, hugging me tightly, tucking my face against his chest with a hand on the back of my head. His lips lowered to my ear and he whispered, "I was teasing you. I'm sorry. I didn't mean to upset you. Forgive me? Sister?"

I nodded, but didn't speak, unsure if I could keep my voice even.

He released me to shake hands with Nico and Deryn.

"Jolie?" Fox whispered.

"Where's Rhys?" I asked.

"Emrys took him inside," he said.

I nodded and headed up the steps, only to have my path blocked by an eager teenage boy. His arms wrapped around me and he spun me around, my feet dangling in the air.

"Jolie!" he exclaimed.

"Gavin," I gasped, clutching his arms while smiling.

He set me down, a joyous smile on his face. "I'm so happy you're here! Come on, food's ready."

"Oh, I don't know if I can eat yet," I admitted.

"You will once you smell the meal that has been prepared," he told me, adamantly.

Nico slid his fingers between mine as we walked down the hallway, pulling me to his side as we held hands. "You look beautiful," he whispered.

"Thank you," I replied, glancing at him curiously. While he did give me compliments, he normally reserved them for when we were alone. He also rarely held my hand.

"What?" he asked.

"You're just not usually so affectionate in public," I whispered.

"Does it bother you?" Nico asked.

"No!" I gasped. "Nico, you know it doesn't. I was just wondering what the change in attitude was from, that's all."

"Almost losing you," he whispered a shadow passing over his

face. "I thought I had lost you and, in that moment, I saw all of the times that I was rude to you or the times that I wished I had expressed my feelings more clearly to you. I'm not generally an affectionate person. However, when it comes to you, I find myself constantly wanting to hold your hand, hug you, kiss you, at least touch you briefly."

"You're always welcome to touch me," I whispered and squeezed his hand.

He kissed my cheek and whispered, "I will keep that in mind."

The dining room was decorated with garlands, poinsettias, gold leaves, and pine cones. It was rustic and charming at the same time. Rhys's mother looked in my direction and scowled. She said something to the servant she had been talking to and walked toward me. I dropped Nico's hand and took a step away from him, so I wouldn't try to hide behind him, like I desperately wanted to.

"Jolie," she said in greeting.

"Queen Adelaide," I replied and dipped my head. "Thank you for allowing us to come enjoy Christmas with you and your family."

"You are family now," she said and sighed. "Whether I agree or think you worthy or not, my son loves you and I can tell that you love him. I wished he would be with a female dragon, but you are not a bad specimen. I would like to speak to you in private, if you can spare a moment?"

Should I go somewhere alone with her? I wasn't convinced she would not hurt me. She loved Rhys and I was definitely not her choice for him.

"Certainly," I replied and glanced at Nico. "I'm going to speak with the queen for a moment. I'll be right back."

And if I didn't come back, hopefully they would come looking for me.

Nico nodded and whispered to Deryn, who was talking with Rhian. Rhian had a slight blush on her cheeks and a huge smile on her face. The adorable teenager must have a crush on Deryn.

"This way," Queen Adelaide said, spinning and causing her dress to flare around her. She was so graceful and beautiful. I followed close behind her, glancing at the pictures on the walls as we went down a hallway I had never used before and into a study that smelled mostly of Emrys.

She shut the door and spun to face me. "Are you truly going to remove your ability to have children?"

Crap. I had not wanted a discussion like this with her.

"Yes," I answered her.

"Why?"

"There are many reasons," I replied, trying to be vague and hoping she would leave it at that.

"Please, indulge me and let me hear these reasons," she said softly.

She didn't seem mad, but I still wasn't sure if I could trust her.

"I'm going to be mated to four different males. Four different clans. I don't want to have a child with one of them and not the others. What if I only got pregnant with a child from one or two of them. Or, even worse, three of them and the fourth never had one with me. I don't want to have one of them never have a child and see the others with their children. Plus, I don't really want children. I've never viewed myself as a person who would have children. There's so much work and they have to be protected. I can barely protect myself right now."

"And my son is okay with this?" she asked me.

I nodded. "They said that if I wanted to have children, they would all love the children I had, no matter who the father was, but it's just too strange for me to think about. What would the children call them? Uncle? Here, little John, this is Rhys, your uncle and mommy's other mate? It's too weird. I don't want to do that. I would prefer to never have children if that is the only option available to me."

"You're certain that you are going to have this procedure done?"

She didn't seem to be judging me, but she also didn't seem to be upset or angry with me either. Maybe she understood.

"Yes."

She sighed and said, "While I would prefer to have grandchildren from Rhys, I understand your reasoning. If you would like to talk about childbirth ever, I am willing to discuss my experiences with you."

"Thank you," I whispered, shocked by her offer. Maybe she had gotten over her initial reaction of hating me and thinking I was not good enough.

"We should return. I'm certain Rhys will be following your scent trail now to make sure I'm not being rude or cruel to you."

"So, Rhys is your favorite?" I asked with a smirk.

She laughed. "No, he's just the oldest, so I spent a bit more time with him than the others. I had alone time with him, while the others never had that luxury."

We walked down the hallway again and almost immediately ran into Rhys.

"Mother," he said in a worried tone.

"I was perfectly nice to her. Not a scratch on her head."

"She was very nice and just giving me some motherly time. Don't be so mean to your mother," I ordered him and poked him in the ribs.

"Great, now you are teaming up against me?" He groaned.

"There you two are," Emrys called. He walked to his wife and kissed her forehead. "I think we're ready to eat now."

"I am famished," she admitted, leaning into him.

As cold as she had been when I met her, seeing her like this made my heart swell. She truly loved Emrys and I knew that she loved Rhys as well. She wouldn't be concerned with my intentions with him if she did not care about him.

"Are you hungry yet?" Rhys asked me.

"A little," I admitted.

We stepped into the room and the scents of the food

surrounded me. A tornado of cooked meats, baked breads, and vegetables swirled around me and made my mouth water. I was definitely hungry again.

Rhys pulled out a chair for me, between Deryn and Nico, and took a seat across from me. I saw Rhian rush to take the seat on Deryn's other side and had to hide my smile behind my glass as I took a drink.

Rhys arched an eyebrow at me, but I just smiled at him and refused to say anything.

As soon as Emrys sat down, everyone began filling their plates with food. I didn't even get a chance to fill mine, Deryn and Nico filled it for me. Fox tossed a bread roll to them to add to my plate and Rhys laughed softly.

"I can make my own plate," I whispered to them.

"We know, but you like to pile your plate high with potatoes and not enough meat. You need to eat more meat," Deryn told me.

"I eat a lot of meat," I grumbled, but instead of truly arguing with them, because they were likely right, I just dug in. Everything was delicious and I could understand the appeal of having chefs at your house. I wanted a chef at my house to cook for me! If we all moved into a house together, we could pool our money and hire one of the best chefs in the world to cook for us.

I froze, my body completely tense at my last thought. Since when had I begun thinking of their money as mine? Since when did I start thinking about having a house with all of us together? It would make things convenient, but we had never discussed that. Should we? Should we all live together in one house? We could have separate rooms still. Or one huge room that would make it much easier for us to share a bed. We could make the entire room a bed for all of us to share.

"What's wrong?" Nico asked, setting his hand on my knee beneath the table.

I shook my head and shoveled more food into my mouth. I

did not want to talk about this right now. I did not want to admit the crazy thoughts going through my head. What would they think about doing something like that? Would they agree? Would they want to find a house for all of us to live in?

I supposed, the thought of being their mate truly hadn't sunk in yet. Yes, the sex part was well understood. Our future though, what were we going to do? Would we find a house to live in together or would we stay in the apartments? Would they want to have one house or would we go to different ones? Would I go certain days to certain houses? Would we have to make a schedule like we had done before?

"Jolie," Deryn said loudly.

I jerked my head to the side to look at him. "What?"

"You cut through your plate," he whispered.

"What?" I looked down and sure enough, I had cut my plate in half. "Oh! I'm so sorry! I didn't mean to. I was just-"

"It's alright," Emrys assured me. "We have more plates."

"What's wrong?" Deryn whispered in my ear.

I shook my head. "Nothing, just got lost in thought."

"Are you sure?" he asked. "We can go outside to talk if you want to."

"No, really. I'm alright. I'm sorry."

Rhys was looking at me with a strange expression. He looked into my eyes and then glanced at his mother and back to me. I shook my head. No, this wasn't because of what his mother and I had discussed.

A servant brought out a new plate and wiped off my place setting, so I wouldn't have any of the pieces of the broken ceramic on the table still. Deryn remade my plate for me and I ate in silence, listening to what everyone else was saying instead of focusing on the thoughts swirling inside of my head.

Everyone finished eating and we continued to another room, this one had a ten foot tall tree decorated with lights, hand crafted decorations, and pine cones. Beneath the tree sat a giant pile of presents. The room had several large couches and we all took seats on it while Emrys stood before the tree.

"Tradition here is to give out presents from youngest to oldest," Emrys informed me.

"Did you bring the presents?" I asked Rhys.

He nodded. "They're under the tree already."

Good. I would have felt awkward opening presents when I hadn't brought any myself for others to open.

"Tonight, however, we are changing it up a bit," Emrys said.

"What?" Rhian grumbled. "Why?"

"Tonight, we want to give Jolie her present first. Then we will resume our normal course of action," he explained.

"I can wait my turn," I assured him. "It's really alright."

He shook his head, picked up a package wrapped in beautiful teal and magenta and set it on the ground in front of me. "Merry Christmas, Daughter."

Kneeling on the ground, I ripped open the present and opened the box. A gasp escaped my throat before I could stop it. Inside of the box lay a transparent piece of paper with a swirling dragon on it. I knew it wasn't just a drawing though. This was the symbol of their clan, the one that they all had tattooed on them once they could prove that they could shift and were accepted by the clan.

"Is this...are you sure?" I asked, looking up at the King and Queen of Dragons with tears in my eyes.

They both nodded.

"May I?" Rhys asked, holding out his hand.

I nodded, speechless, and handed him the piece of paper. Unlike tattoos done by machines with ink, this was done by magic. Rhys turned me to face him and looked down at my body thoughtfully. Finally, he turned me and pulled down the right shoulder of my dress, baring my shoulder to him. I kept a tight grip on the front of my dress so that it wouldn't drop lower and cause me to flash his family. Rhys pressed the paper to my shoulder blade and whispered in a language I didn't understand. A brief zip of pain shot through my shoulder and then warmth spread from it until it engulfed my body.

I could feel them. All of them. I could feel all of the dragons in this room and beyond. I was part of their clan.

"Welcome to the Clan of Dragons, Daughter," Emrys said with a wide smile.

Rhys kissed my tattoo and the little bit of pain that had stayed, disappeared. After fixing my dress, I stood and walked to Emrys, throwing my arms around his neck and hugging him tightly. He wrapped his arms around me and whispered into my ear, "Even if something happens between you and my son, now you will always be part of my clan. You will always be my daughter. You will never be alone and never be cast aside."

"You're going to make her cry," Adelaide chastised him. She pulled me away from him and kissed my cheek. "Welcome to the clan, Daughter. You are officially our princess and will forever be so, unless you take over ruling and become queen."

That did not sound like something I wanted to do any time soon, but I didn't say that. I just hugged her and said, "Thank you."

"Alright!" Emrys said with a clap of his hands. "Let's open the rest of the presents."

I took my seat on the couch beside Rhys and didn't stop smiling the entire night. Accepted. They had accepted me.

Everyone loved the gifts I had given them, especially Gavin who swore he would wear the bracelet I'd purchased every day.

We said our farewells and drove on to our next destination. Rhys ran his fingertips over my shoulder, over the tattoo, as we drove while looking out the window.

"Did you talk to your dad about what happened?" I asked, even though I knew they had.

"Yes, he said it is because I've become lazy and just relied on it to happen. I've got to get back to doing things on purpose and not on habit. He's, of course, right."

"Well, I'm glad it's just that," I said with a sigh. I had been worried something might be wrong with Rhys.

He kissed my cheek and whispered, "I'm fine, love. And, even if I were dying, you have my family to support you now."

"What are we, chopped liver?" Fox asked with a scowl.

"Yes, she'll have you as well," Rhys chuckled.

The time with the mages was a somber affair and I wasn't the only one glad to be done when we climbed in the car two hours later.

"Sorry," Nico whispered. "Dad's not been the same since the Summit."

"Because of me?" I asked.

"Because of himself," he snapped. "Because he was so willing to sacrifice you despite knowing how much I love you and how much the others love you. Despite knowing what Dan and Emrys feel for you. He realized what a terrible decision he made and he's not sure how to atone for it."

"Is that why he gave me such a huge present?" I asked, looking at the card in my hand. He had pre-loaded a credit card with one thousand dollars and told me I could use it for whatever I wanted, since he wasn't really sure what I wanted or needed.

Nico nodded.

"Well, you'll have fun with the pack," Deryn assured me. "Dad pulled out all the stops for you."

"You guys really didn't have to go through all of this for me," I whispered, feeling embarrassed.

"Dad heard that you hadn't really enjoyed a true family Christmas and immediately went into action. I could not have stopped him if I had tried," Deryn told me. "Plus, you know how much he loves you."

I did. Dan had been the first to decide I was good for his son and had claimed me for his pack immediately. Though, Emrys had been the first to officially claim me.

We pulled to a stop in front of Dan's house and twin whirlwinds of fur bounded around the truck, barking and yipping for me to get out. I stepped out and they tackled me to the ground, covering my face with puppy kisses.

"Hello, nieces," I said laughing as they continued to greet me.

"Girls," Dan said in a chastising, but kind voice.

They stepped off of me, sat on their rumps, and looked at me with wagging tails. Deryn pulled me up and I wiped my face off on the bottom of his shirt.

Dan pulled me into a hug and kissed my cheek. "Daughter, I have been waiting all day for you."

"We told you we would be here at this time," I reminded him.

"I know," he admitted, "but I had hoped you would come sooner."

"Jolie!" Sharla exclaimed, rushing forward and pulled me out of Dan's arms and into her own.

I hugged her back and kissed her cheek. "Sharla!" I exhaled.

She kissed my cheek and then pulled back to look into my eyes. Her hand whipped out and she twisted my ear harshly, making me cry out in pain. "If you ever sacrifice yourself for me or Martin again, I will skin your hide!"

"Sharla," Deryn growled, stepping forward.

I held out my hand to him and he stopped.

"Sharla," I whispered, seeing the tears in her eyes. "You know that I could not let Martin die. I could not let him die and allow myself to live. I would not be able to look at you or the girls knowing I had let him die. "

"You almost died!" she snapped at me, growling softly, but her grip on my ear released and she buried her head in my neck. "He told me how they found you."

"I'm alive," I whispered and hugged her tightly. "We are all alive and that is what matters."

"Don't you ever do that again," she ordered me, her growl vibrating my entire body.

I stepped back from her and shook my head. "I can't promise you that," I said honestly. "If Martin is in danger and I can prevent his death with my own, I will always place myself in danger."

"You're supposed to let me die for you," Martin said, wrapping his arms around me from behind.

I turned around and hugged him tightly. "There was no way I could let that happen."

"You're so stubborn," he grumbled into my hair.

"That's enough," Dan ordered us. He pulled me away from Martin and put his arm around my shoulders. "Come on, let's go inside and start this party right."

Dan led me inside, but then took me to his office and shut and locked the door.

"Dad?" Deryn called and knocked on the door.

"Give us a minute," he ordered Deryn, the order carrying power enough to make Deryn leave.

"What?" I asked Dan.

"They're right," he told me.

"Who?"

"Sharla and Martin. You cannot sacrifice yourself like that."

"Dan, what would you have done if they said to sacrifice yourself or Deryn dies?" I asked him with hands on my hips.

He growled and turned away.

"Exactly," I said and pointed at him. "I could not let them die. I love them. I had been in relationships with them. I could not let them die. I would do it again. I don't care what pain I endured. As long as they survive, that is all that matters!"

"You matter!" he yelled, the wolf showing in his eyes. He paced back and forth in front of his desk a few times and then turned to face me. "You are not just a human girl. You are the Princess of the Four Clans. You are the Queen of the Four

Princes. You are my daughter, though not by blood, but that does not matter to me. You are important to me. You matter to me. Do I want to lose my son? No! But, I don't want to lose you either. I hope I never have to worry about losing either of you. If there is ever a time where you must choose between you and Deryn, I hope that you choose yourself."

"Dan!" I gasped. "He is your son. Your prince-"

"And you mean the world to him. If he loses you, I fear that he will fall into a darkness that I will not be able to pull him out of. When your connection was severed, he collapsed to the ground, like a puppet with their strings cut. He collapsed and cried. My boy never cries. He has never cried in his entire life! Not even as a baby. He would whimper or fuss, but never cry. Your connection was cut and that hard-ass wolf cried and wailed. I feared the worst. I feared you were dead from his reaction. I tried to comfort him, but he was inconsolable. The others were much the same. I have known those four their entire lives, Jolie. I have seen them together and seen them in battles and in times of joy. I have seen them with females, some they thought they might love. I have seen them face down enemies I did not think they could defeat, but they did. I felt my heart breaking for them when your bonds were cut. They thought you were dead. They thought you were gone from them forever. They were desperate, unthinking, and began to rush around to look for you. We had to sedate Deryn. Please, do not tell him I told you. He was shifting uncontrollably. He tried to attack me. He was so beside himself in grief he could not even form sentences."

"Why are you telling me this?" I demanded, tears in my eyes attempting to stream down my cheeks.

"Because, I want you to know how much you mean to them. I need you to know that if you sacrificed yourself to keep them alive, it would eat at them for the rest of their lives. They would never forgive themselves. You are the only thing that matters to them. You are the most important thing to them. I understand the desire to protect them. I'm not saying you should not protect them if you can. Just, please don't sacrifice yourself like that again."

"I will do my best," I replied.

"I almost killed him," he told me, fists clenched.

"Who?" I knew he didn't mean Deryn.

"That stupid fucking Mage King. I wanted to rip his head off and Emrys was right there with me. Had you died, no one could have stopped me. I would have killed him. Nico seemed close to doing it himself. I've never seen him attack his father before, but that night, he sent his father flying into the castle wall and told him if he ever put you in harm's way again, he'd take his place as king."

Holy shit!

"When did this happen?"

"The night you were returned to us," he answered.

The night I came back basically dead. I'd barely survived.

"The princes are powerful beings," he whispered. "More powerful than the kings. They're the most powerful any of us have ever seen and we aren't quite sure how they became so powerful. When someone is that powerful, they usually lose their humanity. But you allow them to keep their humanity. You keep them humble and remind them that there are people to fight for. People who need their help."

I teared up again at his words. I thought I made them weaker, not stronger.

"Promise me, Daughter. Promise me you won't sacrifice yourself like that again," he whispered, setting his hands on my shoulders.

"I promise I will do everything in my power to stay alive," I answered.

He sighed then chuckled. "I suppose that is the best answer I will get from you. Come, let's leave these serious discussions for later."

I nodded and followed him to the living room where we found the twins in wolf form wrestling with Deryn in human form.

"That's something we had never seen before," Dan whispered to me. "He loved children, but he did not engage with the pups often. Now, he plays with all of the pups, letting them jump and climb on him and playing."

Deryn looked up and his wide smile wavered a moment as he took us in. The girls turned to see what he was looking at and rushed towards me. I held out my hand, making them slide to a stop before me. "Shift," I ordered them.

They shifted and stood before me in matching red dresses. "Auntie," they said in unison.

I got down on my knees and hugged them. "Hello, girls."

"We've got to go," Martin told the girls.

"I'll come see you tomorrow," I promised them. "I have awesome presents for you two."

"Yay!" they yelled in unison, hugged me once more and followed Sharla and Martin out of the house.

"They're very fond of you," Deryn said behind me. "They never want to talk to me about anything other than you."

"They're great girls," I whispered.

"Come!" Dan ordered us. "Time to eat."

"I can't believe how much you've eaten today," Fox said to me.

"I know," I agreed.

"What did the old man want to talk to you about?" Deryn asked, keeping his voice low while Dan talked with Nico.

"It's personal," I whispered and tried to walk away, but he grabbed my arm gently and stopped me. "I'll talk to you later about it," I promised.

"You're upset," he whispered.

I turned to look him straight in the eyes, rested my hands on each side of his face, and whispered, "You are amazing. I love you, Deryn."

He blinked twice and said, "I love you too, Jolie."

❀

DAN HAD GIVEN ME A TATTOO AS WELL, MAKING ME AN OFFICIAL member of the pack. The little wolf was on my left shoulder blade and it was a bit strange being connected to so many people at once, but as we drove back towards our apartment complex, their minds faded a bit into background noise.

Deryn taught me how to block them completely and that was a huge help.

Once home, the guys stood in front of the tree, all looking down at the one present from me.

"Sit," I ordered them.

They obeyed, taking seats on the couch.

I picked up the present, fumbled with the bag, and pulled out the four black boxes.

"Tricky!" Fox exclaimed.

"This was your dad's idea," I chuckled.

"I don't doubt it," he grumbled.

After handing each of them their boxes, I sat on my knees in front of them and smiled. "Open them."

They lifted the lids and all of them stared at it in shock.

Dropping the front half of my body to the ground, I bowed to them. "I'm a lowly human girl. I don't have powers, unless I borrow yours. I don't have much money. I'm not the most beautiful woman in the lands. I don't have much of anything. But, I do have a heart that beats only for you four. I love you four more than anything else in the world. I'm not worthy. I'm far from worthy. I'll never be worthy. However, I can't deny my feelings. I love you four. And, I have one thing to ask. Will you become my mates?"

I had rehearsed the speech for hours, but it still didn't come out quite right. I just hoped they knew what I was trying to say.

"I accept," all four said at the same time.

I looked up and the four of them put the bloodstone beneath their left eye, between the eye and their cheekbones. It melted into their skin until it was part of their body, the crystal showing with a slight glow from the magic and blood within.

Mates. They were my mates. Now and forever.

All four bowed to me and said, "You are my queen and my mate from now until the end of time. None shall separate us. None shall come between us. You are mine and I am yours. My heart, my body, and my soul are yours. I shall touch no other female. I shall love no other female. You are mine and I am yours. Forever. This vow I make you, my mate and my queen."

The magic surged through us all and I cried fat tears of joy, hugging and kissing each of them. We weren't perfect. We weren't going to be safe from danger and problems. But, we had each other and that was all that mattered. And, tomorrow I would have them add their blood to my bloodstone to put under my eye, finishing our bond.

"Forever," I agreed.

TO CONTINUE READING THE HER ROYAL HAREM
SERIES, PRE-ORDER ROYALLY ELECTED (BOOK THREE):
https://books2read.com/re3

Alys of Asgard

Phoenix Possessed

Tiger Tears

Sybil Deceived

CONNECT WITH CATHERINE BANKS

I really appreciate you reading my book! Here are some ways to connect with me:
www.catherinebanks.com

Follow me on BookBub:
https://www.bookbub.com/authors/catherine-banks

Join my newsletter for deals and snippets:
http://Catbanks.co/newsletter

Like my author Facebook page:
http://www.Facebook.com/CatherineBanksAuthor

Follow me on Twitter:
http://www.Twitter.com/catherineebanks

Follow me on Goodreads:
http://www.Goodreads.com/catherine_banks

www.Turbokitten.us
www.Turbokitten.us/catherine-banks

Purchase items handmade by Catherine:
http://Etsy.com/shop/TurboKittenInd

Printed in Great Britain
by Amazon